THE
ENTWINING

THE ENTWINING

RICHARD CONDON

RICHARD MAREK PUBLISHERS
NEW YORK

Library of Congress Cataloging in Publication Data
Condon, Richard
The entwining.

I. Title.
PZ4.C746En   [PS3553.0487]   813'.54   80-14981
ISBN 0-399-90089-6

For the four Condon women

When we drink and when we dine,
When we lust and when we pine,
When we're born, or life declining,
The present writhes with past entwining.
                    The Keeners' Manual

THE
ENTWINING

1

The minutes swam by like sharks. The silence was astonishing, as if the birds were holding their breaths. She waited for Charles to swan up the drive in his small, garnet car, his red-faced man driving, having sped all the way to her twelfth birthday with another special present from beautiful, dead Mama.

She rocked contentedly on the main veranda at Rockrimmon; a long, blonde child with Eskimo-style cheekbones and navy-blue eyes. The year before, Charles had tethered a brown-and-white piebald pony to a chair at the breakfast table. She came into the room, stared at the horse speechlessly, turned the luminescence of her freckles upon Charles, and made a beautiful popping sound with her lips.

"Your mother was horsey," Charles said.

"Oh! So shall I be then." She mounted the pony from a chair and rode it bareback out of the house through the kitchen past Mrs. Willmott and her helper, Rose. "Jean!" Mrs. Willmott yelled. "That horse will make an unsanitary mess!"

"It isn't a horse," Jean said as she rode by. "It is a very hygienic pony." Rose held the door open and she rode the animal out into the yard. Charles strolled out after her. "I shall call her Jezebel," Jean told him. "Unless she is a stallion."

Rockrimmon was a large Palladian house in eastern Connecticut. It had a forest, lakes, lawns, summerhouses, planned walks, shade trees, flowerbeds, and greenhouses. It was a prodigal bravery in building, providing space for all the things with which later generations had stuffed it. There was a polo field left from her father's day, and an underground bowling alley. A swimming pool had been placed as if it were God's notion of a mountain tarn, but it leaked. Rockrimmon needed six servants inside, two tutors (Miss Knauerhase and Miss Garfunkel, whom Jean thought of fondly as twins who joined together at the intellect, at birth); sixteen gardeners; Miss E. Hunt, gymnastics teacher; librarians and technicians in Grandfather's immense library, which was a building in itself; and Charles, Jean's guardian, who arrived every Thursday afternoon from New York to spend the weekend with her and did not return to New York until Monday morning.

"Why not conjugate German verbs in your head while you wait?" Miss Knauerhase asked.

"Why not? I am thinking of Charles."

Charles Coomber Cantwell was senior partner in the law firm, now called Henstell, Masters & Cantwell, founded by Jean's family. Jean had never considered how much she loved him because he was always near. Charles had been a young lawyer with her father, and Charles had not only known Mama, but had been her lawyer and her executor, although Jean knew that was not the only reason Charles always remembered her birthdays. Once every month, at three o'clock on Saturday afternoon until five o'clock on Sunday afternoon, he took her to New York in a large limousine driven by his red-faced man, Stinnett. They stayed in his house which was on the East River in Beekman Place. They walked almost everywhere in Manhattan; saw the sights together, the shows, the galleries, the shops, the people, and never had less than a marvelous time.

Charles was very good company. He rarely got cross, and when he put his mind to it, he could be *very* silly. She had never had any family except Charles. Daddy had died eight years ago in Europe and Mama had died while Jean was an infant.

She had once overheard Mrs. Willmott say that Mama had died of a wasp sting in the deep gorge of the Sik, stronghold of the ancient Nabataeans at Petra, but when she had asked Charles about that he had snorted and said, "They don't even have wasps in Transjordania." He must have spoken to Mrs. Willmott about it because Jean never heard her mention Mama again.

Charles Coomber Cantwell had several personalities. He was able to seem to think just a few years ahead of Jean, whatever age she was.

When she was six he was like an adored "big" friend of eleven to her, and as they both grew older, he contrived to stay young with her, just a helpful bit ahead of her. But, Jean aside, he was a complex man, a brilliant lawyer who had spurts of periodical vice among the fleshpots; who periodically drank heavily. He was also a man who had such a massive feeling for his own identity that he would not, by as much as a gesture, speak or move or live in relation to other people so as to ensure his popularity. There were dozens of men and women who could prove that he had no humor or interest in humor. Yet Jean, two newspapermen, four of his mistresses, one waiter, three barmen, and his own houseman, Stinnett, thought he was hilariously comical. He could be epigrammatically witty or satirically bawdy. But for most people he didn't need to show any more than what they could see, because he was a beautiful man. He was tall and elegant so that his old and once very expensive clothes seemed to have been painted on him by some *trompe l'oeil* master. His face was both sensual and angular; the planed and sculptured angularity emphasizing the bold protuberance of his slightly thyroid-popped eyes and the fleshiness and balance of his mouth. He was effortlessly magnetic to women because of his beauty—a quality which women will frequently accept if it is accompanied by some other useful things. He was mostly uncommunicative with casual people, which lent him wisdom's aura, defying them to find him silly. He was rich, a fine attribute, but he was also generous. And he had the gift of never needing to keep the acquaintanceship of any of the women he had loved, or they his, after they had decided to part. This accomplishment alone had most men in awe of him because it showed no inconsiderable flash of genius. Other men paid alimony or listened to long and dismal harangues on the telephone in the small hours of the morning. Charles Cantwell made women happy. They were happy to have discovered him against all competitive demographic odds.

They were ecstatic that he was not married. They achieved a great fishing bank of bliss during all of the time when it was spiritually and carnally satisfying to be in love with him and—without either expensive presents or hangovers—when they parted it was as though he had been laundered out of their yearnings by the best of the mind-control teams of the CIA. He never married.

The reason he never married (he was a loving, and—by demonstration—a monogamous man) was probably because nature abhors continuing perfection. Great change and monumental character—be it in flora or fauna—only come out of greatest conflict; endless harmony in existence is inimical to this. Because he had had it so good in every other experience with women, Charles had it worse than bad and longer than forever with one woman who, loving him beyond sanity, not only refused to marry him but bolted with another man whom both of them had always held in a sort of amused contempt.

So he settled on short bursts of vice and for sudden bouts with booze and, although few were ever aware of these, he was never happy again—which is to say, simply, he was unhappy for the rest of his life.

If it had not been for a last testament which made Jean his ward (Jean was an orphan with the sort of fortune that almost demanded she be raised by Wall Street lawyers), he would not have survived. He would not have survived as a lawyer because he would have gradually drunk much more than he did. He would not have survived intact as he did because women and the law were his only diversions and he would have gone too far into excess to try to change the boredom which so narrow a scope might have forced upon him.

But the caprice of the dead woman who had been married to one of his law partners marooned him unexpectedly upon a world he had never seen or imagined; then the responsibility of Jean Henstell was handed to him, which he came to consider an act of God's mercy. A will was read and he was named her legal guardian. He saw her first when she was about one hour old. He held her in his arms and was unable to understand why he should have feelings of love for her. After nine days of constant talking with the infant's mother, it became known that she had to return to Switzerland because her husband was ill and because the Phony War was about to heat up almost at once.

"She is already provided for stupendously by her grandfather's estate," Jean's mother had said. "But, what with this war about to happen for real, Josh on his part and I on mine have drawn our wills in her favor. She owns this place, the big house in New York, and all the rest of the claptrap."

"Some claptrap," Charles said reverently.

"You'll know better than I, probably, how to see that she is raised well. But, for me, let her have languages, music, and the law—and for heaven's sake promise you will hire an actress who will make sure she will speak like a woman and not like a hen."

"How long do you think this war will last, for heaven's sake?" he asked her.

"Oh, we'll be back. She will have a mother. I am only saying these funereal things because people don't last forever."

She went away at 9:57 that night—he never forgot the moment—and she never came back again.

Charles approached the problem at first the way any experienced lawyer would protect a ten-day-old, combustibly rich client: he interviewed baby nurses and hired two of these, although when she reached six and the time came to cast about for an equally gifted nanny he did not hire one because Jean had advanced to a point where few nannies would be able to follow her. Besides, Cantwell wanted the job himself, and he filled it from Thursday at noon, every week of the year, until Monday morning at seven. It was not difficult to persuade the doctor who delivered her, a medical wizard named Abe Weiler, to visit Rockrimmon for a weekend every two months to keep her well, because Weiler had no other access to such wine nor the opportunity to glut one of his interests in sculpture—Houdon busts. Weiler was, even then, a distinguished American doctor. Internationally he ranked just below Aesculapius.

Both men realized very early that Jean was a child of immoderate intelligence, wide interests, and unusual mental capacity. Together they led her along through time carefully but boldly, and she responded to all the signals until, at five, she discovered the prodigious Henstell Memorial Library, which was seventy yards away and straight off began to take over her own education.

She could read and write at three. At five, Cantwell brought in a teaching governess, but within four months the woman said Jean should be taught with more advanced methods because she was inhaling innocence and exhaling knowledge. The woman told them sadly that she was holding the child back. So Cantwell retained *two* advanced tutors with quite high IQs of their own and graduate backgrounds as teachers, to supply the unorthodox methods. They were called Knauerhase and Garfunkel. They taught Jean to speak sound French, Italian, Spanish, and German in eleven months, then let the child settle in to polish her skills while they moved her into higher mathematics and music. By laying down directional syllabi, they allowed Jean to teach herself history and literature out of the great stores at the library, then held oral and written examinations in all subjects every sixty days.

Charles told them he wanted the child to have a mind prepared to accommodate the tonnages of the law when she reached an age to study it. Knowing that such things are best taught against the give and take of other minds, he was determined that Garfunkel, Knauerhase and, importantly, himself, must talk to her and listen when she spoke.

Weiler said, "If anything she is too sane."

"Adolescence will take care of that," Cantwell said grimly.

Jean was fortunate that Cantwell was as sane as he was, or he might have contrived one way or another to keep her at Rockrimmon until, in her twenties, she would have been forced to run away to escape him and find the world.

Charles Cantwell was Jean's all-in-one combination of surrogate father, best friend, and advocate. They were parts of each other; supporting, complementing, enhancing and exchanging strengths whenever one cried out for rescue by the other.

Charles had raised her—and Miss Knauerhase and Miss Garfunkel—in the best good manners. She was a linguist. She was on her way to developing as a mathematician, and was already a sound musician on the piano, cello, and the double-action harp (as patented by Sébastien Erard in 1810). She owned 8.7293 percent of the third largest bank in the country; a residual interest in one of the leading law firms in Wall Street; all of Rockrimmon; and a few less formidable possessions.

The library which had been built and amassed by her grandfather was connected to the main house by a tunnel, paved with green, pink, and white tiles, for use on inclement days. And there Jean spent her unscheduled time. She was an habituated student; a committed scholar.

The library contained over 600,000 items: books, manuscripts, musical scores, prints, films, slides, and records. It was the largest privately owned archive in New England. Her grandfather, the illustrious Thomas Henstell, had established it as a research center for archival techniques. The library was not open to the public but was available by appointment to scholars, graduate students, and administrative librarians.

Jean asked Miss Hadley what Mama had looked like. Miss Hadley was the chief librarian, a woman who had introduced her to such vocabulary-expanding words as *tump* and *cicatrix* and who had insisted from the time Jean was six that she must seek to be able to use her various vocabularies as well as Woodrow Wilson had used his. No matter how busy she was, Miss Hadley always did her best to smile at any mention of Mama. "You look like her, dear," she said. "She had golden hair and eyes *just* like yours, *deep blue* with tiny diamond chips floating about in them. She must have had freckles like yours when she was your age, but when I knew her she was a statuesque blonde woman with rare olive skin which seemed to be dusted across those thrusting cheekbones with roses. You will allow that was *very* unusual."

Jean had never seen a photograph of her mother. Everyone else in the family had been painted in portrait by this or that fashionable painter, but not Mama. Charles was able to describe her with moving beauty. As soon as she was old enough to think about it at all, Jean knew that it was better to be able to assimilate all the lovely descriptions into her consciousness and be able to reconstruct without pictures the sweet face and form which had been Mama in her own indelible way. Mama had had all of the physical features which Jean intended to possess some day. A handsome bosom held by a commanding but unrigid carriage; *so* important Miss Hunt had proved to her. Mama would have had long, straight legs, and when she was feeling naughtily beautiful, she would fill sheer, high, black stockings with them. She wasn't certain about Mama's bottom. She had seen some quite comely women with wide bottoms, but since her own was small and very flat, then that was the way Mama's must have been. Mama's teeth would be very white and even and her hands soft, narrow, and long, the better to stroke one with. Both Charles and Miss Hadley agreed entirely upon Mama's height, and Jean had been assured by Miss Hunt that if she applied herself to special selective exercises, her body would achieve the ideal which Mama had set forth for her.

From far off, she heard the sound of Charles' garnet Gozzi sports car crossing the bridge across the brook which was less than a half mile from the house. She stood up. "Charles has come," she said triumphantly, as if Miss Knauerhase and Miss Garfunkel had doubted it. The tutors stood, craning. "I was able to get the book for him," Miss Knauerhase said. "He will be so pleased."

"What book?" Miss Garfunkel asked sharply.

"Just a book."

The small garnet car came whooshing up the approach. Jean squealed with pleasure and ran down from the porch to stand in the driveway like a matador facing a bull, her arms held rigidly behind her at her sides, one knee partly bent. She tried to glare as the car was dominated to halt almost at her feet, but she grinned instead.

"Oh, Charles!" she said with all of the ecstasy of her twelfth year, "what did Mama think of for *this* year?"

2

Charles unfolded his long legs and got himself out. His merry eyes were sly with birthday power.

"Quite a haul for you this year," he said. "You have been awarded your mother's diaries."

"Diaries?" Jean said blankly, not disappointed but baffled.

"Your mother was a very interesting woman."

"Her *diaries!* Oh, Charles! What a wonderful present! Good morning, Stinnett," she called out across the car to Charles' man.

"Good morning, miss."

Jean looped her arm through Charles' and they strolled out across the wide lawn to a bench which looked out over the valley below the house.

"Happy birthday, old bean," he said.

"It has been. Miss Knauerhase spoke to me in German throughout breakfast this morning."

"Both ladies are quite pleased with you. Beginning Monday they will be getting you ready for college entrance examinations."

"*Whaaaat!*"

"Oh, yes."

"But where?"

"It is not widely known around here that I am a trustee at Smith College. In Northampton, Massachusetts. So, out of loyalty to the old

16

school bloomers, and with some extraordinary marks from you on the college entrance examinations, we should have you installed on the Smith campus in just about a year."

Jean stared out across the valley, looking grave. "It is a responsibility," she said.

"So is everything."

"Northampton is so far away."

"Oh, well. It's high time you saw more of the world."

Jean was excited. She hadn't been sealed up as a recluse at Rockrimmon. Every summer since she had been eight years old, Charles had taken her to a different country in Europe for six weeks to practice languages. She had met a lot of people, but the idea of testing herself against other girls day after day after day was thrilling. Then it hit her that Miss Knauerhase and Miss Garfunkel would have to be left behind without anything to do.

"What about the Whiz Kids?" she asked.

"They'll find something, or maybe we can help them find something."

"They must be very rich," Jean said. "I am sure you pay them well and I don't think they have left here in seven years, even in the summertime."

"Let's go in," Charles said.

"What for?"

"I have my birthday present to you in the safe in my study."

"I cannot *stand* it."

"I wish we could do something about showing you your mother's diaries, but they are locked in boxes inside a chest which is inside the trunk of my car. And, by the terms of your mother's will, the keys to that chest, and those boxes, and quite possibly each diary, were sent by registered mail from my office yesterday morning—as indeed your mother's instructions specified—to the head librarian in that Henstell Library building over there."

"How melodramatic of Mama!"

"Oh, she was melodramatic all right."

"But it makes the diaries even more fun. All right. We must proceed according to plan. First we go to the safe in your study, then we go to demand the keys from Miss Hadley at the library."

"Hadley doesn't work on weekends," Charles reminded her. "She is off from noon Friday until noon Monday."

"An assistant will be there."

"Your mother's instructions were firm. No one but Hadley may turn those keys over to you."

"But it is too suspenseful, Charles. I will explode with the waiting. And you won't be here by the time Miss Hadley returns on Monday."

"The diaries weren't meant for me. Strictly a mother-daughter affair, message from the grave, sage counsels from another time."

"You don't intend to read them after I have read them?" Jean looked puzzled.

He leaned over and kissed her under her ear. "Look, darling child," he said gently, "you weren't born when she wrote those things, but she must have yearned to be able to talk to you. So I'm sure those diaries are very special to the intimate dreams a mother has for her daughter. She was right to lock those diaries up into boxes within boxes. Her will states that, 'in the event of my death before the twelfth birthday of my daughter, the large carved camphorwood chest which contains such infrequent diaries as I have kept, and which contain the counsel, warnings, and opinions which I wish to convey to my daughter about this life, shall be delivered to her by my executor on my daughter's twelfth birthday and, so that these records which I am most desirous of conveying to her shall remain a matter which shall be confined between her memory of me and herself, the aforesaid executor shall convey the keys to the chests and containers of this record to the head librarian at the Henstell Library, Rockrimmon, for delivery to my daughter at the earliest opportunity.' "

"Pretty awesome," Jean said.

"Yes. I believe your mother was distantly related to Edgar Allan Poe."

They went into Charles' study, a thirty-foot-square room whose walls were paved floor to ceiling with books. There was a large snooker table in the center, close to a large Florentine desk. Charles went to the section of the bookshelf where the spines of books on "Security" were stacked and opened the section to reveal a safe.

"What's the combination, again?" he asked.

"Zero start," Jean said solemnly as she had for many years each time he asked her to help him open the safe. "Then 3-18-15-4."

"You have a good memory," he said, swinging open the safe's door. He reached into it and came out with a black Nikon camera. "It is not only loaded with color film," he said, "but a reasonably clear booklet of instructions goes with it."

"Oh, Charles!" Jean exclaimed with enormous pleasure. "There is nothing I would rather have wished to have!" She blushed. "Excepting Mama's diaries, of course."

3

When Jean's lessons were over at four o'clock on Monday afternoon (Garfunkel: Celestial Navigation), Jean walked purposefully across the lawn to the library building quite prepared to do her duty by Mama and to read every page of the diaries. It was not that she was reluctant to learn about how her mother thought and felt, but diaries of days long gone contrasted so strongly with the news that she would actually be a student at Smith College in just about a year's time—news so packed with excitement about what had not happened yet—that she went to find Miss Hadley with more resigned patience than real eagerness.

Miss Hadley was expecting her. She took an envelope which had been sealed with heavy green wax out of the top drawer of her desk. It was thick enough to contain keys, Jean thought. Miss Hadley asked her to sign a receipt which was written on the printed stationery of Henstell, Masters & Cantwell for "One green-wax-sealed envelope addressed to Miss Jean Henstell."

Jean thanked Miss Hadley, who asked her how her vocabulary development was coming along, and Jean told her that she had just added the word *pinguescent* that morning.

"Good word, pinguescent," Miss Hadley said.

Jean returned to the main house with the green-wax-sealed envelope, going directly to her own apartment on the second floor of the house, facing the wide valley. The camphorwood chest was waiting on a side

table. It wasn't at all a large chest, about two feet long by one foot deep
by ten inches high. Jean broke open the envelope to find that it contained four numbered smaller envelopes. She took the key out of envelope number one and tried it on the chest, which opened. Inside were two
wooden boxes, each with a lock. One box was marked 1, the other, 2. She
shook the key out of the second envelope and tried it in the lock of box
number 1. The box opened. A large, thick, leatherbound diary in the
color of amethyst lay in the box. The excitement of the next thing to
actually meeting her mother flooded Jean as she touched the diary.
Breathless to know the woman, she lifted the book carefully out and
opened it at random.

The handwriting was strong, small, and intellectual; very clear to
read. The pages were written in black ink. The passage to which Jean
had opened was undated. She riffled backward through the pages; all
were undated. Puzzled, she returned to where she had opened the book
and, standing in the mid-October afternoon sunlight, she began to read
the first words she had ever known her mother to have actually written.

If you could have seen the *fustaat* of the King—the old king. Its
roof was a clear night sky with thousands of gleaming stars appli-
quéd to its ceiling. It had been made in Egypt in lofts where a thousand skilled men labored to make palaces of silk and canvas which
held so many rooms that it took more than 100 camels to carry the
royal family's tenting. The king's own tent complex, where I sat
with him, was so huge that it had taken 193 artisans 9 years to cut
and sew. But, oh my dear!—the *carpet* in that tent! Its body was silk
but its design—on 8400 square feet in a silken tent which was 120
feet high—is a design which has entered their legend and poetry,
politics and art. The design was of a formal garden of blooming
flowerbeds, watercourses, fruit trees, lawns, and blossoming
shrubs. The carpet had gravelled paths which were sown with gold
nuggets. Flowers, fruit, and birds were worked into that design
with pearls and every kind of jewel. The wide outer border was
solid with *emeralds!* I tell you, my dearest, when the sun was
allowed to shine in upon that spectacle, it was transfixing. It proclaimed power and resources. It overwhelmed ambitious nobles, the
governors of provinces, and the ambassadors from foreign courts.
But it also symbolized the fact that it was the king's first task to
guarantee, and to compel, the return of spring. The carpet prefig-
ured Paradise—which is their word meaning walled park—so it

also had religious significance. That single, vast carpet signified deliverance from the harsh desert.

Please try to understand the tremendous honor the King was paying to your mother by permitting me to sit with him in his great *fustaat*. Women simply do not *exist* with such people as these, dearest. Women are servants and must remain totally invisible. But the King wanted to show the extent of his gratitude to me as a geologist, a gesture which I considered not only a gallant salute to me, but a tribute to my science.

Jean was exhilarated. She closed the book and took it to her desk. She sat down, opened a drawer, and found what was left of a chocolate bar. She opened the book at the beginning and began to chew and to read.

These diaries are for my future daughter's eyes. Should anyone else come upon them let him close the book in shame at having invaded my memory which is now my daughter's sacred possession. As curses were placed upon the invaders of ancient tombs so do I place a curse upon man or woman who on reading these words does not close the book at once and forevermore.

I wrote these diaries all during my pregnancy, hoping and praying for a daughter. How I rejoice that a girl was born to me, a girl whom I place in Charles Cantwell's trust while I go off to an uncertain future at my husband's side in warring Europe. Had my baby been male I would have burned these diaries. Their legacy is for a future woman's eyes only.

Her hand trembling, the child turned the page.

FOR MY DARLING AND GLORIOUS CHILD

There are two things I must say, then I must say them again and again as you read through the account of how life happened to me.

1: Control your life. To do this you must control yourself. This never ends, waking or asleep. When you have mastered control of yourself you will then have the power to control others and to control events; ironically, even time may be controlled by using every moment of it to learn control itself. Say to yourself: I must take control and keep control so that I may help to realize the true meaning of women's existence.

2: Do not trust most men. You will be able to trust your given nature to *want* men, but after they have served that purpose, impress upon your mind—*sledgehammer* it there—that vileness and deceit, cruelty and destruction, are the nature of most males. Classify their qualities. To abide with men you must *control* them, my darling, and to do this you must control the events upon which they build their aspirations. To control yourself is to learn to control men. To control men is to control your environment just as the new settler in a strange forest must subdue that environment so that a good life may be sustained.

When you finish reading this introduction will you go straight off to the head librarian to obtain the biographies of Alexandra Kollontai, Ch'iu Chin, Louise Michel, and Flora Tristan? Those women were *revolutionaries* in the women's struggle for liberty. They *forced* control upon themselves so that they could help achieve women's equality with men.

Ch'iu Chin said, standing on a mountain of truth in a man's world, "Concubinage is truly a hell on earth which competes with the hell of the dead."

When you are old enough to look about you, dearest, you will become aware of the millions of women who serve the men in their counting houses. What are these shamed women but concubines of the industrial revolution? Who is going to make revolution for them?

Jean felt helplessly torn and confused. What is she trying to tell me?—that men are bad? Charles isn't bad. Herbert the butler, John Moran the head gardener—they certainly aren't bad. What sort of control did Mama mean beyond the control which I've been taught? Who are these women? What have they to do with me? But Jean knew that her mother would not have gone to such lengths to see that her daughter received such statements so long after her death unless she had known many, many things that Jean herself did not know or hadn't even dreamed about. Jean would have to keep reading on and on, then read it all over again until she grasped what her mother was trying to tell her. She went back to the diaries.

Kollontai fought fiercely within the Russian Bolshevik Party to make even revolutionary men accept that women's struggle for freedom was part of the class struggle. That she was a general's daughter and a great beauty she considered disadvantages. Yet she

could write: "Love, with its many disappointments, with its trage-
dies and eternal demands for perfect happiness, still played a very
great role in my life. . . . "

But *then*, darling, *then* she wrote:

*We of the older generation would have been able to create and
achieve much more had our energies not been fragmentized in the
eternal struggle with our egos and with our feeling for one another.
It was in fact the eternal defensive war against the intervention of
the male into our ego, a struggle revolving around the problem-
complex: work or marriage and love. We felt enslaved and tried to
loosen the love bond. And after the eternally recurring struggle with
the beloved man, we finally tore ourselves away and rushed toward
freedom. Thereupon we were again alone, unhappy, but free to pur-
sue our chosen ideal . . . work.*

Was Mama warning her that it was better to work than to fall in
love? Jean asked herself. But why couldn't anyone work *and* fall in love?
There must be invisible traps waiting. Mama had been a full-blooded
woman, Charles had said so. She would have known men as lovers—but
if the result of having lovers was bad, why keep on having lovers after
one has been disappointed with the first, and if everyone *knew* it was an
impossible idea? She just could not yet get Mama's warning that one
had to make a choice between work or having lovers. The diaries were
baffling. Perhaps Mama misjudged when she decided that I would be
ready to understand what she needed to tell me just now, Jean said to
herself. Perhaps I am failing her. Perhaps these books should have been
held back from me until I was finished with college, then the second set
given to me after I was married. But Mama knew! She had seen it all
and she knew that whatever it was she needed to warn me about needed
to be told *before* I left Rockrimmon and went away to college. She is
trying to help me. I must help her to help me by paying attention.

Louise Michel fought at the head of a men's battalion in the
French Commune of 1871. She was one of those tempestuous revolutionary spirits the world has rarely seen. Take her as your model,
dearest girl, if you cannot find another. Her memory is surrounded
by superlatives. She was a poet, a novelist, a teacher, and an inspir-
ing orator. She said—in every sense directly to you, sweetheart—
"We *expected* to die for women's liberty." She said to a courtroom
filled with men: "Since it seems that every heart that beats for
freedom has no right to anything but a slug of lead, I demand my

share. If you let me live I shall never cease to cry for vengeance. If you are not cowards, kill me.

Can this kind of thing possibly be what happens to women when they go into the world? Jean thought anxiously. This is certainly very much of a woman's matter and is between Mama and me, but I wish somehow I could talk about it with Charles. But he must have read these diaries because he has already set down the rules that what Mama has written here is only between herself and me. But why can't men tell girls about women, and women tell girls about men? Why has Charles never married? Did he learn—does everyone know except children—that men and women when they are combined are dangerous for each other? Was Mama so desperately unhappy with Daddy that she needed to write these *books* to me to warn me about control and men and the belovedness of work and conflict as a barrier between men and women? Miss Knauerhase reads the Bible to me. In the Bible they are just people, not this division of men against women and women against men. They have joys and sorrows and they work together and they work separately but there was never any plan for a division between them. But Mama knows. And Charles knows or he would have married. And the Bible was written about another country in a different time. The world changes by changing the people in it and obviously where we are now could be a perilous place for the unwary. Mama loves me and she is warning me.

Jean read and reread her mother's diaries at every free moment before she went away to Smith College. She read them as if they were the only food she would ever digest. Mama knew the secrets! Mama knew where life was to be found in the mind and in the heart.

It was not until Jean had read both volumes twice, and with increasing attention to them, that she realized why they were not dated. Had Mama dated them, the last pages would have ended sometime in the year when Mama's life had ended. Jean became certain that her twelfth-birthday present had been incomplete, that there had to be other diaries and other truths that Mama would have wanted to share with her had she lived.

At dinner one evening during the summer of 1951, served on the veranda at Rockrimmon, Jean said to Charles, "Y'know, I have the feeling that Mama wrote more diaries than just the two I got."

"You do?"

"Y'see—she—well, I just know it and I *feel* it."

"You happen to be right."

"What?" Jean was more astonished, by a long, long way, than she would have been had Charles told her she was wrong.

"You remember I told you once that your mother was distantly related to Edgar Allan Poe?"

Jean nodded, chewing.

"Well, she was even more closely related to Phineas T. Barnum. There are four volumes and you have two."

"Four!"

"I am to deliver the second two volumes when you graduate from Smith—and considering everything I suppose that could mean that your mother expected you to graduate from college when you were eighteen or later."

"How come?"

"Well, it follows, doesn't it? She designed everything to fit her needs, after all. She made up her mind on what you would be ready for at twelve, then she held out the rest until you were ready for that part of it."

"Gosh—those last diaries must be pretty wild stuff," Jean said.

"Your mother was pretty wild stuff," Charles answered. "Say—incidentally, I got permission for you to live off-campus—you being so young and all that—"

"Charles! How could you! Good grief, are you sending the Whiz Kids with me?"

"No, no! Nothing like that. You'll have housemates and you'll certainly mingle freely with any other students you choose and you can enter into any campus activity you choose. But the dean thought it would be best considering your tender age if you lived away from the dormitories."

"That isn't fair!"

"Well, hell, Jean," he grinned, "I understand those dormitory characters at Smith use some pretty rough language."

She whacked him with a cushion.

4

Before Jean went away to college she was deeply involved with and pervasively dominated by her mother's increasingly intimate presence. The powerful images of the advice and accounts of the crowded diaries took over within her mind because the cautions and insistences, the urgings built upon the yearning for someone who is not there, are mystically more powerful than the influences of those who are there. Mama was a metaphor of Jean's longing for her, of the sweet expansion like that of a musical note of the girl's wish for her mother, and to become like her mother. Mama was not there except in her warnings and instructions, therefore there was no person with whom Jean could grow disillusioned. Instead, through her years of change from childhood, to girlhood, to young womanhood—and later into maturity—Jean's vision of her mother was locked within the blinders of her mother's absence, but captured and enthralled, as a fly in amber is enthralled, by her mother's essence. Jean had not grown up with her mother and therefore was unable to grow away from her. Distant or dead, Mama had nonetheless returned to claim her child in a logical and loving manner so that the girl could not find the exits to grow up and escape the imaginary, the unreal fealty which Mama had thrust upon her. A living mother yields up her children to adulthood. A mother made invisible by death, but whose voice whispers on in fascination and shock, never can.

Jean stayed on at Rockrimmon, working with Miss Knauerhase and Miss Garfunkel, playing with Charles Cantwell, and finding a full and separate life inside her mother's diaries, until she went to college. She had read Mama's diaries in their entirety three times before she went away, but there were many passages in them, marked with paperclips, to which she would return again and again until she felt she knew them well enough to lock them into their boxes and leave them behind. She looked forward to reading them all again each summer when she returned home.

My dearest child: You are my child, so you have a mind and I am certain that you know by now from all that we have "discussed" in these diaries, that women are the psychic minority which is oppressed by male (and female) capitalists. As you get further into this philosophy you are going to find that this capitalist oppression certainly began long ago when an utterly deluded world overthrew its female deities and replaced them with the exploitiveness of our brutal male gods. The lame duck exception is the Virgin Mary, but I do not see *her* doing much to alleviate women's conditions.

Sweetest girl—please investigate this—*who ruled the Phoenician theogony?* To save you the time and trouble, I will tell you that the answer is Mot (Mud, the Earth Mother from whom the languages have found such names as mother, madre, Mutter, mère). MOT which grew into MOThers Day! Who nurtured the Sumerian theogony? It was Nammu, the *goddess* of the primaeval sea. Who ruled the ancient Greek theogony before *men* designed that farting, bilious, and venereal Zeus? It was Gaia, the Earth Mother—*Zeus' grandmother!*

Remember as you prepare to go out into the world, among thieving men and kind men, that the heritage of all time has made you their equal *in all things of the mind and the spirit, in all rights to property and place.* If men are successful as draught animals and weight lifters where you are not, then be happy to leave those sweaty exercises to them.

Go back to Ch'iu Chin, sweetie, that immortal Chinese woman revolutionary, for the badge which emblazons a greater truth, the *superiority* of women.

> My body does not attain
> In prominence to those of men;
> My heart verily transcends in ardor
> Those of men.

* * *

I urge you after you have satisfied your soul by confirming the substance of this information, to range across the library to such splendid books as James Bailey's *The God-Kings & the Titans* and Robert Graves' *The White Goddess*. I am citing male writers to prove my point. They are writing about women, but they speak with *facts* not prejudices. Graves *says it all*, my darling! Lodge these words into your memory and never forget them. ". . . invaders from Central Asia began to substitute patrilinear for matrilinear institutions and to remodel or falsify the myths to justify social changes. . . ." *Social changes?* What was changed, overthrown through millennia, and entirely destroyed by my lifetime, was the ascendancy of women—the watchful, rightful ascendancy of women, embodiment of the religions, the greatest myths of humanity, overthrown. Its place was taken by hairy, sweat-thick male savages whose reason for existence *at all* is only as the messenger boys for seed. They delivered the seed, touched their forelocks when they were given their tips, but it was and will always be the women who manufactured the life upon this planet and therefore have the *holy right* to supremacy over it. Men! What is their puling intellectual homosexuality but an escape—as Mr. Graves so bravely points out—from the ascendancy and the power of the Goddess?

Oh, darling! How my own life—and what it might have been—would have been different if an *equality* of Goddess with God had been maintained. So much more important for all humanity, which really wanted and needed the *ascendancy* of the Goddess!

I write this before my child is born so that one day she may know the truth. I sought life. I had lovers, I won recognition, I tore equality out of their grasp, I married and I made you. But before I knew any man joyously or in shamed pain, I knew the man who drove my mother to the ledge of a window sixteen stories above the street and sent her turning, spinning, screaming, to fall upon a fence of iron pickets which pierced her dear body so deeply that other men with acetylene torches had to come across the ice and through the blizzard in that city to lift and rip her poor, broken body from those spears.

Year after year I had listened to his steel voice cutting into her, raging like a piece of rogue machinery. I can *still* hear her voice answer softly, then even more softly, then becoming scraps of sound, denying everything he shouted at her only because she was a woman and he was a man.

Time and time again I went to her. I *begged* her to go away with me because he *hated* us and we didn't want him. She would not go.

A night came. They began the sounds again. His voice was terrible. I darted into my mother's bedroom and shrank against the wall with my hands pushing into my ears so that I could not hear them. There was a half-light from the moon and from the city. She came rushing in, going past me. I could hear his heavy feet coming after her. She threw open the window and climbed out upon the ledge. "Mother!" I screamed. "Mother! *Mother!*"

She turned. She stared into my eyes with a horror that I should be witness as she slipped upon the ice of the ledge and fell backward and downward out of my sight. I screamed. I could not stop screaming. (My God, am I screaming as I write this?)

He—my father—stood on the threshold of the room staring stupidly, his eyes turning from the empty window ledge to me.

5

Jean's shared quarters in Northampton were in the house of the most distinguished lady of the town, Miss Nancy Neil, in Bancroft Road on Paradise Hill, which was about two hundred yards from the quad on the highest ground in Northampton.

It was a very romantic house, Jean felt. For one thing Miss Neil always seemed to be in Italy with her lover, and also because Jenny Lind, "The Swedish Nightingale," had once lived two houses down the road.

Jean lived with two students, Alexandra Fowles and Ursula Baggot, and with Mrs. Ryan, housekeeper, and Mrs. Moore, demon gardener, until the young women were graduated two years later. Alex and Ursula were entering their junior year when Jean arrived to begin what the college had decided would be her sophomore year because her grasp and accomplishments were much in advance of the freshmen and yet she was too acutely young to be admitted as a junior classwoman.

Jean worked hard to try to achieve the physical and social development of the other girls at Bancroft House, but her years were still against her. She arrived armed with many exercises from Miss Hunt as well as teeth braces. Her posture was better than the others', otherwise progress was slow.

She arose each morning at 5:45 because she liked to study in the mornings. She also liked to study in the evenings and in rowboats in the sunshine during the spring and autumn months.

She declined irregular French verbs as she brushed her hair. Her bedroom/study at Neil House had a four-poster bed, straight-backed chairs, and bookshelves on each wall, fitted from floor to ceiling, forcing the bed out to the center of the room. An antique mahogany easel displayed a large painting of Paradise Hill before it was so named, by William McCarry (1717–1797), an ancestor of Miss Neil's, and a broad worktable on which books were neatly stacked at each corner. It was more like the room of a fifty-year-old scientist than that of a very young girl.

Alex, aka the Slut, and Ursula were several years older than Jean. Alex had the *look* of a thoroughbred. She wore clothes so well that women stared after her. Males assumed that she was a tycoon's daughter, and much of the money Alex borrowed from Jean was to lend to men. She was the belle of West Point, Harvard, Dartmouth, Yale, and Princeton, and she had scandalized her two housemates by bringing home a pudendum alive with crabs. "He was such a nice guy," she told Jean. "He was sloppy and he ate in bed, but he had a marvelous disposition."

"How do you rate lovers, Slut?" Jean asked her.

"How do you mean?"

"Well, do you use the Von Gebelmann Measurement Statistics which tend to state that length is strength or are you more unduly subjective than that, using the Arbeit Clock for elapsed time within the vagina?"

"No kidding, kid—are there really systems like that?"

"Did you ever take Comparative Religion 2?"

"No—do they have stuff like that? At *Smith?*"

"That's not the point. What grading system do you use on your lovers?"

"Kid! You're five ways a virgin! How can you even follow stuff like this?"

"Straight A's and four years in two."

"Oh—yeah. Right. Well, I grade them on their capacity, not how they make love. I mean, you could be climbed by some hot Italian guy who takes himself very seriously in the sack—one of those cats who knows all the moves—and I could rate him like 3 on a scale of 10 because love isn't mechanical, is it, kid? Love is love. It is *feeling*, not a sensation. If you have the feeling the sensation has to follow, doesn't it? I mean, this guy at Princeton who gave me these crabs had so much feeling that I just wept all the time he was transferring them to me. He put feeling first. He didn't know the first thing about how to *make* love, kid, he just felt love and he made you feel it."

"God, I hope it happens to me like that—when it happens—if it happens—but without the crabs."

"It will if you want it to."

"Every time?"

"No."

"Why not, Slutsie?"

"I am finding out something about myself. The more guys I sack the less feeling I have. That's no good."

"Why don't you stop?"

"*Stop?*"

"For a little while. Until the feeling comes back."

"Because I *need* men, kid. And I can make them need me. The sex is all right. I mean, it's enough fun, but—wow!—you can't beat that need."

Ursula Baggot loved Jean because when they met, just before Jean's first term at Smith started, Jean was still twelve years old. Ursula had three sisters at home in Hong Kong who were older than that and she had been homesick for them for two long years. The American aunt who had left them each enough money to be educated and maintained at Smith had not provided more than one round trip ticket out and back, so Ursula stayed on at Northampton, working through the summers. After Jean arrived she spent the summers at Rockrimmon, steadfastly refusing any money and paying for her keep by mowing lawns and pulling weeds during the hours Jean was in the huge library. Ursula was a pale young woman with the glistening black hair of her Oriental mother and a dazzling smile in a sweet face.

"What are you going to do after graduation, Urs?"

"I will be able to go home."

"But Hong Kong is so far away!"

Ursula grinned ruefully.

"You could bring your sisters here. Charles and I will help. They are all going to have to go to Smith anyway so they might as well all be at Rockrimmon."

Ursula patted her hand. "I love you because you are good, Jean. My sisters belong in Hong Kong and so do I. They will not be coming here at the same time. This is what college is about. It is a place for friends to part."

She thought Jean would become a beautiful woman and was worried about her not accepting that as a responsibility. She insisted that Jean must struggle with all her might to live up to the majesty of her intelligence and the gift of the beauty which was soon to be.

"But as opposed to *what?*" Jean asked.

"I mean, you don't become just another woman shrieking about the rights of women."

"Hey! You *know* how I feel about that."

"Yeah? Well, for what *you* want either men will have to change or it will only be something written into some law. No, ma'am! You've got to do great work and set great examples."

"Oh—*drat!*—there are about two billion men and more women than that. History screams that if there is ever going to be any equality it will have to be legislated, because men clearly can't be reeducated."

"Do *you* think men are our enemies?"

"Well—not *all* men. Charles Cantwell is certainly not an enemy."

"Do you know *any* men who are the enemies of women?"

"I know what I read!"

"There are no individual egos in this, Jean. There is only one vast human organism with a bottomless appetite. Men and women are already as organically equal as the heart is equal to the brain. If one fails, the other dies. Nothing can legislate the appetites of such a colossal single organism. Each tiny cell of it is called a human being. The only definition of the human comedy, for heaven's sake, is that each of these tiny cells believes she or he is sacrosanctly individual, surviving apart from the other tiny cells of the great single organism. It's a mockery but it does help to pass the timelessness."

"You can well believe that," Jean grinned. "You were a sophomore cell a whole year longer than I was."

"Then are you going to march in the demonstrations and beat old men over the head with umbrellas? Are you going to get yourself tattooed and wear trousers, and slap your thigh laughing whenever you fart? Will you shave every morning? Maybe even get yourself an obedient little wife, buy some kids from an orphanage, and roar out 'Where are the broads' at the annual sales convention? What do you want? To be the one who sweats the fear into the underwear or be the one who sends it out to a laundry? Can you break your heart and imagine that you are, at last, very old, and then be able to say that you wanted to be the equal of men or will you say that you are content and proud that men hoped and tried to be the equal of you?"

Jean gazed at her friend steadily and gravely. Her great pavonine eyes were as open and willing as her youth. "When I am very, very old," she said, "I hope I will be content and proud if I can have lived by one half of what my mother taught me."

Charles Cantwell received an honorary doctor of laws degree from Smith College on the day Jean was graduated summa cum laude. After the ceremonies, they strolled for a while across the college lawns, and Charles asked her what she thought she would be doing next.

"I've thought about that," Jean answered. "I want to do what my mother and you would want me to be doing."

"Your mother? You can't know what your mother would have wanted, can you?"

Jean had not discussed the diaries with Charles since she was given them. For one thing, Charles didn't seem to want to discuss them when Jean tried to bring up the subject, needing badly to talk to him about so many of Mama's startling, complex, and confusing—to her—points of view. Then, after such a long silence of working out for herself her acceptance of Mama's "new" positions, Jean had at last decided that it would keep Mama more alive for her if the diaries remained her own secret. She was convinced also that Mama wanted it that way.

"I think I have a feeling for Mama," Jean said. "I mean she *did* give me her diaries, and I *do* have her example."

"Example?"

"She was a good geologist."

"A geologist," he said. "Do you think you want to study geology?"

"I want to be a lawyer."

"Why? Because the family firm is there?"

"Not entirely. But that's part of it—you and the family firm—but I want to be a lawyer as a stepping-stone to politics."

"*Politics?*"

"I'm going to see that equality is enforced between men and women."

"All women equal with all men? And all men with all women?"

"Under the Constitution, Charles. Not by unwritten laws which govern individual marriages or—well—passions."

"That's one of the weaknesses of the law. It can't get a handle on passion."

"Not only the law is disjointed. There are so many more women than men, but men try to deny our equality when we, as the majority, could be denying them theirs."

"Then equality is the main thing? You don't see it—as your mother might have seen it, for example—as the inevitable consequence of the toppling of religious goddesses, or of the need for the total control of men so that they can't continue to control and oppress women? You don't think the denial of women's rights has been an eight-thousand-year-old conspiracy?"

She sat down abruptly on the grass, her hands trembling because she thought he had found the diaries. "Where did you get those ideas?" she asked shakily.

"Why?"

"They sound like something my mother might have said. They are like her. Like her diary."

"Maybe. But they're also some of the most banal ideas some women like to preach. And, in the context of confusing solutions, some of the silliest."

"Well, Charles, _I_ don't think they're silly."

"You'll find out."

"I don't want to talk about politics anymore. Tell me about Mama."

He nodded gravely.

"And I don't want to talk about Mama after today, Charles. I don't want to forget her but neither do I want to talk about her."

"What do you want me to tell you?" he asked gently.

"Everything."

"There isn't time for everything. I knew Joshua Henstell, of course. We were together at the firm. What I knew about your mother before she ran away to Europe with him was that she had been wildly in love with another man."

"How did you know that?"

"She told me."

"Why would she tell you a thing like that?"

"I suppose she decided she had to tell someone. Anyway, you have to know more about Joshua Henstell," he said.

She thought about the diaries in a flash, and all they had told her about _him_. But Charles couldn't be expected to understand all that. What Mama had had to say about Joshua Henstell must remain a secret. The truth about her father had to be kept secret.

"In Dr. Weiler's opinion Henstell was dying when he left New York to join your mother when they went to live in Geneva. He had been feeling poorly for years."

The diaries hadn't told about this. The diaries had had much worse things to say than this, she thought.

"Instead of looking for the truth from Weiler, he let himself be treated by an old classmate, a shaky general practitioner called Dr. Norman Lesion, after whom the luminously prestigious Lesion Institute is named."

"But Lesion is one of the great healers!" Jean exclaimed.

"He's the sound track for a Donald Duck movie. But he gave Josh the jargon to explain his bad health away—things like 'florid neurologic signs'—but Abe Weiler says Lesion never made the connection between the mental and the neuromuscular symptoms to get a diagnosis of endocrine disorders. Lesion handled Josh like he was any run-of-the-mill hypochondriac with depressions, anxiety, and tremors."

"No matter what, the Lesion Institute stands there today!"

"The Lesion Institute got itself named after him because his wife left it a fortune. Lesion's own gift really has been to take on perfectly sick patients and make them into corpses within the required three years— and his prognosis for Josh was to send him off for some head mapping. He told Josh he couldn't be better medically, that the neuromuscular weakness was just a response to psychic stress."

"Why are you going into such detail?" Jean asked. "I didn't ask you about my father. I asked you about my mother."

"Your mother's story is locked into Henstell's."

She sighed. "All right."

"Josh believed everything Lesion told him because he had been agonizing over your mother for two years. But she had hardly recognized that they were living in the same city. So Josh believed he was caught in psychological stress and he accepted the fact. It was easy for Lesion to send him from shrink to shrink to deal with his deepening disease. He finally went to Abe Weiler. Weiler is such a good doctor that he will never have an institute named after him. He ran Josh through pathological test after test at the New York Hospital, and he was deeply puzzled. Sure, he told himself, young Henstell was a psychological mess. But what was that today, after all? No worse than a bad cold, and as easily curable. He pored over the records which he had kept on Josh since Josh's birth, but he got no further with that than he did with the tests. In the second week at the hospital, he got Josh to recall that he had been given X-ray treatments for a football injury at prep school and Weiler began to run that down."

Jean *knew* how her father had died, and no one else except herself and Mama knew the truth. She loved Dr. Weiler, but he didn't know, he only thought he knew. She remembered the diaries; she listened to Mama's voice.

With a slowly grinding realization, and then with despair after she had read the shocking statement in her mother's diary, she had made herself understand what kind of a man her father really had been. Mama held nothing back.

Your father worked with Dulles in Switzerland during the war, but during the early forties the Secret Police assigned him to Iran. His work was desperately sinister and there was *nothing* romantic about it, even viewed through the eyes of a breathless young woman. He was charged with bringing down foreign governments, arranging assassinations, and betraying lives. Oh, yes! He did these things for "high" reasons, of course. But companies, and men, and governments always profited on his side of the bargain and he left hopelessness behind him on the other side. Joshua Henstell seemed to be without any feelings for people who had less than five million dollars.

These things are hard for me to write. He was your father. I loved him, God help me. But since these diaries are insisting that you live by the truth, then you must have the whole truth and never mind the cost to me.

But, for reasons which will shortly be made quite clear, and even if nothing else in these diaries is to remain a secret, this is a family secret—yours and mine, for we are the only family with the right to cherish and guard it together. I say to you that even Charles Cantwell must never know what I am about to tell you because even though by the time you read this I will be far beyond the recall of the law and its penalties, Charles is first a lawyer and therefore an officer of the court. Despite all such prattle from me, you will understand at once why *no one* but us can know what I must now tell you.

To begin again I shall repeat that I loved him even while I watched him being transformed into a corrupter and a murder broker for our Secret Police. My background would be called today Iranian, I suppose. I was raised by my mother in the pride of our Persian heritage. We still had family there, and as it happens—as these things always seem to happen—my family was on the side which opposed the goals of my husband. I can tell you this much, dearest. Two families had bred the stock of shahs and kings of kings, but the stock which your father's people put upon the Persian throne was not one of these, but of a gutter stock, the offscourings of an Iranian army sergeant. *My* family fought your father for our *historic* and *traditional* rights to the Persian throne.

I was told what were your father's political and dynastic intentions in Persia by our people, so, in my capacity as an oil geologist, I made the excuse to follow your father to Iran.

Joshua Henstell coolly arranged the murder of the three male members of my family who could have risen to be seated upon the throne of Persia for what the SP looked upon as straightforward, practical political reasons. It was my duty to pay them back an eye for an eye and a tooth for a tooth. I went to him at the bar of the SP hotel in the capital and he was overjoyed to see me. He wanted to take me upstairs where we could make love, but I told him that I had news so important that it would drive even the thought of *that* from him. I told him that I had found an ocean of oil under the ground, far to the east of Iran, and that if we moved properly during such a time of political turmoil, we could possess this. Well! He came *alive* with greed. No more talk of love. He demanded to be taken to the area and shown what I had found. We left aboard a small two engine SP plane within the hour, myself at the controls. I guided him down to the most remote part of the eastern desert and I killed him there. I buried him in the soil of Persia, releasing him from his life of treachery and destruction. It changed nothing. The SP replaced him, the juggernaut rolled on, and their puppet was placed on the throne anyway.

Now that I have told you this I can almost hear you crying out for vengeance for the murder of your father by your mother. But after you think about all of it, I know you are going to see that the only true vengeance must be taken upon the stupid men who seduced your father into becoming a stupid criminal. It is the *men of power* who are the enemies—not your exploited and discarded father.

They sat on the broad lawn of the campus at Smith, each wearing cap and gown.

Charles was telling the resistant Jean what Dr. Weiler had told him: "We had to get a better case history. A long time ago it was fashionable to irradiate benign thyroid nodules until they found out that the X-rays were changing an adenoma into a carcinoma. Those early neck X-rays were the keys."

"Weiler discovered that Josh could bend his thumb back to its wrist! So he ordered a serum calcium test, an EKG, and a slit lamp. The serum calcium elevated. The EKG showed a shortening of the Q-T interval. The slit lamp revealed opaque material in vertical lines both parallel and vertical to the limbus. Josh went to surgery. After that he seemed to get better, but Weiler knew the condition had advanced to the lungs and the liver.

"So he congratulated Josh on winning the battle, and Josh left for Geneva to join your mother. He calculated that Josh had about two years to live. It worked out to be three."

"Charles, *why* did Mama leave a man you say she was wildly in love with to marry my father?"

"I wish I knew, Jean. I never understood that part at all," he said.

6

At her graduation from Smith, Jean was too young for admission to law school, so she persuaded Charles Cantwell to let her work for a degree in international law at the University of Geneva, in Switzerland. He was reluctant to let her go but he couldn't think of a better plan so he saw her settled in Geneva where, for the first time in her life, she was alone. She was alone in a new country and alone with the second half of her mother's diaries, which had been given to her after graduation. She read them less omnivorously, but with consuming curiosity, because she was alone to explore a beautiful city, so new to her.

She lived in a four-room apartment on the cathedral hill of Geneva which overlooked the lake from one side and gazed up at Mont Salève from the other. She could walk to classes, auctions, down the hill to movies or cafés, or to anywhere else in the perfect city. She went home to Rockrimmon each Christmas, but stayed happily on in Geneva for all the rest of the year, touring Europe in the summer holidays with Charles.

She took the bus to Cologny only once to see the house her mother had lived in. The proprietor of the grocery directly across the street on the Route de Capite remembered Mme. Henstell. "She was so beautiful," he said. "I have never stood directly before such a beautiful woman." There was no need to go back again.

She thought Geneva was the most romantic city in the world. It was where Lenin had plotted the Russian revolution, where Mussolini had cadged drinks and slept on park benches. It had a Hell Street, a Blonde Lane, and the telephone directory listed twenty-one Hugs and nine Kisses. Uniforms other than Swiss or the Salvation Army were barred by law, including priests' and nuns' habits. The city maintained a one-man submarine to destroy the weeds which grew on the bottom of its lake and one 124-pound stripteaser for each 1437 inhabitants. Where else, she thought, did butchers display great bouquets of fresh flowers in their windows to mourn the passing of their stock in trade? *Frankenstein* was written here. Casanova had lived here. Marvelous! And the food was so delicious! Augustin de Candolle had developed his theory of the evolution of plants in Geneva, which had inspired Darwin to apply the theory to animals. On a quay in Geneva the empress of Austria, mother of Rudolf of Mayerling, had been stabbed to death by an anarchist. Even more romantically, it was here that Jean gave away her virginity.

In the autumn of 1958, when Jean was twenty, she was eating brasatino and taglierini at Roberto's in the rue Madeleine, when a beautiful, small-boned young man with skin the color of scotch and soda sat down in the seat facing her. It was a crowded restaurant. She was a student, a rich student, who much enjoyed Roberto's, the greatest Italian restaurant between San Francisco and Bologna. After smiling blankly at the young man to assure him of her permission to share the table, she paid him no attention but went on eating and reading a paperback copy of *Finnley Wren*. She heard him order a double prosciutto. She admired him for that because the silver platter would take up all of his side of the table. Then he went to work on a carafe of Valpolicella. They remained in repose until the ham was served and she was just finishing off the brasatino. He said, in French, "May I speak?"

She nodded.

"I have been following you for two days and I don't think I can bear it any longer unless I speak to you."

"Two days!" She answered in French.

"You won't ask me to leave?"

"Are you a student?" she asked, fluttering her eyelids.

"I am at Le Rosay. But I have not been back since the day I saw you reading at the Café du Commerce."

"What is your name?"

He paused delicately. "It is a complicated name."

"Are you—Indonesian?"

"I am Prince Chaiyaphum of Thailand."

"Oh!"

"How old are you?"

"Well"—she decided that eighteen would seem very young to him—"I am nineteen."

"I am nineteen."

"You don't look nineteen."

"Since I have been in Europe, I can see that even my father would not look nineteen here. You are the most interesting girl I have ever seen."

"I *am*?"

"I feel very close to you."

"Isn't that wonderful ham? Did you know that they go personally all the way to Parma to buy that ham, about seventy enormous hams at a time?"

"May we spend the afternoon together?"

She thought of Mama's words: *You must control the men in your life because if you do not they will control and oppress you.*

"I want you to go back to Le Rosay right after lunch because you must be in trouble enough as it is." She tried the sentence on because it wasn't in any way how she felt. His homage excited her. His eyes confirmed everything he had said to her, and Geneva was *proving* it was a romantic place, but she knew that if she were going to design her life so that she was always in control she had to begin that way from the start, with the first man she had known who wanted her. Still it was vital that she try to see his point of view. Seeing the other's point of view was one of Mama's cardinal rules of control.

"It is impossible for me to be in trouble," he said. "I am Prince Chaiyaphum."

She held up her hand, looked directly into his eyes, and said shakily, "If you will return to Le Rosay as soon as we finish lunch, I will go with you to the Gare de Cornavin and I will agree to meet you for lunch on Saturday."

"The Gare de Cornavin?"

"The railway station."

"A limousine takes me to Le Rosay."

"Very well then. Finish your lunch, take your car, and go."

"You are angry? If you are angry I will take the train."

"No, no, *no!* All I want is that you get back to school as quickly as possible."

"I am not nineteen. I am only seventeen," he said.

"You look eighteen—truly."

"Where will we lunch on Saturday?"

"I think we should lunch at the Parc des Eaux-Vives."

"Is it grand?"

"Oh, yes!"

"Are you a shopgirl? No, of course not. I followed you. Do you work at the university?"

"I work there all right." She giggled. "I am a student."

"Then we must have lunch at some place which is more intimate."

"Why?"

"I feel very intimate towards you."

"You sound very nice when you speak like that."

"Where is it more intimate?"

"But—I don't know."

"We must have a place which has rooms upstairs."

"*Rooms?*"

"Lightning could strike both of us at once. That has happened. I have read of that again and again." He shrugged sadly. "It probably won't happen, but we should be ready."

"But—"

"I will find the place. May my car come to fetch you at one o'clock next Saturday at wherever you live?"

"Does it have a royal crest?"

"No. My people rent the car."

"Does it have a Thai driver?"

"Oh, no! You wouldn't want that. It has a safe English driver who is also the bodyguard."

She gave him her address in the rue Théodore de Bèze. They each had zabaglione and espresso, paid separate checks, then he kissed her hand and left.

She was ready when the bell rang on Saturday at one minute to one. She had dressed carefully in tones which made the most of her natural colors. She had been thinking too much about what she might permit to happen that day and had more than half-convinced herself that she *must* attain the experience of sex so that she could judge proportionately the other things that were massing into her life. The prince was quite beautiful and also certainly pleasantly clean. She aroused him, she knew that. He was a gentleman about everything, and what could be more propitious than that for the total spiritual protection of the first affair of one's life—indeed perhaps the last! She had to see this as an opportunity, as if she were really trying to live up to her mother's words and trying to control men so that she could control events.

She came down the stairs full of anticipation when her heart jumped at the sight of the man who was holding the main door open for her. He was a tall, dark-eyed gypsyesque-looking man. Not like any gypsy she had ever seen, but like Heathcliff or the gypsies cast in operas. He was as long and as thin as a coach whip, and as she came down the stairs ever more slowly, as she stared down at him and he up at her, she saw an erection rising on him.

"Mademoiselle Henstell?" he asked. He had a very cultivated voice, but he was neither Swiss nor French, she knew. The prince had said his driver was not a Thai so she answered in English. "Yes. Are you from Prince Chaiyaphum?"

"Yes, milady," he said and grinned.

She swept past him, then he darted past her to open the door of the enormous limousine. Before she got in she said. "Where are we going?"

"The Hôtel du Cerf in Hermance, milady."

"One moment, please, I must tell the concierge." She swanned back into the building, closing the door between them. She did not seek out the concierge but stood calmly recomposing herself. She summoned up Mama and control. She needed control more than she had ever needed it, in fact perhaps for the first time. The man stank with sexuality; he was very beautiful. She decided several things in a very short time. First, she would get into bed with Chaiyaphum to set her virginity aside and not be a child when she decided to take this man who drove the car. Next, she would carefully begin to control him so that each succeeding development would be installed correctly and when the time came to terminate, she would be the terminator. She went outside. As soon as her hand touched the main door it opened.

"Will the prince be waiting at Hermance?" she asked.

"Yes, milady."

"Then I shall ride in the front seat with you so that we may chat. You may call me Miss Henstell."

"Thank you, Miss Henstell."

The limousine drove out along the south side of the lake toward Hermance, fourteen miles away at the French frontier. Jean asked many questions which the driver answered. His name was Thane Cawdor. He was English, age twenty-five, an actor who was temporarily at liberty because he had wanted to tour Europe, working his way country by country, before he went to the United States. No, he would not go directly to the United States. In a few months he would return to London to make a name for himself in the theater so that he would be *invited* to appear in the United States. He would do one full theatrical season in New York, then allow himself to be moved on to the film business in California.

"Have you planned beyond California?" she asked sweetly.

"Yes. I shall take the money which I shall amass in California and move to some place in Dorset where I shall establish a facility which will restore classical motor cars and manufacture their replicas. I am a very fine actor but acting is a layabout's business. My only interest is in saving and driving and rebuilding motor cars—beautiful, enormous, almost unattainable motor cars from times which will never come again."

She felt her control over him slipping but she did not know what to do about it. "Ah—*that* is why you are the perfect servant," she said, remembering his vanished erection. "You were *playing* the perfect servant."

"No, milady, I was not. I do things well. That is an article of faith with me. That is why I will be able to live as I have just outlined to you, ending my time somewhere in Dorset among exquisitely revived motor cars which I will by then, and at last, be able to buy and restore to their places. Has milady ever been to the Hôtel du Cerf?"

"She has not so been, Cawdor," Jean mocked.

"Their *omble* is first rate. They do a nice rabbit in mustard sauce."

"Where will you be while we eat that?"

"I shall have my lunch at Aniérès where a man, using a blender and some beer, makes the best omelet I have ever had."

"I love omelets," Jean said.

"Here is Hermance," Cawdor said. "That is the Hôtel du Cerf."

The prince had arranged that luncheon be served in a suite from which one could see the lake if one had the time. He had caused a magnum of Pommery '49 to be chilled. There was caviar and small jugs of potato vodka from Estonia if Jean would prefer that. He was quite amazingly changed, as though he had been memorizing books on the techniques of courtship and seduction, and she found it overwhelmingly pleasant. As he plied her with champagne, caviar, and courtliness she was able to contrast him with the chauffeur and could not remember two men who were more different.

"Their *omble* is first-rate here," the prince said, "although I must tell you that they also do a nice rabbit in mustard sauce." She wondered whether he had been taking instructions from Cawdor or Cawdor from him. Imagining she saw Cawdor's movements, she wondered whether the chauffeur had drilled him or aped him.

"Let us have another glass of wine and more caviar," she said. "We wouldn't want to get drunk and lose control though, would we, Chai?"

"Did you call me Chai? How very good of you. My friends call me Chai at school."

Cawdor had told her that. "This is what I have been thinking, Chai," she said, feeling a supreme moment of control. "We are both quite young and although I speak only for myself, we must both be inexperienced. I think—if we are to be honest with each other—that it could be that we are both interested in finding out about sex. Is that true, Chai?"

"Oh, yes, indeed it is true!" he squeaked, and his voice emerged as if three mice were swinging on his vocal cords, ringing the changes.

"I suppose men are different from women in that they cannot help rushing into sex, but for the woman—well, the fact is, Chai, courtship was invented not only so that people could grow to know each other better, but to ensure that the *most* and the *best* of this unborn sexuality be sharpened by the equity." She wasn't sure she understood what she had said any more than he seemed able to.

"I am not sure I understand."

"I am saying that I *do* agree with you—in the experience, or the experiment you have in mind—but I say we must give it more time, Chai, so that we may make it better when it happens."

"I have no ready frame of reference for this," he said. "But your wishes must command me. If we are agreed to achieve that which we both wish fervently to achieve, and if it is altogether better for it that we delay this for just a little while longer, then I am of one mind with you."

She felt a stab of keenest disappointment in him. She had not expected such a response. She had assumed instinctively that a certain amount of negotiation would lead in a gradually passionate path toward the completion—she had not expected him to *agree* with her. But on the other hand she had to admire him for such a show of understanding and of courtesy even if she didn't know what to do to change its course back to the launching of their passions.

They both decided on the *omble*, and the prince himself opened the chilled bottle of Le Montrachet '47 which he had brought from school. They chatted formally about safe topics and the prince made several witty jokes, but behind her gaiety, behind her decorum, Jean realized overwhelmingly that she had fallen in love with the prince's chauffeur.

7

She was besotted with Thane Cawdor. She waited during six days of silence, then, at a quarter to seven on a gloomy Thursday night, Chaiyaphum appeared at her door. She was so enraged that it was the prince and not Cawdor that she wanted to throw him down the stairs, but her mother's teaching prevailed and she kept control.

"I admire you more than any other woman," Chaiyaphum said, handing her such a bouquet of flowers as would have made any floral tribute rushed down to the stage at the end of a Ziegfeld musical appear as though plucked from a slum windowbox.

"As I admire *you*, Chai," she made herself reply, because she did admire everything about him including his kindness and his honesty.

"Just as we were growing to the moment when we might have ignited each other's souls with passion," he told her, "I have been called back to Bangkok for political reasons."

"Bangkok?" She had forgotten he was a Thai. "You are leaving Geneva?"

"Yes."

"But what will happen to"—she almost said Cawdor's name, but the control her mother had helped build into her kept that back—"to our love affair?"

"It will live on forever inside of me."

Alarmed, she detected an erection beginning to fill his narrow trousers.

"Let us pray," she said, falling to her knees. "Let us pray that we will live on in each other's memories." That did it. The swelling behind the trouser wall diminished.

"I am not a Christian," he said, "and it would be inappropriate to pray to two different gods. I came to say goodbye. The plane will leave in one hour, five minutes."

"You must hurry!"

"Before I go, I want you to have this friendship ring," he said, passing her a small box. "As you look into it, the stone will mirror your memory of a glorious day beside the lake; Au 'voir—ah—"

"Jean."

"Jean."

"Au revoir, Chai." They moved to each other, stood closely, held each other in their arms and kissed. He put on his hat, opened the door, and left.

The Geneva airport was eight minutes from the center of the city, so it was not until twenty-five minutes later that Thane Cawdor was at her door.

"Shall we have dinner?"

"*Dinner?*"

"I have the car until the garage opens tomorrow morning. We could go to Carouge or all the way out to Aubonne if you want to."

"I—I'm not hungry."

"What's your first name?" he asked softly, moving close to her.

"The prince didn't know, either."

"He told me you never said. And there was no reason for you to tell me."

"There's no reason to tell you right now, either," she said hotly. "For heaven's sake, do something! Rip my clothes off! Fling me on the bed! *Do* it!" She had the shaking feeling that she had lost control, but there was no time to analyze.

They remained besotted for an entire year. They held calid carnal celebrations in such places as telephone booths, garages, on grass, in hammocks, on billiard tables and countertops. He showed her every move that he thought had ever been developed and which he had accumulated with the greed of a randy chipmunk guarding his nuts in (so far) six countries of the world. When he knew he had taught her everything and then moved in to polish all of that, her superior intellect and appetites invented fourteen more applications and conjunctions of their passions and stamina.

Following the tiny tap upon her instantly shatterable hymen came continuous inundating orgasm upon orgasm in celebration of youth compounding itself, ultimately to be reduced to one such cold word as love: as when the poets apply it to Pelleas, age twenty, and to Musaeus' Leander, eighteen, to the hot-eyed Juliet, thirteen, and to Longus' Chloe, age fifteen. It was a *tremendous* year for youth in the rue Théodore de Bèze. It was even more of a tremendous year for mooning, sighing, glassily-staring romantic love.

They swore to belong to each other forever and never to leave or to lose each other. They fought heartbreakingly over less than nothing, then wept copiously with gratitude and joy when they made up, to swear eternal understanding again. It was the most glorious year of their lives. Then it was over as suddenly as it had started.

Thane got a playscript in the mail which he read aloud to her, making her sob with the power of his voice and his art. He accepted the part. He got a telegram. He had to go to London. He wanted very much to say goodbye but she was in class when he had to leave so he slipped a note under her door and barely made the plane.

When she was twenty-one, Jean moved from Geneva to the Yale Law School. She returned to the United States a reasonably intact young woman who had acquired two more languages, Russian and Japanese, and a degree cum laude in international law. She was a lovely girl with hair as yellow as fine Meursault, clear rose-dusted olive skin and sea blue eyes. She had long, beautiful legs whose thighs could have been models for Lysippus, and she lived convinced that she controlled all of herself and both the men who had ever touched her.

At Yale she was editor of the Law Review and was elected president of the Law Society. She earned a rarely pursued doctorate of juridical science, so it was not entirely only a matter of ownership or nepotism that she was asked to join Henstell, Masters & Cantwell. Two years later she was an established Wall Street lawyer, a specialist in international cartels/conglomerates and their international taxation problems.

8

Because the partners thought she was too young and beautiful to take too readily apparent a place in her family's law firm, Jean was assigned to do the backup thinking for many of the other lawyers—and there were 274 people in the firm. Charles Cantwell managed to watch her work without hovering over her. She was, as when Thane Cawdor's mistress, a prodigy of both reach and accomplishment. Within twenty months, in several important ways, the firm revolved around her. She knew more about more kinds of law than the specialists, but her mind was so keen and her memory so orderly that she could take on arguments both in and out of court. Gradually she bearded the lions, took on the heavy clients when moments of difficulty or danger appeared, and took their breaths and their considerable fees away. She grew as a consultant lawyer for the principal partners. A prodigy, she was instantly recognizable as a legal Mozart. Charles Cantwell was so proud of her collection of the scalps of client, adversary, and opposing lawyer hanging in the longhouse from her time in the firm, that he told her he estimated that in five years' time she would not only be raised to a senior partnership in the firm but would have her name repeated in its title.

They were dining in an Italian restaurant in midtown Manhattan when he told her this. She leaned over and kissed him tenderly when he had said it.

"Charles," she said, "in five years I'm going to be in politics. I'm just getting my feet wet now."

"*Politics*? *Politics*? Do you have any *idea* of the things you don't know about in this world? *Where* in politics, in God's name? They're nothing but sharks and self-seekers! They'd have you for breakfast! And what the hell do you *need* a sordid business such as politics for?"

"Easy. Now, take it easy, Charles. You're asking me questions and I must try to answer them."

"You're goddamn right you'd better answer them."

"Remember commencement day at Smith? I told you about this then."

"You were a child! I—I took it as I would have taken a little boy telling me he wanted to grow up to be a bullfighter."

"Charles, did you ever think about the fact that men have considerably more rights than women?"

"Jean, for heaven's sake, you are an exceptional lawyer with a simply tremendous future in one of the most important law firms in this country!"

"Help me to explain, Charles. Answer the simple question of whether you think that men have considerably more rights than women."

"What the hell does that have to do with politics?"

"Oh, Charles—play the game!"

"All right. No. I do not think men have more rights than women."

"Can you defend that position?"

"Men pay more for being born men. They die sooner, for one thing. They're forced to live under the tyranny of an organized, perpetual money hunt. By God, they have to *work*."

"And the women? Tell me about the women, Charles."

"Jean, we can't be talking about the occasional women who pretend to compete with men for jobs and murderous glory. I think we're talking about most of the women in this world—the ones who raise the children, make the homes, and hold the families together. And that is sacred work. Sacred work."

"What about them?"

"Who?"

"These sacred workers."

"Well! They damned well aren't squaws anymore, are they? At least they aren't in this country. They don't have to ruin their beautiful teeth chewing hides to make soft leather for their men, do they? You're damned right they don't! They cool it in a soft world of laborsaving gadgets, and as the media show, they use the leisure to let their children become malcontents or worse. They are the spenders in our society, the bottomless-pit consumers, and they spend the money their men bring home from those idealized concentration camps called their jobs."

"What about freedom?"

"What do you mean?"

"I mean women are people and that's *all* it's all about. Time! Ha! Laborsaving devices! You should be ashamed of yourself. To have this great gift of illusory time which you talk about, under the terms of which it is conferred—if it is there to be found at all—is to accept being a child forever, Charles, a slave. Don't you understand what everyone else with intelligence understands by now? Women are people. That's all. Anyone or any sex that doesn't control his or her own life is a slave and a thing. How can it possibly matter to a human being who also happens to be a woman that if some man—all right, her dearly beloved—gives her a washing machine and all that alleged time you were snorting about if she has to live where, how, why, and when the man tells her? She has nothing to do with deciding that she must automatically be cast into the lifetime job of washing machine, vacuum cleaner, microwave oven, walk-in freezer operator. And anyone who doesn't have a part in deciding how she is going to create her life is some kind of a nonhuman. Well, they keep telling us that the culture has created the history of man, so I'm going into politics so I can build a megaphone big enough to tell all of them that the culture has created a history of *women* and man."

"Jean, listen to me. I am a specialist in banking law. As you know. So I can tell you that politics is a rough and brutal and dirty business. It's no place for you."

"Practicing law has hardly left us gently reefeened and lily-white. Darling, don't fight me. This is no snap decision. I've been thinking about it for half of my life. Help me. You *can* help me. You know all the movers and shakers and I have to have a few dozen favors you've scattered out there which are waiting to be returned."

"I'll help you because I can't stop you," he said grimly. "But don't expect me to agree that you're doing the right thing."

"I won't." She smiled. "Not tonight. Tomorrow will be time enough to agree with me."

A grin broke across his face "By God, you *really* look like butter wouldn't melt in your mouth."

"I never really understood that expression. Wouldn't one have to be absolutely *frigid* for butter not to melt in one's mouth?"

"Oh, horsefeathers! All right. How have you figured it out? How are you going to get into politics?"

She beamed at him. "Well," she said, "I've been thinking about a machine to create cash for the people who can do the most to advance me in politics. To me, that seems the best way to get started."

"What people?"

She smiled. "Politicians. I've already started, Charles. I've hired the people I'll need. I've rented seven thousand feet of floor space on East 40th Street and a pretty good-sized warehouse in New Jersey. I've leased the best computer for the job. It's cost me about two-eighty so far, but it's going to be the best investment I ever made."

"What about practicing law?"

"The computer runs everything and nothing will suffer downtown."

"But—what *is* it?"

"I hired Joseph Fater."

"I don't know him."

"He's the demographer. You *do* know Tom Buckley?"

"The Nixon campaign?"

"That's the one. I hired him, too."

"Why?"

"We've developed a system for locating potentially favorable blocs of voters and a way to raise big campaign money painlessly."

"How?"

"The voter locating combines attitudinal polling, computer technology, and a rather sophisticated use of census data. Anyway, you'll just have to believe that it costs a lot less than television campaigning. I'm going to call it Voters' Research and Development."

"How do you get the money?"

"The computer needs four operators and a supervisor," Jean said, grinning wickedly at Charles' intensity. "That's seven with Fater and Tom Buckley. I hired two behavioral psychologists to formulate the questions. There will be about fifteen boiler room people to start, working the phones in the warehouse in New Jersey. Then I have two solid young lawyers who are hipped on political processes and three aggressive PR people. The rest handle the office. Seventeen altogether in New York and about nineteen in New Jersey."

"What do they *do?*"

"They raise money. I bought 2000 reels of magnetic tapes which hold the names and incomes of about twenty-one million people and organizations—unions, clubs, trade associations, you know—who at one time or another have contributed to political action whether from the left, right, or center."

"Twenty-one *million!*"

"Oh, that's nothing for *this* computer. Before the next presidential elections we're going to raise more than fifteen million dollars from those tapes," Jean said happily.

"Hell! The next presidential election is years away. Who are you going to favor—or are you sane enough not to answer that?"

"We don't have to *favor* any candidate, Charles. My PR people will be there to keep telling the candidates that I'll be waiting with a lot of money for them. They'll come after me. Then I'll tell them what *I* want. Candidates need money. They all need that easy money."

"That sounds just a little corrupt, doesn't it?"

"Corrupt? Charles, it's normal procedure for American politics." Jean showed that she was offended that he could think otherwise because it made him seem naive. "It's what *every* candidate for every office from the presidency down to dogcatcher made into our political culture. Corrupt! It's the way the whole country prefers that things be done. They *want* a system in which every candidate suborns himself *before* he is elected. It costs one tremendous gang of private money to get elected to *anything* in this country—and I'm running for the big stuff."

9

Jean met Ames Spano on a deserted beach of the Seychelles Islands. The meeting was either inevitable considering the distances they had traveled separately to get there, or, considering the endless expanse of that deserted beach, unavoidable. When they each saw the other for the first time it was across more than a half mile of tropical sand which formed a velvet processional carpet, held in place by a pavonine sea on one side and tall stands of palm trees on the other.

Ames Spano had the sun in his eyes. He could not have been able to see more than a shimmer of what was approaching him. Jean saw a tall, godlike (as Apollo was godlike), beautifully formed man in the far distance, whose silver hair had been transformed into a crown by the sea and the wind. They stared at each other from far off, from where it was still safe to stare and conjecture, and kept advancing into each other's lives slowly, moving across the wet-paved sand, feeling the heat of the sun and their imaginations.

He was a radiant figure—from far off and then from closer and closer. She wished for an instant that this had been the presence of her fate approaching in a glorious form, deeply bronzed, his strong body contrasting ridges, lines, and plates of muscle and bone—her fate journeying across the time allotted to her, to dispose of the rest of her life.

When his older eyes, taking the sun, could see what she was, he felt many things he could not admit having felt so precipitously before. He felt lust. A startled admiration of her beauty followed. He knew he was looking at perfect youth and that he was permitted to lust because God had arrayed the world with youth as the decoy reward for he who desired desiring.

As they came up to each other he was going to bow and say good morning. She intended to wave and utter something banal such as, "Getting pretty crowded, isn't it?" Instead when they reached each other it seemed obvious to both that he was all the males of the species and she was all the females in the world. Each held out both hands, they allowed their fingertips to touch. Each studied the other's clear eyes gravely. They sat down on the sand together. He said, "Another lovely day."

She smiled at him.

He said, "I've never seen a bathing costume like that before."

She was filling a *tanga,* a string bikini of solid parrot red against golden tan skin.

"Costume?" she asked. "Are you English?"

"I used to be."

"What are you now?"

"The documents say I'm an American, but I feel English, American, and everything else that people are."

"Even black?"

"Oh, yes. If the blacks in my neighborhood in New York had the money to spare, they'd be right here."

"I'm from New York. Shall we introduce ourselves? I'm Jean Henstell."

"I am Ames Spano."

"I think that's about enough for the first day, don't you?"

"Enough of what?"

"Vital statistics?"

"I agree to a point. Are you married?"

"The woman is supposed to ask that."

"Why?" He was surprised to know that.

"In all literature they do."

"Oh, that."

"No. I am not married."

"Neither am I. Were you ever married?"

"No."

"I was married for six years twenty-eight years ago," he said. "Do you read poetry in different languages?"

"Some of them."

"Spanish is the language I like."

"It's a masculine language—in the way French is feminine."

"The people who need the most who live near me speak Spanish. Not that I see much of them."

"Why not?"

"Oh, circumstances."

"Are you a psychiatrist?"

"No. Heavens, no."

"I'm a lawyer."

"A law student?"

"Yes. But I practice law."

"Lawyers are strange people. Do you find that?"

"As a group, yes. Not as crazy as surgeons, but tilted. A surgeon wants to separate bone from muscle, organs from cavities, but lawyers want to separate money from money."

"Yes," he agreed, "that is how I found them. Someone else must do the living before they can practice their art."

"This society wouldn't last long without us."

"I suppose not. But I never thought I would be at peace talking to one. And, even if it were conceivable to get that far, I could never have imagined lying half naked beside a nearly naked lawyer in a string bikini beside the Indian Ocean."

"What do *you* do then?" she said, irritated.

"I am a clergyman."

"For Christ's sake!"

"Oh, definitely."

"In *Har*lem?"

"No," he said sadly. "I am pastor of the St. Grace of Wherry church."

"The Felsenburshe church on Riverside Drive?"

"Yes."

"How did you get *that?*" she marveled.

"My late wife was a Felsenburshe."

"Oh."

"Funny, isn't it? I have a vocation. I am *called* into service. I feel that powerfully. Not called, that is, by a government or a bank, but by my God. I accept that with peace. I had a church among the Zuni as a medical missionary in New Mexico. They need anyone's help. They are alcoholic or venereal or tubercular and—I don't need to add—very poor. They needed someone like me to take their side. I had six years with them. I should still be there but I met Carla—my wife—who was quite willing to live among the Zuni. But her family felt reluctantly that her health wasn't up to that kind of work. So when the pastor of St. Grace's died it fell to me as Carla's husband to become the pastor of the most fashionable church in the United States."

"Are you unhappy?"

"No, no! I don't recognize that condition. It is something to be tucked inside popular songs. Life is too dimensional for people to settle for being happy or unhappy. I merely lack enough peace, that's about the size of it."

Jean had never thought of anyone choosing to be good. It was a difficult concept for her to adjust to. She had been raised in a society which manufactured entertainments to be the total morality of their audiences, delivering visions of people who were consciously bad. She felt she could understand evil. Her mother's diaries had been imploded by her father's evil. For Ames Spano to seek out good deeds and as unflawed a life as might be their consequence nearly embarrassed Jean.

For some time she tasted his character with skepticism. He made love to her when they returned to New York, about two months after they met. Not only was he an inept lover at first (which changed her point of view since his ineptitude made him more human and less professionally saintly), but he brought to the act of love a commitment which until then had been alien to her. It was the commitment which proceeded out of his determination to approach making love to her as he approached all of the other things in his life—with devotion and mission, with open-eyed calm gentleness and without pretense. But he was not a passive man. He led her running deeper and deeper into sex, headlong as it were.

"How good that you are a young, healthy creature," he said as she lay in his arms. "All glands function for you as companions. You aren't stained by repression because you are an unashamedly sexual woman. I take no credit. It has been a long abstinence for me."

"Do you mean," she asked with horror, "that you have had no sex since your wife died?"

He roared with laughter. "No, no! Not at all, my blessed nymph. I have had sex whenever it seemed to be either the necessary or the delicious thing to do."

"How? Where? The organist? The choir ladies?"

"We have an all-boys' choir."

"You didn't!"

"No. I'm too tall, really. But a deaconess once slid her hand under the belt of my trousers without warning, to seize my member. We were standing eye-to-eye in a manner of speaking, in the vestry. She was defiant. I was curious. I remember telling myself that she was God's creature with all the attendant needs as I thought also about the valve at the base of my penis which is deaf, dumb, and blind but which, under requisite stimulus will open itself to flood the penis chamber, swelling it out of proportion. I asked her a straight-out question. 'Do you feel love for me, Mrs. Thompson, or is it that you would like—allow me to say it the once, Mrs. Thompson—to fuck a clergyman?' She withdrew her hand. The valve closed itself. We are still friends."

Jean sat upright in bed, her eyes popping, then she began to laugh unselfconsciously for the first time since they met. When she quieted down and rested back in his arms again she said, "Why didn't you ask me that?"

"Because you love me," he answered.

He was a man who was a supplicant for material things. He absorbed them all greedily, as they came and kept coming from her, then demanding more. They were married two months later. When they had been married for six months or so she began to regret, resent, then to hate the stark fact that long, long before, he had decided he could marry only rich women. At the beginning of their second year of marriage this corrosion was burning her too painfully to be ignored so she turned it into a confrontation. She told him that he was a fortune hunter, that his vocation was to possess everything his wives' wealth could buy.

He considered that carefully. "You are half right at least," he said. "That is, I am and have always been a fortune hunter; bankers don't need to be, nor, I suggest, lawyers. But clergymen are the people they meant when they wrote so cruelly 'as poor as church mice.' My father was a dedicated pastor in Semley, which is a hidden village on the Dorset-Wiltshire frontier. My mother was—if possible—even more sweetly devout and admirable than he. But we were so *poor*. Dear God, when I think of what we ate and what we wore; of how they worked and what they got for it! The fact is I fell short of accepting their own estimation of the fulfillment of their lives. They would tell me we were more fortunate than other people because it had been given to us to be allowed to serve. I thought about that all through my youth, praying that our blessed condition be changed only slightly so that my mother need not die of malnutrition and my father not be blown away on the first autumn wind. I had their faith. I *knew* they were right. I wanted to serve as they had served but I did not want to die early and without dignity. In those days, you see, my darling, the people who lived well *believed* that the saintly pleaded to be undernourished and demanded to be protected from comfort."

"Ames, I am *deeply* sorry I put you through this."

He ignored that. "The way I saw it, Jean, was that a clergyman *must* have a wife. But I could also reason just as purely that he did not have to have a poor wife. I began thinking like that when I was eight years old. I worked and I prayed and I thought and I prayed to burn that message into my consciousness. By the time I was ordained and I sought my mission in New Mexico it was with the self-knowledge that since it was my choice to serve the Zuni, who were poorer even than I, then I must be twice richer. As it all happened, I believe it would have been an impossibility for me to fall in love and to marry a woman who did not bring to our marriage the things which I could not bring to it—freedom from worry and indignity. So, if one must have money to cushion that sort of life which I prefer, then it had to be a lot of money to balance the pain and hardship. I thank God that I met Carla when I was a very young man. I thank God that I have you." He shrugged.

Jean was weeping, cleansing herself of the months of trouble she had stored away. She clung to him. He held her closely while he spoke to her. "I loved her insanely—as I love you. Deeper than deeply—totally as love is meant to be felt—as we love, my dearest woman. But you must see that I could not have loved her, nor could I have loved you, if either or both of you had been as poor as my mother."

10

Two days before her wedding to Ames Spano, while she was concentrating deeply on the installation of legal safeguards into an international industrial agreement, at a time when her outer office well knew she was not to be disturbed, Jean's secretary burst into her room saying "Miss Henstell! Thane *Caw*dor is on the line and he says he *has* to speak to you."

"Thane Cawdor?"

"Thane *Caw*dor! The movie star? *Racing Stud!* You saw *Racing Stud,* Miss Henstell?"

She stared coldly at her otherwise sensible secretary because only the information had penetrated, the emotional realization of what the woman had told her hadn't reached her yet.

"Ask him to call back in twenty minutes."

Then it hit her. She knew she needed twenty minutes before she spoke to him—on her private phone—because, no matter what, she knew that a chain of women from the switchboard to her own phone would be listening in.

She closed her eyes and thought of Ames Spano's goodness, but it didn't work. It had been so long. She could hardly remember his face. She had avoided his films because they were only two-dimensional shadows of him, in no way real. She poured cold water into a cut-glass crystal tumbler and, switching on the spotlight over her desk, stared into its clarity and thought of Mama to bring her psyche together and to concentrate the clarity of her control. Her clitoris was thlocking like a flamenco castanet. Her breasts had swollen until she feared that her nipples might knock the vase of flowers off the side table across her desk. Everything was opening and expanding. She forced herself to think of Cawdor as a grimy garage mechanic, not as a movie star. Again, thinking of Ames' saintliness brought no restraint whatever.

Surely the way she felt was the way *men* felt and reacted when a female sex object to whom they had been relentlessly conditioned suddenly made herself nakedly available? If only women felt this way, as she waited to speak to him, then the movement was going to have quite a few years more to suffer before achieving truest equality. The thought of mass surgery flashed through her mind. Surely, the in*tell*igent women would rather be freed from this overpowering bondage, the humiliating bondage of the need for men? Surely this majority of women would, with bliss, submit to a simple surgical operation which— if it existed—could free them and thus guarantee equality?

Then the annealing memory of the diaries came back to her. Mama had never instructed her to do anything other than to enjoy men. Mama had welcomed her needs for men, but she had separated that physical need from the human need which must take precedence over all needs: the right to the dignity of equality with men.

The intercom buzzed. Jean flipped the switch.

"He's on!" Miss Fernley-Whittingstall said breathlessly.

Jean picked up the phone. "Thane? How are you? Are you in town? Where are you?"

"What is this?" he laughed. "Are we buying or selling?"

"I thought we might meet for lunch." Her voice trembled with embarrassment at her knowledge of the chain of eavesdropping women who were panting into telephones.

"We work through lunch. How about dinner?"

"Let me call you back."

"I don't have another twenty minutes to spare."

Jean took control. "There are a few actor-simple women hanging on this telephone line," she said sweetly and had the pleasure of hearing at least one click, which she was sure was not Fernley-Whittingstall hanging up. "Tell me where you are and I'll call you right back on a more private line."

"No, thanks. Give me that number and I'll call *you* right back." Submissively, she felt, she gave him the number.

The private line rang instantly. "Okay," he said. "How about dinner tonight?"

"Thane?"

"What?"

"I'm going to be married in two days."

There was a silence. Then he said harshly, "Aren't you married *yet?*"

"All right."

"Then I take it dinner is on for tonight?"

"Yes."

"Good. 3725 Waldorf Towers. About nine." He hung up.

She left the office at five o'clock, an hour and a half before her usual getaway time, took no work home with her, and settled in to get ready to affect Thane Cawdor, big movie star. She supposed he was thrown into contact with many commercially beautiful women in the course of his work, but they couldn't have made any impression on him because she knew she had heard hunger in his voice. He had never married, insofar as she knew or had read. He was probably still very much in love with her.

She felt the vaguest kind of unease about Ames. When she allowed it, her thoughts about him became impossible and she rejected them because she had *not* taken actual vows with him yet and it was a silly thing to have regrets about any future Thane, a future which would be about two hours long on top of one of Mr. Waldorf's beds. It would not be disloyal or unfair to Ames but only a natural continuation of what she and Thane had done the last time they had been together, she convinced herself. There had been no chance for finality in Geneva because he had been called back to London so quickly. They *deserved* the dignity of finality even if it was going to happen years later. If this had come up next week, she knew, it would have been impossible. But it wasn't yet next week and she owed it to Thane to consent to see him for one last time.

She was quite dazzlingly beautiful when she saw the final results of all her labors. She had been massaged. The man had come over from Alain di Parigi to make sure her makeup was right and to comb out her hair. She wore a black chiffon dinner dress with a lot of diamonds because she supposed actors liked diamonds—almost everyone liked diamonds. At twenty-five minutes after eight, fully set out and very much pleased because she realized that Ames would understand and even have done exactly as she was doing had he had a love affair of such long standing before she had met him.

She made herself a very dry martini in her apartment on East 35th and worked out how late she could afford to be. To hell with that! she decided suddenly. Men didn't plan things like that, they either viewed an appointment as an oral contract or they were early or late. She decided to arrive on the stroke of nine as a measure of camaraderie and out of respect for what they had had in the past.

The Carey car picked her up at ten minutes to nine and drove her to the Towers entrance of the Waldorf on 50th Street. She went directly to the 37th floor, and was looking for the floor sign which would direct her to 3725 when she was stopped by a rough voice which called her "Young lady."

A middle-aged, Italian-looking man with a pleasant face and a large stomach was seated at a card table at the corner of the floor where he could watch two corridors. He said, "Maybe I can help you?"

"I don't think so."

"Who you lookin' for?"

"I am looking for 3725."

"He ain't back yet."

"Who ain't back yet?"

"You Miss Henstell? Right? It's okay. He wants you to go right in and wait. Order whatever you want onna phone. Also, he's gotta big bar in there. They got held up."

"Held *up?* You mean detained? Where? And how do you know that?"

"I'm one of his security men. He's makin' a movie. It ain't easy, lady."

The door to 3725 was open. She went into the large living room. She looked at the flowers, which were in more profusion than at any funeral parlor. She looked out the window at Park Avenue, then at a silver-framed picture of Thane as Gork in *Shine of Planets,* which never seemed to stop playing. Oscars were portable that year and Thane's two Oscars were on the mantel, all of it, she supposed, to make the place seem more like home. She went to the bar and poured herself a Perrier over ice. When she had finished drinking it, she looked at her watch, then went out to the elevator bank and pushed the down button.

"Whattsa matta, young lady?" the security man said.

"Tell Mr. Cawdor I was here, please, but that I had to leave at"—she looked at her wristwatch—"four minutes past ten." The down elevator arrived. She got into it and the door closed. She had maintained control over the entire possibly humiliating situation. She could hardly bear the disappointment, but behind it there loomed the undeniable happiness of the realization that she was going to marry Ames Spano the day after tomorrow. She hailed a taxi and went back to her apartment in Murray Hill.

11

Jean and Ames Spano were joined in marriage by Archbishop Paul Empey of Washington, D.C. (known affectionately as "the president's parson"), in a private chapel at St. Grace of Wherry's church. Charles Cantwell gave the bride away. Canon Kullers was the best man, and the British consul in New York, Sir Alan Brien, was the third witness so that he could create and sign an official-looking document which would be essentially British and which Ames could send with respect to his grandmother in Pickering, Yorkshire.

After the ceremony all repaired to an eminent Chinese restaurant on West 126th Street for the wedding reception. Archbishop Empey got tipsy. "It means so much to me to be among my friends, away from Washington," he burbled gently. "I permit myself to relax in this manner."

Canon Kullers drank nothing, glared at the tea, which was reflexively served, and told them that a cardiac specialist who had to be nameless for his own protection had told him that marijuana was the ideal specific for the tensions which produced heart disease and that he wished to ask the archbishop if the Church would consider undertaking its own intensive research into this subject so that lives might be saved.

"Good heavens, John," the archbishop said unsteadily. "Narcotics? Are you wishing the shepherds to turn upon the sheep? Oh, never! No, no, no. Never, never!"

Jean felt she was ecstatically happy.

* * *

The newlyweds moved into Jean's flat on East 35th, in a rather special compound of private houses called Matsonia, which Jean owned. That aspect of it pleased Ames, although he was not altogether sure about the space provided. They had only six rooms, but on the other hand he didn't feel there was a suitable hotel in the city either, at any rate not since they had torn down the Langdon.

Fortunately, Jean had inherited a house on Riverside Drive at 119th Street (very nearly adjacent to St. Grace's Church) from her grandfather, Thomas Henstell ("the Patron Saint of Wall Street Lawyers"), whose years had been those of ever-available domestic staffs. The house had thirty-two rooms.

Jean redesigned the house and had it rebuilt into a glossy-magazine layout of twelve rooms including a gymnasium and a swimming pool with a sauna perch. The restyled house could be run with two servants. There were elevators; chutes; intercoms; walk-in refrigerators and freezers; rare paintings imbedded into concrete walls within temperature-conditioned steel frames covered with carved woods and connected with burglar alarm systems which were as advanced as the state of the art would allow; a microprocessor whose floppy disks held all of Dr. Spano's sermons; any paragraph, any phrase of which was capable of being switched in or out into new messages to be automatically typed at 550 words a minute; cybernetic kitchens; heating/cooling/garbage disposal systems; advanced total security grids sensitized throughout the house which were checked three times a week against each other by a bonded electronics company.

Units of each two rooms were protected from fire in other two-room units by automatic fire doors. Dr. Spano had his figure skating rink in the large cellar near the $74,377 wine investment, also protected electronically.

"I have my wine hobby, of course," Dr. Spano would tell guests. "I don't drink much of it, but I taste quite a lot."

Dr. Spano had become something of a wine authority concerning acidity in clarets, and had taken sharp exception on more than one occasion in prompt letters to The Living Section of the New York *Times* when he felt that the editors had accepted the statement of some Bordeaux shipper which he knew to be in error. He read aloud from copies of these letters at dinner parties at home. Jean kept a card file of which guests had heard which letters so that he would not seem to be repeating himself.

"The total acidity of Bordeaux red wines varies between 3.8 and 3.5 grams per liter, expressed in sulphuric acid, in most vintages," he would recite. "This is significantly higher than *Le Vigneron's* figure of 'commonly less than 0.5 per cent.' I feel as well that *Le Vigneron's* comments regarding tannin are equally questionable. New wood can give to wine primarily ethanol, soluble lignins, hydrolyzable tannins, and the acids related to vanilla. These compounds differ significantly from the condensed tannins native to the must, coming mainly from the pips. The use of succinic acid in tasting demonstrations is dubious procedure as it does not provide a true acid flavor to the wines. Citric, tartaric, and malic acids are much more useful."

He always finished at a crescendo so the dinner guests always knew that the time had come to applaud. However, although Dr. Spano enjoyed bringing his guests the pleasure of these wine parlor games, he personally had been dabbling with psychotropic drugs ever since experiencing the revelations peyote had exploded within him when he had lived among the Zuni. He knew the psychotropics were the future. "Name the psychic state you want and there is a psychotropic drug which can put you there," he explained to Jean, indirectly accounting for the vast increase of his sexual prowess in performance upon and around her. What had transformed him was a pill derived from brain peptide which he did not share with his wife because patently there was no need whatever for that.

"The equivalent of religion—and mass political conduct—is tied up in these drugs, Jean. There won't be much resistance to them. When anesthesia was introduced people thought it was grossly unethical to eliminate pain. Anesthesia is a psychotropic. All these drugs will block pain, and no existing law prohibits the development of drugs that might stimulate such transcendental processes. They are here *now*. They act only on specific receptors of the brain, as a key acts upon a lock. Pain, pleasure, fatigue, exhilaration, religiosity, and memory are tied to specific receptors. I tell you, Jean, the next God who comes to earth is going to have to bring a trunkful of brain peptides with him."

Jean wondered why such a model of a man needed these things to shape himself into such a variety of disguises. She thought about this for many days and decided prudently to ascribe all of his beliefs in his needs for such things to his wistfulness about wanting everything that had been denied to his parents. When she had finally convinced herself of this she found it easier to forgive him his interest in psychotropic drugs than to forgive his interminable speeches about wine acidity.

The huge house on Riverside Drive had food and luggage storerooms, a workshop, and a photographic darkroom in the cellar, as well as a vault where emergency cash and Jean's collection of jewels were kept. It was an extraordinarily modern house; totally safe from the world beyond it. Jean felt privileged to have provided it because Ames had much anxiety about their security. "We live too near Harlem/ the river/ three out of five New Yorkers are paranoid/ the police are indifferent, not to say criminal." Nor did he feel safe about the capabilities of the fire department of the near-bankrupt city. He had instant statistics on murder, burglary, rape, arson, bombing. He really felt they should be living on the two top floors of the Olympic Towers, in midtown, where security needs were given total priority, but he realized sadly that a pastor must live within his parish to maintain credibility.

Henri and Louise were the permanent staff. Henri bought, prepared, and served the food and had secretly agreed with Dr. Spano to wear a concealed sidearm, for which Dr. Spano made sure he was licensed, while working. Henri was a former banker who had become deeply entangled in the gastroporn movement which was sweeping the country, some say in protest against Richard Nixon.

In Henri's case it had all started with a casual Christmas subscription to *Gourmet* magazine which a former mistress had sent him as a gift. This had led him directly to an attempt at making turkey loaf, because it looked so beautifully delicious in the color photograph, stuffed with broccoli and accented with mushroom sauce. To make turkey loaf properly Henri felt compelled to obtain a Cuisinart food processor (because Mr. James Beard and Mr. Craig Claiborne had them) which inevitably led to a KitchenAid mixer, an electric pasta maker, and to the importation of an English AGA cooking stove. These essential pieces of gastroporn equipment had pulled him, as if by a steel cable spooled by a donkey engine, to commission the great Ronny Jaques to design and install a $91,000 kitchen which had electronic woks, an overhead camshaft shish kebab grill, a ceramic Bar-B-Q, a laser beam Quik-Kook apparatus, a gas rotisserie, a solar-powered pasta extruder, a nine-level electric baking oven, and an automatic doughmaker—most of it operated by three microchips—plus 803 cookbooks and a brick oven.

Henri taught himself execrable kitchen French and wore a *toque-blanche* at all times (except in bed) behind the locked doors of their apartment in Yorkville.

He went broke with the addiction. A hooked cook, he could not stop. To be able to finance a protracted cooking-for-the-freezer program— for what could have been called a drive-in freezer which had been converted from their former living room and which could hold 8932 pounds of frozen food—this cuisine-committed banker even considered working nights as a short-order cook at a McDonald's but, through the providential agency of Dr. Spano, was saved from the dishonor.

Henri was a devout parishioner of Dr. Spano's church. When, in lieu of a cash Easter offering, he placed four perfect *crèmes brûlées* in the collection plate, Dr. Spano instantly concluded that the man was suffering from either a financial or an identity crisis or both. He went to the banker. They had long talks, and then three afternoons a week for almost two months, they prayed together on the floor of Henri's kitchen in seven-minute bursts. Soon after that, and at a time when domestic servants were becoming almost impossible to find, Henri resigned as vice president of his bank and Dr. Spano hired him and his wife as a domestic couple.

Dr. Spano worked hard at St. Grace of Wherry. He had his christenings and weddings. He had the brilliant sermons to recompose; the maintenance of his copes and chasubles to supervise. There was the sacramental wine to be kept at a constant temperature. But he also kept right up with his strenuous schedule of visits to the ill and elderly, never sparing himself. He developed a Youth Center at the church which became a model for the bishops of the synod because Jean was such a strong organizer. He was an exemplary clergyman because he wanted deeply to ease the way toward salvation for his fellow man. He discussed these things with Jean, fully resigned to the garishness of the sins of his flock, but with Christian forgiveness of the plenty and painlessness with which his flock was blessed even though these had the effect of separating him from them.

"I visited Mrs. Coulart today," he said with a sigh to Jean. "She is ninety-one. She still maintains that amazing house at Seventy-ninth and Fifth. It must have forty-five rooms with a decorator-placed oxygen tank in every one of them. The same size staff care for her alone as was there when the house was filled with Coularts, and they are augmented by two day nurses and two night nurses. She has a day doctor and his son, the night doctor, but she is a good sleeper so he is not often inconvenienced.

"Mrs. Coulart is a wonderfully hospitable old woman. She insists that I call at tea time. Quite a high tea, I must add—Colnbrooke sandwiches, potted hare, Montpellier butter, port wine sauce, cods' roe, syllabub, publishers pudding, elvers, fat rascals, Gosforth girdies—and something which I would dearly love our pious Henri to learn to make— Northumberland ale jelly, for which a pint of old ale is mixed with a quart of jellied stock, a pound of sugar, the juice of four lemons and the grated peel of one, a stick of cinnamon, and the beaten whites of four eggs. It is all boiled together for fifteen minutes, then strained till it runs clear. A wonderful Chinese cook who has been with her for forty years does all this. The servants and the medical staff have to eat all of it, of course. Mrs. Coulart lives on vintage Krug."

"Still, you do love vintage Krug, dear."

"Oh, yes. I nibble on this and that and we talk about sex. We strain to remember Mrs. Coulart's sexual adventures of the decades past. We speculate on what sex would have been like with the late Ronald Colman. We ask Nurse One and Nurse Two about their sexual proclivities, and they are forthcoming, always apologizing to me first, but explaining how *good* it is for Mrs. Coulart. I would surmise that the visits to Mrs. Coulart's house are the least bleak of my rounds. The other parishioners want to talk about Ronald Reagan or the tax law."

"You really ought to cultivate some hobby, Ames," Jean said. "Something which could keep you busy while you make these calls."

"But such as what?"

"Well—photography, for instance. Think of all the things you would have to photograph if the camera had a flash attachment. The art treasures of the Coulart house alone would be worth an album."

"Jean, really! Mrs. Coulart would immediately ask me to photograph her in the nude, then move right on to ideas such as hiring young men to create fleshy tableaux with her."

Jean smiled gently and patted his cheek. "You could learn to develop things like that yourself. We could install a darkroom."

Ames did acquire a camera, and Mrs. Coulart did yearn to pose for him exotically, but the day doctor forbade it because of the dangers of thermal changes. However, Ames did do some pretty things with the camera and turned out some rather nice metropolitan studies which Jean's family's bank arranged to have presented to the Museum of the City of New York, in whose archives they still rest. But Ames ached with uselessness. He became ill occasionally, then more frequently, both winter and summer. Jean worried so much that she hated to send him off to church in the mornings.

Finally, unable to stand it any longer, she established the Charmian Foundation for him, in honor of the memory of her mother. And, to Ames, it was like being an innocent man awaiting execution for whom a pardon had been granted. The Charmian Foundation was a virgin thing, submissive entirely to what Ames or his wife would wish to do with it, but Jean thought it best that she keep it.

Ames' health restored itself almost immediately. "Because of you," he said, "life is no longer linear to me. It has become an exultation, speeding me off centrifugally to universal fulfillment."

"Dearest," she said, "we *all* want religion to remain a fantasy; it could not survive otherwise, could it? But you, a theological scholar, cannot seem to fathom that. You insist that religion exist only in the reality of self-sacrifice and service. That is a neurotic impulse, but if I don't do something about it, your vocation is going to destroy you."

"Do you really think so, pet?"

"You look simply terrible, Ames."

"Oh, I hate that. It depresses my older parishioners so."

"I can't give you peace of mind, Ames, but I can give you, with this foundation, the chance to wash the feet of the poor for the rest of your life."

"Oh, my darling! Darling, I will never be able to make this up to you. There will never be enough words to thank you."

"Thank me by staying well and strong, Ames."

"But can it be done?" he asked her helplessly.

"Yes! Money *can* build a bridge to the poor. And not two miles from this house there exists poverty and degradation such as even Washington, D.C., has never seen. And—if I can only do it—it won't just be for the two of us and the poor, but a fitting monument to the memory of my mother, with you as its guardian. Oh, Ames! What an effort it can be! We will have the bank have the city condemn blocks of land in the worst part of Spanish Harlem or the South Bronx, then buy it for a song! If there is local resistance at first we will bribe all the neighborhood gang leaders and the other opinion makers in the community, pay the police regularly for their cooperation if necessary, and perhaps distribute free marijuana until we have everyone behind the project, really cheering for you."

"I must say, you certainly make it sound wonderful."

Jean endowed the Charmian Foundation with $50,000. She asked each senior partner in her law firm to persuade their principal clients to instruct *their* foundations to endow the Charmian Foundation. Within four months, the Charmian was funded into perpetuity with $9,236,749.41. With this, together with the Charter of the Foundation and the standing of Ames Lally Spano, pastor of the St. Grace of Wherry church, Jean was able to secure an additional $1,290,822 from the State of New York and a flat grant of $5,000,000 from the Welfare & Social Service Agency of the federal government by an Act of Congress.

Jean's cash contribution was a charitable donation deductible from her income tax. So while the $15,000,000 gift she was able to offer her husband had not cost her very much, the thought was there and the sentiment was hers entirely. Dr. Spano's gratitude was a beautiful thing to see. At last he was going to be able to serve where it would have meaning for him.

Psychotropically, he switched immediately to Urugunine, an extract of natural coconut and synthetic sapin. This lifted him as on a cumulus cloud to a heaven of exalted saintliness and forgiving, even messianic, unselfishness. But this new psychotrope made him loving about people *generally*, as opposed to the effects from the brain peptides, which had intensified, so specifically, his sexual concentration on the *individual*, a response which Jean had come to appreciate so greatly since their early-on (joint) sexual experience.

12

As soon as Ames Spano was thriving as the Saviour of the South Bronx, Jean settled into effecting her entry into politics. For some time she had had it in mind to begin her upward swarming from a base at the New York Police Department. Beyond playing professional football or perhaps taking the heavyweight title, she decided there could be no more macho public institution than a police department because of the ratings of the 119 cop shows on television.

Although (as it happened) she and Ames had been playing bridge with the police commissioner for more than a year because he was enthusiastic about the work of the foundation, and although he admired Jean, it had not occurred to him to offer her any kind of a job. In fact, if he had his way there wouldn't be any policewomen at all. He thought even office work was too dangerous a police assignment for women.

To implement her plans Jean had a long meeting with Charles Cantwell, who among other things, was legal counsel to the bank her grandfather had established and which was one of the five leading banks of the country. Jean always referred to the bank as "we" because she owned almost 9 percent of its stock in well-placed, well-concealed parcels.

"God knows 'we' are well connected in Albany, Charles," she said, "but where aren't 'we' well connected? I am going to need some golden handshaking and I want to be sure I am shaking the right hands. I have everything worked out. The party boys won't have to do any thinking, thank God. I know the first two political jobs I want but I need the first to get the second. I don't want just political influence, Charles. I have to have a clear understanding with whoever it is who controls the nominations."

"Give me an idea of what you want, please, Jean."

"It's simpler but more direct than how we raise money by computer."

"Okay. All right. Tell me. I'll run with it."

"There are two ways for me to make a political contribution to buy the kind of results I want," she said. "If the contribution is made by check, then the amount is limited by law and the money has to go straight to the party's bank account so no one really gets incentive. How can an inside boss become my bosom friend *that* way? So cash contributions are best. The second rule is that the buyer has to know in advance what she wants when she makes the buy because one contribution gets one favor—and one big favor costs one big contribution."

"I'm *with* you, Jean. But what do you *want?*"

"Don't laugh, please, Charles."

"Is it funny?"

"It's funny and it's easy."

"What is it?"

"I'm not asking to be nominated for election yet. All I want—right now—as one-half of what I'll be buying, is the appointment as deputy commissioner for legal matters in the NYPD."

"What in heaven's name would anyone want that for?"

"Charles, I love your tailor, but I can't wear his suits. But every voter in the country thinks of working in the NYPD as a real man's job. And I will lay on the PR to make sure they wallow in that impression."

"But—what *for?*"

"I'll come out as a young woman who is doing a great and marvelous job inside a stereotyped man's world. We'll see that they think of me as being tough, smart, and anybody's equal in the city administration. Then comes the second half of what we'll be buying. After a year or so of that, we'll be ready to let them hand me the nomination for lieutenant governor."

"Why do you need any of this? You're a fine lawyer in a nationally established firm. None of it is as important as what you are doing."

"Just rungs on a ladder, Charles."

"Or a quagmire."

"No. We are going in through the bank. The people I need in politics don't really need my money but they all need the bank. The bank is the fountain and the source—right, Charles?"

"And where are you going from lieutenant governor?"

"Well, no governor needs a lieutenant governor hanging around. I'm going to spend most of my time traveling and promoting New York State across this country while I visit with just about every national committeeman and kingmaker there is."

"*King*maker?"

"Oh, please don't go worrying about *that*, Charles. I haven't even come *near* to figuring that out yet."

Everything was conducted anonymously, the bank handling the passing of the money and the bank chatting with clients in businesses such as real estate, trucking, contracting, and insurance, whose sometime executives were professional politicians.

Twelve days after Jean and Cantwell met at the Auberge Suisse, Police Commissioner Mitgang took Jean to lunch at a fairly dingy Thai restaurant on Houston Street. When they were seated he said, "You look different here than across a bridge table."

"That's because I'm so surprised! This is sure crazy food." They were eating soft turtle in red gravy with a little fried python on the side.

"The Thais know how to eat."

"But fried *python?*"

"This has gotta be the canned stuff. But wait'll you taste the lobster on sugar cane. You'll take the next plane to Bangkok."

"Do you come from an old Thai family, Commissioner?"

"Well, of course I saw *The King and I* a couple of times. Then, a long time ago when I was a sergeant, I hadda go out to Bangkok to bring back a cop killer. The day I got there he got the mumps and couldn't travel—at least not with me, if you know what I mean—so the local force took me out to eat for almost two weeks. That did it."

She thought of her dear Prince Chai, who didn't have to depend on canned python. "Did you ever know a Prince Chaiyaphum when you were there?"

"Was he a cop?"

"No."

"I only knew cops and waiters."

"You are converting me."

"Lissen! You take a place like the Chao Phya Paradise. They feed six thousand people at a time. They got two hundred cooks and five hundred waiters. They run garbage cans in and outta there like baggage out of an airport. And everybody gets a cold towel. You gotta try their black pomfret in plum sauce."

"What are we waiting for? Let's go."

"You're probably wondering why we're having lunch, but you're too polite to ask."

"I did wonder about that, Commissioner."

"The mayor had a terrific idea," he said glumly. "They wanna put a woman executive in the police department."

"You mean—like a precinct captain?"

"Jesus, no—I mean like a deputy commissioner."

"But how could a woman fill a job like that?"

"She'd have to be a very good lawyer."

"But—"

"Lissen, Jean—the job would be yours in a minute as far as I'm concerned, but I told the mayor somebody must be nuts if they thought you'd give up your kind of a law practice to come into the department."

"But what job *is* it?"

"Deputy commissioner for legal matters."

"What would have to be done?"

"Well he—or she, I mean—provides the legal advice to operate the department. Just like any big company lawyer. You'd have to supervise any proposed legislation, serve as my legal adviser, suspend from and restore members of the department to duty, handle the search warrant applications before they go to the courts, advise the guys in the field on law interpretation, attend the courts as directed, place cops on modified assignment. . . . that's the general idea anyway."

"Staff?"

"About eleven supervising attorneys and about twenty-three other lawyers with maybe nine or so clerk-stenographer-typists. Everyone who works there is a police officer. They gotta make a lot of court appearances. And they handle all the wiretap requests, which is tricky stuff, but the most time-consuming job is analyzing the ten or twelve thousand pieces of legislation affecting us which are introduced each year by the state legislature and the city council. We gotta have opinions on everything, and Legal Matters is there to do it."

"What happens to the man who has the job now?"

"He's okay. The mayor is handling that. He's going into the corporation counsel's office with a seventeen-percent raise. Not bad."

"I'd have to be sure that *you* are offering me the job, Commissioner. Not the mayor."

"You can be sure. I'd be tickled and honored and everything else if you just considered it."

"Then I'll do better than that. I'll accept."

"Say—that's terrific, Jean."

"Just call me Commissioner, Commissioner. When do I start?"

"Like the first of the month? Is that enough time?"

"It's perfect."

"I hope we can find enough for you to do. Pass the sour crab claws."

"Which are they?"

"Right there. Next to the fried plakapong."

13

When Jean Spano became deputy commissioner for legal matters she was thirty-two years old. She had been married for eight years. Her Voters' Research and Development, the political money-raising machine, was six years old.

Her marriage had not produced any children. At first she had been too busy creating the house on Riverside Drive for Ames while she attended to her law practice. Immediately after that came the unexpected Charmian Foundation. When she began to talk to Ames at last about their having children, he became quite upset.

"Don't you see the *self*ishness of talking about having children of our own right now when God has shown us a way to nurture, and heal, and teach, and provide for hundreds, perhaps even *thou*sands of children whose needs cry out to us to give them a chance in this life?"

"Are you telling me we are *never* going to have children of our own?" Jean demanded.

"I didn't say that, Jean. I only pointed to where our duty lay."

"You may have your duty. You certainly have become very big on duty. But I don't see having our own kids as a duty—it's more of a fascination—and an obligation, if you have to have it that way—to provide children whom we can train to possess, and be responsible for, what we possess. I mean, next to cloning, I would have thought a man like you would be *wild* to get on with reproducing himself."

"I am not against the idea, Jean. But I must have more time."

"How much time?"

"It is a matter, really, of when we will be ready. We have to be really prepared for the sobering significance of parenthood."

Her reputation as a big-time lawyer had preceded her into the NYPD. The fact of her sex was ignored. She was regarded as a technician having special skills and was accepted by her own department charily. Her first action was to call a meeting with the eleven police officers who were the supervising attorneys.

"We'll work best together if we all know the rules," she told them. "I don't intend to reorganize anything that works in this department. If it doesn't work, that's a different matter. Okay? Logical. So the first thing is to appoint two senior and two junior supervising attorneys to write the brief which will lay down what they consider to be the positive factors in our operation. In the same brief, they'll outline the negative factors. I know you don't have the time. You're all overworked. But it has to be done. Wasted motions may have been accumulating here for a hundred years. Maybe longer. Captain Melvin will make the assignments. Whoever is elected, please get the brief started tomorrow morning. I want it the Tuesday after next, then I'll take it from there. Thank you. Very much."

That was the first meeting, and she had almost been the cause of a mutiny, but that had to be expected.

The brief, delivered on time, was about 78 percent adequate, she estimated. She added the other 22 percent on her own. She called the supervising attorneys into another meeting after she had distributed copies of the final brief to them and told them how pleased she was that they had not made their grievances about the changes contained in the brief public property, and had not bothered the commissioner with them.

"They wouldn't know what we were talkin' about, Commissioner," Captain Melvin, the most senior attorney, said. "And even if they could, it's not their business to think that lawyers don't know what they're doin' better than any of them, you know what I mean?"

She marveled. The mystique which protects every lawyer is painted on while we sleep through classes at law school, she thought. It keeps the rest of the world on its knees, applauding lawyers. "Well, I certainly approve of that, Al," she said. "Have you all read the final brief?"

They rumbled assent.

"Any objections?"

There was a silence.

"This may be the last chance, gentlemen."

"If we have an objection, Commissioner, by common agreement here, it's that it's too bad all the men in the job before you didn't stop to think of all the makeweight that had piled up in the legal matters department."

"A housekeeper was needed, Al," she told them, "and we all know a woman is best for that."

They laughed heartily, believing every word of it, and she invited all of them, with their wives, to dinner at Beefsteak Charlie's one week from Saturday night.

Among the less revolutionary things her brief had interposed was the installation of a nonlawyer, a police officer who would serve as a liaison with the rest of the department on matters that would spare the lawyers in the department from using time that could be best used to do the avalanche of legal work.

Jean cleared the assignment with Commissioner Mitgang, who said he'd get back to her. He talked it over with the chief of detectives, Joe Maguire. He said, "If you had the time and if you were interested I'd let you read what the woman is doing with Legal Matters."

"She knows her bidniz?"

"Like she's gonna save maybe a hunnert and semmenty thousand and get maybe thirty percent more work out." Mitgang grinned. "In fact, I am thinking where I can find some smart woman to do your job."

"My mother-in-law always said she could do my job," Maguire said. "So? I am catching on. What does the new commish want from me?"

"She has a very efficient idea. She wants to have somebody assigned to her who isn't a lawyer but who knows his way around the department, inside and out, so that her lawyers can make things work better for every division because he knows what buttons to push and who to talk to."

"A detective?"

"Yeah. A sergeant maybe. Only don't think only of somebody you wanna move outta someplace. Think of somebody who knows, who fits the job."

"Well—tomorrow morning be soon enough?" They were eating white and green cappelini at Romeo Salta's and drinking well-chilled Verdicchio dei Castelli di Jesi, a wine which found distinction with cappelini the way Salta's could make it.

"About nine-fifteen," the commissioner said. "Don't come yourself. And don't send him to me, fahcrissake. Tell whoever it is he is now working for her and give me a memo on it."

"How come we're eatin' Italian tonight?"
"The Thai joint is closed on Thursdays."

Detective Sergeant Umberto Caen was forty-three, white, male. He had been in the department since he was seventeen years old, claiming to be eighteen. He had walked a beat in Harlem, where he had some great connections. He had been in plainclothes on the vice squad in Times Square. He had been a detective on the waterfront squad, and when he was pulled for duty in Legal Matters (to his fury) he had been plotting how to get himself back in Harlem, but this time on the narcotics squad.

Caen was what long-haired kids and demonstrators thought of when they said the pigs. He was, in his own inverted and unempathetic way, a cop in every pejorative sense of the word. His name sounded vaguely French or Italian, but he was iron Irish-American, because his mother saw to that. His father, whom he never remembered having seen, had been a newspaperman in central New Jersey. His mother had added up the sum total of his vanished father, all newspapermen, and particularly those from over the river, at dinner every day of his life. She also did a pretty good job of convincing him that women were the born chumps and losers of the species, and because of the way his mother set herself up with her son, Caen soon learned to think of all women as eternal marks—perfect patsies there for his personal convenience.

So Umberto Caen used women. He had contempt for them behind the maximum charm he could summon up, which was mainly between his legs. He was like a professional actor to whom the faceless audience was something out there to be wooed and fooled and won, then used, because that was how his mother had always arranged it as the price of letting him have what he wanted whether it was a piece of candy or fifty bucks. He was forty-three years old but he still lived with his mother in Washington Heights. He went home whenever he needed a rest and some home cooking; he wasn't there most of the time, but with Mom was where he lived.

He was called into his lieutenant's office at 8:45 in the morning by the simple expedient of the lieutenant's being lucky enough to get him at home at Mom's at half past seven and tell him where to get his ass and when. The lieutenant ran a tight ship aboard the burglary squad, where Caen was rated highly on gems and jewelry thefts, and handled the hotel unit.

"Jesus, what *is* it?" he snarled into the telephone after he had hung up. He had carried the heat as protection for a truckload of hot Yves St.

Laurent clothes the night before, clothes that would be on sale right off iron racks on the four corners of 50th and 51st streets on Fifth Avenue by the lunch hour. But that was the captain's bag. The lieutenant was hot about something, but he didn't sound like it was something he was going to aim at Caen. So he shaved, listened to Mom about the shit they were putting on television, then took the Eighth Avenue downtown.

"A beef from some citizen, Lieutenant?" he asked as he went into the small office.

"Should there be?"

"No. But that was all I could think it coulda been."

"You know what, Caen? The chief of detectives called me at my house in Bay Ridge at seven this morning just to tell me that he was transferrin' you outta here. Wasn't that nice?"

Caen's heart leaped. Somebody had come through! He was going to make Rich Man in Harlem!

"No kiddin'?"

"For real. And at exactly nine ayem, the chief wants to see you sittin' in the office of the deputy commissioner for legal matters so you can report to her for duty when she comes in."

"*Her?* Duty? What are you tellin' me, Lieutenant?"

"You're now the connection between Legal Matters and the rest of the department. Except spare your old buddies, you hear?"

"Lieutenant, what the fuck do I know about Legal Matters?"

The lieutenant smiled sourly. "Joseph Aloysius Maguire himself okayed it."

"But *what*? What is this?"

"Where you been? You don't know a woman runs Legal Matters?"

"I'm supposed to work for a woman?"

"Caen, you got about twenty-two years' time. You wanna quit?"

"What kind of a woman?"

"Whatta you think? A Wall Street lawyer, a reformer, and—it figures—a triple libber."

"A libber? I hate libbers. They're all dykes."

"You'll get used to it."

"How did *I* come inta this? How come the chief picked *me*?"

The lieutenant stood up.

"Holy shit, a libber!" Caen said, and got out of the room.

She made him wait outside her office until 9:25, but he held his temper because she was a deputy commissioner. Then a woman cop came out and told him to report to Captain Melvin.

"Who's that?" Caen snarled.

"He's *Captain* Melvin," she said. "Does that answer your question? Follow me." She led him through a labyrinth of desks. Holy shit, he thought, I am now a fucking white collar worker.

Melvin bumbled on at him. They're going to make me a fucking lawyer, not a cop, Caen thought dismally. Melvin explained the job—an errand boy between the lawyers and the rest of the department. But something told Caen it could be worse. The job could have advantages. A deputy commissioner had muscle, and he knew he could handle her. He decided to go to Delahanty's on Saturday and sign up for the night course for the lieutenant's examination. Then he would settle down and get to know Spano.

When he got home to Mom's that night he went through his strongbox to find a piece of jewelry he had jerked off the chest of a whore on Eighth Avenue. It was a nice little trinket. It looked like gold. It was nine-carat gold with a fourteen-carat wash; libbers' jail jewelry in the design of a tiny padlocked jail cell door, hinges, and heavy grille. It was lucky, he decided, that he never threw anything away.

He took it with him to the office the next morning. At half past two he told the woman cop outside Spano's door that he wanted to see the commissioner when she had the time.

"What case?"

"Whatta you mean?"

"What case do you want to talk to her about? I gotta log it."

He thought about the papers on his desk. "The Skutch case," he said. "Special sessions next Monday."

"I'll call you," she said.

He got into Spano's office at twenty after four. But at least, he told himself, she's gonna see me on the same day that I asked.

"Sit down, Sergeant," she said without looking at him. When she was finished what she was doing, and she took her own goddamn time, she said, "What about the Skutch case?"

"I hadda say something for Officer Schrader's log," he said, unpacking all the charm which had worked for him like magic on the vice squad, laying it out in front of her like a salesman's samples: a toothy smile, a boyish manner, and a fine balance of diffidence and arrogance. "I wanted to talk to you for a coupla minutes, that's all. We have this thing we are both innarested in—my mother was a friend of Alice Paul."

"Alice Paul?"

"You know, the founder of the National Women's Party in 1913?

The   one who wrote the words to the Equal Rights Amendment?"
"Ah! Alice *Paul.*"
"Yes, ma'am. My mother and her were very close." He fumbled in his
pocket. "She designed this pin and gave one of the first ones to my
mother, God rest her soul." He put the pin down on the desk in front of
her the way a cat might bring a mouse to the feet of its mistress. "I
thought you might like to have it."
"Why, Sergeant—how very kind of you."
She picked up the pin and looked at it carefully. "An historic symbol,"
she said solemnly. "Thank you. Thank you very much. I shall treasure
it."
She looked into his face for the first time and shivered involuntarily.
It was a thick face with heavy-lidded eyes and a pulpy, slack mouth. It
seemed to her to be an image of the fearful men whom her mother had
written about in her diaries. He was enormous, which accentuated his
maleness. He was repellingly handsome in a brutish way, and suddenly
she imagined she could see him standing in front of her—matted hair,
sweat, huge, dangling genitalia, and long muscular powerful arms
hanging at his sides or scratching at an itching anus. She imagined she
could smell him—the strong smell of ammonia and fresh bread, an
acrid stench, mingled with beer and some aftershave like Opium, and
cheap cigars, the kind of cigars that came in a box which said, "A large
percentage of the contents of these cigars is pure tobacco."
The imaginary sum of him overwhelmed her—rank, dank, and stink-
ing, unreasoning maleness—and her own body was reacting like a lone
switchboard during a surprise air raid. This was the enemy. This was
the leering lurker whom all women had to fear or dominate. Her legs
would not support her. She sat down as slowly as she could. How would
Mama have handled this? she wondered. Would she have sent this Kod-
iak back to its trainers in some out-of-the-way cage and make sure he
was forgotten there or would she have seen and accepted the challenge
to her control which he flagrantly represented? Jean didn't know. She
couldn't think with the man standing there behind that awful smile, a
disingenuous shiteater's smile. And that brass pin lying on the desk
between them.
She forced herself to look at the folder on her desk, the only way she
could think to dismiss him.
"Don't mention it, Commissioner," he said. He turned away and
moved toward the door. She looked up under her eyelids and saw his
long, broad, ropy back under the light summer suit and, in the background, the wide leather couch. She fantasized herself under him on

that couch, her knees drawn up to her chin, her legs locked across that back as it plunged the enormous ram into her. She swiveled around in her chair, facing a wall, and picked up the speaker of the Dictaphone, hearing the door close as he got away from her.

14

Alex Fowles, Jean's former housemate at Smith, found it impossible to avoid reading about her in the media because of the population of press agents who were busy crafting her fame. Alex telephoned her at the NYPD and was invited to lunch the following Saturday at Rockrimmon.

Saturday was Ames Spano's day of rest. Sunday was his heavy day because he still preached at St. Grace of Wherry church, thrilling the congregation as a genuine (and famous) slum missionary. He spent every day at La Casa, which was what the community it served called the Charmian Foundation, cheering up postoperative patients who had been shot, knifed, or battered in family quarrels, or chatting with the American and overseas press.

Monday to Friday were Ames' days of fifteen-hour service at La Casa. But on Friday, sometimes as early as eight in the evening, he would fall into the back seat of the Rolls Phantom and let himself be driven to Rockrimmon where he just plain let the staff spoil him with good food and the fine company which Jean assembled. There was always a festive luncheon party on Saturday. They also raised fair amounts of money for La Casa that way.

Faith in the media is the only constant faith, Ames (secretly) knew. People had been trained in how to think by the media, trained to think of Ames Spano as a celebrity saint (and his stunning young wife as his acolyte). Importantly, he was a *rich* celebrity saint, so people wanted to be near him—and his food and wine—on one of the loveliest estates in Connecticut (even if the swimming pool did leak). At those Saturday lunches, Ames was the sun, Jean was the moon, and the guests decorative plants who bloomed checkbooks as their blossoms, keeping their faces turned toward the light.

Alex Fowles was a bred social climber, the way winners of the Grand National are bred for steeplechasing. She had never seen anything quite like the Saturday lunch. To her, dazzled, every guest was celebrated: rich jockstraps, elegant hoodlums, actors who starred in nighttime TV series, publishers from the 10016 zip code, potent astrologers, doctors who had written dieting books which had been forty weeks on the bestseller list, women who shrieked and women who murmured, a former minister of the Irish Republic, a glistening matched pair of sexologists, and a very heavy insurance man. The combined cost of the womens' shoes alone, she thought, had to be over $4500. There was a wonderful cocaine-brightness over most of them. It all combined to give her the warm feeling of a hustler who knows that some of the good luck could rub off on her. She stood mired in luck plus the smarts plus clout, and she was certain the day would have to end by doing her some good.

Alex had just come back from a run-of-the-mill divorce in Alaska where her husband had sold the lower end of the GM line. It had been a very good marriage and a very good divorce. After nine years of a marriage with a Happiness Content just under 7.13 percent of the national average, they had discovered that he liked Alaska and she didn't or—at least to be fair to both of them—that she would be happier in Philadelphia.

Apart from the fact that Ames Spano was Jean's husband, which would have made any man more attractive to Alex, she was put off by the knowledge that he was a clergyman and some kind of freak social worker. But she had seen his face in print many times, so she was able to single him out of the luncheon crowd and introduce herself to him before she could find Jean.

"Dr. Spano? My name is Alex Fowles. I went to college with your wife." Alex had the knack of seeming to be wealthy, which pleased Ames, and he admired her bone structure. She had the clear, outgoing, honest speech to which he had always been drawn whether it came from a former resident of Mayaguez or a stringer from Agence France Presse. Genuinely believing she was rich, because she had known Jean at Smith, he assumed Jean had dredged her up for the lunch with her checkbook, so he was warm and charming, knowing that financial benefactors expected that, if not deference; that they always responded to treatment as equals. Not that this was any difficulty. He was drawn happily to the woman.

"Were you a child prodigy too, Mrs. Fowles?"

"Miss Fowles. My husband and I agreed that I shouldn't be expected to use his name after the divorce."

"What was his name?"

"Hitz. MacDonald Hitz."

"Hitz and Fowles? Rather like a baseball score, wasn't it?"

She tried to laugh. "No one ever said *that* before."

"Our family name was originally Spanner. We were Yorkshire people. One of the Spanners—a long time ago—converted to Catholicism and eventually made a pilgrimage to Our Lady of Fatima. He thought he was in Spain, dear thing, and he was so affected by the exotic nature of what he saw as holiness that he changed his name legally from John Spanner to Juan Spano."

"*Sluttie!*" Jean's voice exploded. She threw her arms around Alex. "How absolutely *mar*velous to see you! How wonderfully well you look! And how good that you found Ames."

"Oh, he is *fas*cinating! He's told me the story about the family name."

"Don't believe a word he says, Sluts. It's his day off and he relaxes with a little lying. The family name was Spinner, changed to Spino, because the man was seeking a barber's license in Livorno, then later generations all thought that sounded too Italian when Mussolini ran the railroads so they changed it to Spano."

"I knew I had that anecdote wrong," Ames said. "What is this name Sluttie or Sluts?"

"Alex's mother's maiden name was Sluttery," Jean said blandly, "but they changed it to Slattery."

It was a successful luncheon. Jean raised $21,693 for the foundation, then, exhilarated by seeing Alex again, got the wonderful idea of calling Ursula Baggot in Hong Kong.

They took turns talking to her. Jean spoke, then Alex, then Jean again.

"You sound down, Ursie," she said. "Is it temporary?"

"Oh—yes."

"What happened?"

"My sisters were killed last year. I get pretty low. This is just one of those days."

"Are you alone?"

"Yes."

"But I'm sure you have lots of friends."

"Oh, yes."

"Did you ever marry?"

"No."

"Well."

"I'm all right, Jean. Really I am."

"Will you come to New York, Ursie? I have a new organization going and I need an assistant who knows how I think."

"Jean, honestly, I—"

"Do it for me, please. Is it the same address in Hong Kong?"

"Yes."

"I'll cable you an air ticket this afternoon."

Alex had her ear to the phone and she was resentful that the good luck had rubbed off on Ursula. "How can she make such awful sounds?" she said, turning away from the noise of Ursula's dry sobbing.

On that same day at Rockrimmon—the day Alex Fowles was exposed to Dr. Spano, the day Ursula Baggot was summoned back from their girlhood—Alex met Peter Cassiman, the most successful insurance broker in a state famous for insurance companies, a principal contributor to the Democratic Party. They were married by Dr. Spano in the small chapel at Rockrimmon four months to the day after they had met. Seventeen months after the marriage, the then senior senator from Connecticut found it necessary to resign because of some mistakes he'd made in simple subtraction in the use of campaign funds and Peter Cassiman was appointed to take his seat. Then Cassiman was reelected. He became a powerful man in Washington and he bored Alex into numbness.

15

Jean was so stimulated by the accident of seeing Alex Fowles again, then talking to Ursie again and getting her to agree to come to New York to work, that she felt even greater confidence that all of her plans were going to come true. Alex didn't affect anything one way or the other. She was just there and she went on her sluttish way. But Ursie was a *mind* and had towering *character*. Ursie could take over the full-time running of her Voters' Research and Development, freeing Jean to concentrate on moving up and out of the NYPD into a dominating, instantly recognizable political position. It would take her about three weeks to break Ursie into the job, therefore in a month she was going to begin to make the preliminary moves to line up the nomination for lieutenant governor through Charles and the bank and the accumulated "campaign contributions" at Voters' Research. She would be ready.

The word ready made her think of Caen. Something had to be done about Caen if she was going to have her mind free to plan and deal. He wanted her. He nosed in and around her office on the slightest excuse. She was in total control. She knew that if she were a man and felt a physical attraction as powerful as this she would just move in and take what she had to have then forget it. Caen was just an animal who dressed himself, after a fashion, every morning. Her mother had been clear in the diaries that if women were ever going to be free and equal they would have to be liberated sexually, as their bodily demands required, in the way men had to be. Perhaps that was what ensured the continuance of male supremacy, she thought. They did not hesitate to move in and take from women.

There had been a time in her marriage, she thought sadly, when she wouldn't even have seen Caen, much less slaver over him. What had happened? She decided that nothing had happened to her, but that somehow everything had happened to Ames. Her husband didn't love her anymore. He had fallen for any mirror he happened to chance upon. And for masses of people. Not just any people. They had to be abjectly poor and exploited to put him into a passionate heat as he had the Rolls glide among them, exciting their admiration for its shininess. It was all too diffuse for her to be able to do anything about it, so she concentrated on doing something about Caen.

The urgent fact was that she had to get Caen off her mind. Just one time with all that sweat and dirty laundry after *she* had originated it, and she would be ready to go to the commissioner and resign, for by then she would have been asked to run for lieutenant governor. Yes. She would line up Caen in some hotel room for one long animal night, because if she didn't she wouldn't be able to think about anything else.

When the luncheon party was over at Rockrimmon and Ames had gone off to bed, she went to consult the diaries on some higher plane than Caen. She needed Mama to tell her what her *real* goals had to be.

Jean took down Volume Three and began to read as Mama explained again that only women were the cherishers and that therefore, as the true conservatives, the political salvation of America was in their hands.

How I dream, awake and asleep, that one day someone who really cares, as I care, will awaken American womanhood and lead this overwhelming moral force, the *true* conservatism which exists on the surfaces of and deep within all women's minds to provide the only defense for our country. Men, the hunters and destroyers, are far to the left of the moral right in the precincts of the American soul.

I would contribute my fortune and follow the woman who would dare to grasp the helm to bring the women of our country into striking unity and thus into the mighty offices where the men of American history have failed.

The women of America have not rallied to save the future because they will not rally around a male leader. There have been thousands of male cynics who have inhabited politics for personal gain, for personal glory, wasting the essence of our country and denying the birthright of helpless children who must somehow cope with tomorrow.

Only the American women can save that birthright for the unborn because only women understand that no one can spend all their resources decade after decade yet still have left the capital to invest in making possible the safety and security of all the years to come.

How I would flame with pride wherever I was—in this world or the next—if my own daughter were eager to wear the sword and shield of American moral leadership and move out upon the plains of Columbia to do battle in the vanguard of the great, conserving, and politically responsible union of the one sex which wants to cherish this country and this great life which God gave to us.

16

Jean used her NYPD wallop and drove the Rolls out on the tarmac at Kennedy Airport to meet Ursula Baggot arriving on the Concorde flight from Singapore to London to New York. Captain Cremers of the police harbor unit went ahead of her to wave Customs men away and to hasten Immigration with a rubber stamp brought out to the car. The two women were manic at seeing each other again.

Ames came home from La Casa for the special lunch which Henri had laid on, first ingesting a genial psychotropic helper which confirmed and heightened his sincerity and merriness. He opened a bottle of Mrs. Coulart's Krug and made a sonorous toast to ensure Ursie's happiness among "her friends on the American continent." Ursula obliged by weeping. Ames held her around the shoulders, chuckling, telling her she was weeping tears of joy.

Henri cooked a stupendous meal which reproduced the entire center spread of *Gourmet*. They drank glorious Bonnes Mares '69, then Urs collapsed with jet lag and was taken off to bed. She slept for fourteen hours, until four o'clock the next afternoon. By the time she was unpacked, bathed, and dressed, Jean arrived and the two women took up their lives again.

In time, they got around to discussing Ursie's job. "We've been building Voters' Research year after year," Jean said. "We have about thirty-eight percent more people than when we started. In the first year we raised seven and one half million for women's rights, eleven million-two for political campaigns, and about two million for other causes. We are up on those figures by thirty-seven percent as of this year. Next year will show a leap of over fifty percent. Now—entirely between you and me—CR has two jobs: to advance me politically and to achieve the Equal Rights Amendment—both objectives being more or less the same."

"Jean?"

"What?"

"I've become a lesbian."

"Why?"

"I'm not sure. But I've never loved anyone but my sisters and you, then I met her—and it happened."

"Isn't it a weird feeling? I mean with a woman?"

"No. Not for me. Not even at first. It was wonderful."

"But where is she now?"

"Dead."

"Dead?"

"She died in the car crash with my sisters. They didn't approve of us. They hated it. She was driving. She may have killed them all. But I love her."

"It's surrealistic to me."

"I can survive because I still have you, Jean. I love you. You've always known that."

"I suppose so."

"I would do anything for you. I would protect you from anything and do anything to keep you safe."

"There is nothing to protect me from, but I'll always remember you said that."

"Men are the enemy."

"My mother saw most men as the enemy."

"But we've taken the only unequivocal position."

"We?"

"The lesbians. We have only one tactical belief: that a woman must either be a lesbian or become a lesbian if the revolution to free women is going to be successful. Because *any* association with men is fraternizing with a mortal enemy and therefore is a sellout."

"Crazy." Jean shook her head. "Listen—be as much of a lesbian as you have to be, but make sure everyone knows you are a woman—okay? And if the ERA is ever going to be passed through politics—and it can't get there any other way—then we have to work with men. You, your job especially, because men are the politics."

"But after we win," Ursula asked. "What then?"

"After we win—at last—men and women will be allowed to assimilate each other's tolerance so that we can sustain what we have won."

"Then you obviously don't see men as the enemy?"

Jean patted her friend's shoulder. "It is one of the few areas where Mama and I don't agree. Not that it hasn't been a trail of tears—but there are worse things. Man's indifference to justice for women is historical. But they were conditioned that way. When we bring about equality through laws which will change their conditioning, and when they understand why the sexes are equal so that *both* can thank God that he made two sexes—when everything has been ironed out and men have been changed, Ursie, there just won't be any *reason* for lesbians."

17

The Charmian Foundation's first purchase for Dr. Spano's dream was four nearly derelict brownstone houses in Spanish Harlem where he could work with doctors, psychiatric social workers, nutritionists, and lawyers until the foundation could complete the building of a fifteen story community center hospital-employment training complex upon a condemned city block. Dr. Spano slept and awoke in psychotropic ecstasy, blessed be Urugudine, and the fevers of his growing national fame. He was able to sleep only four or five hours a night, and abandoned even the memory of ever having had any interest in sex. Jean was shaken by physical loneliness. There was no way to reclaim his interest, because he had flung himself into the organization of a maze of social services from English-language phonetics to the cultivation of community gang leaders, while he kept ingesting Urugudine for saintly insurance.

Jean worked with him in Spanish Harlem four nights a week, chattering their language in staccato bursts, never dressing like Lady Bountiful, but like El Padre's woman. In the interests of her own career, she made certain that La Casa stayed above politics. It stood for her husband's life committed to her mother as witnessed by *People* magazine.

Gradually Dr. Spano grew away from his work as pastor of the St. Grace of Wherry church, finally agreeing to stay on there in an honorary capacity. Within four years he became the tame saint of Spanish Harlem. Large additional funding was offered to him to establish his methods in different parts of the world. He began to talk about "greater service"—about doing much more. For example, as he would tell anyone, there were thousands of people in the Central African Republic who were afflicted with river blindness caused by the bite of the *Simulum damnosum* fly.

"And Bilharzia is *rife*," he would say. "And they are not only blind, they are starving to death. In Bangui the people walk, play, defecate, bathe, and launder their clothes in the same water, and they die very easily. On top of that most of the population has a ravaging strain of gonorrhea, yet the women produce an average of seven to twelve children in their lifetimes. They die from a whole population of diseases— every one of them eradicable. We ought to be doing something about this."

But by the time her husband had reached the level of thinking about doing something bigger in places which were farther away, Jean was activating her long-term plans to enter national politics. She considered that she had already gotten him what he had wanted and that her own chance had finally come. If he wanted to serve more than he was at present, there was plenty for him to do inside the United States; there was no reason to move into anonymous jungles to do it.

Patiently she explained all of this to him. He protested loudly and bitterly that he *had to* serve in countries where no other possible salvation existed. The United States was cured and decontaminated when compared to Central Africa and almost all of Asia. For several continuous days he made strong arguments. She listened to all of them. Only when he began to repeat himself for the third time did she move in to cut him down.

"Ames," she told him, "I have merely transformed your life, and—if you could hear yourself and see your eyes—you would know you have become a mirror raper and a clipping junkie. I got you everything you wanted. Four dozen times you have told me I have saved your life. For what? To run off to Africa to be a carbon copy Schweitzer? I need you here so that your work can set off my work, and for a man who wants deeply to serve, you *know* that's where you can serve best."

"Why do you need me here?" he asked in his saintly, psychotropic way.

"Because the American Bar Association has had three good meetings with Franklin Heller. Can you follow that? Heller looks like he will be the next president. Heller is considering appointing me as his attorney general, and when he does I will accept. When I accept we are going to have to spend most of our time in Washington—at least I will—and by the nature of American politics the attorney general of the United States can't have her husband off wandering around the world helping outcast foreigners when he ought to be home helping his own."

"As you wish," he said with deeply forgiving overtones.

"If you can't understand this any other way, Ames," she told him, "try it this way. I am going on and up in politics. We can have no rocking of the boat. Is that clear, Padre? That is a family decision and we don't need to talk about it again."

18

Estelle Chantage had been a client of Henstell, Masters & Cantwell for many years before Jean arrived there, but as with most everything else, she made it her business to hear about Jean's talents as a lawyer. And, when Bennett F. Reyes retired from the firm to lead the Trace Elements industry, Mrs. Chantage asked that her files be transferred to Jean's accountability. Mrs. Chantage owned the most considerable international cosmetics company in the world. She was a tough lady, but while she laid the whip on the backs of her employees, she was solicitous of people such as Jean who told her how to use her money and lessen the cruelty of her taxes.

Mrs. Chantage owned a house wherever the beautiful people and the "movers and owners" gathered. She entertained them all, whether they spoke the same language or not, including some very odd people indeed, counting the overworld, the underworld, and the jocks of all nations. She appreciated that Jean would never accept an invitation to any of these galas. "After all, baby, your husband is a very revered man."

Jean did dine with Mrs. Chantage alone at her New York house, which was two large houses knocked together, situated across 51st Street from St. Patrick's Cathedral. The house was a free interpretation of a *palatium Ducis*, an exuberant carnival of a house permanently intended to swing its style perspective between a belch of grandeur and the design on the outside of a calliope.

The dining room, forty by fifty-five feet, was lined with statues of naked putti. Profusions of baroque paintings hung on each wall, and the furniture was upholstered in contrasting species of Russian fur.

One evening after they had finished the monthly legal counsel dinner, the rugged lady suddenly asked Jean anxiously, "You getting much, honey?"

"Much what, Mrs. Chantage?"

"Nooky."

"*Nooky?* Does that mean what it sounds like it means?"

"Certainly—so?"

"That is none of your business, Mrs. Chantage."

"They all say that. Are you compatible in the bed with your husband?"

"What's the matter with you tonight?"

"So how are you doing with your husband?"

Jean sighed. "My husband—"

"He's competing with the saints, right?"

"Well—"

"So what is the hangup with him?"

"I think about going into politics, and he thinks about becoming a missionary in Central Africa. We can't have both."

"So in the meantime you're not getting any relief—right?"

"Relief?"

"Nooky."

"What a word."

"Lissenna me, Jean. I'm no chicken, and I had arreddy four husbands. What I got, I hadda make inna man's world and kind they're not. I decided a long time ago that I'm not gonna let anybody who works for me ever get close enough to stab me with his fleshy dagger. Nobody is gonna have *that* on Momma. But I'm a healthy woman, you know what I mean? When I need it, I need it bad. So what do I do?"

"What *do* you do?"

"I call a certain telephone number, of which I got three, and they send a nice stupid young stud over. I am waiting for him in a suite in some West Side hotel. I bang him a coupla times, then I slip him a hundred bucks and I never see him again. Believe me, that solves it for me so it could solve it for you!"

"But, Mrs. Chantage!"

"What?"

"The danger!"

"What kind of danger? You mean like clap?"

"Well, certainly that too. But I mean men like that could kill you just to get money and they certainly have it in their minds to get money if one has to pay them a hundred dollars."

"Jean, lissenna me. Learn. If a guy is a whore, that's what he is—a whore. If he had the nerve to rob money from people that's what he'd be doing. People do what they feel safest with, and all these guys got are big numb pricks which they can keep going as long as you can keep going. Then they take the hundred and probably go out and spend it on sex."

"I should have realized it, but I never *conceived* that *men* did that for a living—the poor devils."

"You thought only women? But it's not only like the system produces whores—men or women. Some people are naturally whores just like there are carpenters and some very fine jockeys and dress designers. They are what it means when people say good-for-nothing. But they gotta eat. And why should only women be good-for-nothing? From my experience that quality comes to men more naturally."

"But how can people like that be one's *lovers?*"

"Lovers? It's nothing but a buncha friction! It's a business thing with these guys. That's their entire inventory, all their qualifications. That is their particular diploma from the Harvard Business School or they don't get any hundred dollars a shot. You want the telephone numbers?"

"As a possible solution to something which is on my mind a lot when I try to get to sleep, I might say yes. But as a practical thing, Mrs. Chantage, and you *know* I am grateful to you for trying to help . . ."

"Don't make a big thing out of it, honey. I am only tryna get you laid in a convenient, disposable way."

"I'll take the numbers, Mrs. Chantage. Thank you."

"I wrote it all down. Ask for Mildred. Tell her Harry Fink told you to call, then give her a phony name and the number of your hotel room. Afternoons are best. The guys are stronger."

Even though she was not unaware of the magic of brain peptides, Jean felt marooned without Ames Spano's body as a four-wall lusting court. She would not take sedatives to get to sleep. She would lie in bed and fantasize about sex with Thane in so many different ways, with the disassociated bodies of men she had glimpsed over the years across crowded rooms. Twice, she almost put through calls to Mildred; once she got as far as hearing Mildred's high-pitched baby voice answer after the first ring. But she couldn't take it any further.

She was amazed that she wouldn't mind the idea of the strange whore invading her body. She didn't even seem to be bothered by the grotesquely shabby business of checking into a matinée hotel where the beds were never cold—at least not in her imagination. She weighed what Mama might have done in her place and how she would have responded if she could know Jean bought whores.

But there was a gross political risk. If she were connected with using afternoon whores in bizarre hotels, that would undo everything Mama had prayed that she would become. Because she wanted what Mama wanted—to soar to the heights of politics—she taught her body that she could not take such a chance for such a nothing reason as a hundred-dollar roll in the hay.

19

Ames Spano became morose and sullen when he was with his wife unless he was on Urugudine extract. From the day she told him that he would not be allowed to extend his gifts of service and charity across the world, his Urugudine-placed saintliness increased his frustration. For two months Jean ignored his sulking, convincing herself that it was a temporary thing. There was a bad flood in the Mississippi Valley and she had the inspiration to ask him if he would like it if she arranged to have the bank bring his willingness to help to the attention of the president and secure for him the appointment as director of the emergency relief activities in the region. To her amazement he said that already had been done, that his appointment would be announced by the White House the following morning.

"How did you arrange that?"

"Through Senator Cassiman."

"You know Cassiman?"

"I married him to his wife, if you will recall."

"Oh, yes. Of course you did."

"His wife has most generously agreed to work as my executive assistant in the Mississippi Valley."

"*Alex?*"

"In twenty days we'll have those people safe and sheltered, fed and healthy."

"How did Alex get into this?"

"It was her idea."

"Ames, I have been paying a lot of odd charge-account items—things like perfume, and little Pucci things, and flowers. Were they for Alex?"

"Yes. For Alex. Nor have I made any attempt to conceal those small gifts."

"Why do you send her gifts?"

"I have every hope I can persuade her to work with me as my executive assistant at La Casa."

Jean grew pale. "You must be stupid—among other things, Ames," she said quietly. "*I* control La Casa—no matter what you read in the newspapers after feeding it to them by the spoonful. Alex will *not* work at La Casa."

"Very well."

"What else do you and Alex hope to do together?"

"La Casa seems to be out. Africa and Asia seem to be out—although I can never be convinced that you do control Africa and Asia, Jean. So I suppose you can see," he said maliciously, "that all Alex and I can hope to do together is to see what we can do in the Mississippi Valley."

Jean and Charles Cantwell had lunch at the Plaza to set the final arrangements for the assurance of her nomination as lieutenant governor. For five months Jean had been wooing the gubernatorial candidate-to-be at a series of dinners for twelve people who could deliver money, attention, and votes. She had discussed in some detail with his campaign managers the fact that she felt she could divert some of the financial benefits of Voters' Research into the campaign. She offered the candidate's managers access to two and a half million dollars (two hundred and fifty thousand of it in cash, packed in a canvas airline bag) if they would pledge to carry out the objectives of VRC contributors, i.e., that New York State was ready to support a woman candidate for the second place on the ticket. They welcomed her on the team by accepting the money and Jean; the nationally celebrated police executive let herself be persuaded to run.

"It's just that there won't be a helluva lot for you to do, Jeannie," Bennet Reyes, the campaign manager, told her. "It just seems to me to be a goddamn waste of talent for a woman like you to take lieutenant governor."

"I don't want a lot to do, Ben. I love New York. I want the governor to appoint me as his ambassador-at-large to sell New York State to the rest of the country."

"Maybe you got something there, Jeannie." He grinned. She would be a model lieutenant governor.

The time had come to take her resignation to Commissioner Mitgang, and to bed Caen. Her plan to use a liaison man between Legal Matters and the rest of the department hadn't worked out. It wasn't anyone's fault—particularly not Caen's. He had invented jobs to keep himself busy. It was just one of the new administrative ideas that hadn't worked. Most of the others had. She listened to Captain Melvin tell her that Caen should be transferred out to where the department could get some use out of his salary. "He's a good man, Commissioner, a lot smarter than he looks. When he was in organized-crime control he made himself into a hoodlum. He knew everybody in the rackets. When he was on the hotel squad the guy turned himself into a locksmith and a jeweler. They say he could appraise a stone as good as a professional."

"He was on the vice squad too, wasn't he?"

"Yeah. The point is—we aren't *using* him here, Commissioner. Let him go back to being a cop. A letter and a call from you to Chief Maguire could get Caen a good assignment. So nobody has to know we made a little mistake bringing him in here. Caen won't say anything. Let him go."

"Very soon, Al. I just want to make sure everything is done right."

Friday afternoon at about four o'clock she told Officer Schrader, who ran the office, to instruct Caen to be ready to go with her to the corporation counsel's office. As they rode over in the cab she could feel his presence the way a Christian martyr could feel and smell the hungry animals before they were released from their cages. She pretended to be checking out some papers from her briefcase during the ride over. They didn't speak. The business with the corporation counsel was over with in twenty minutes, while Caen waited in the anteroom. As she and Caen left the building together he said, "Hey—was there something you wanted me to do, Commissioner?"

For eleven months he had tried to sweat her out of his skin. He had had extraordinarily cruel fantasies about her, getting even with her for ignoring him like he was dirt. He would ride home on the subway obsessed with her, trying to figure out some kind of a handle he could use to grab her and throw her out of his life.

As the months went on he had transferred what he wanted to do to her to the bodies of other women. He sought out the real masochist freaks in the business, but it did nothing for him. Then he tried talking to known libbers as if they were all a snake pit of intellectuals. They argued bookies, junk, singers, pop songs, death, baseball—anything. He got nothing out of it. Then he found a young girl, a very nice, pretty girl who lived on 167th Street and whose father was an inspector in the internal affairs division, so Caen wasn't about to get kinky there. He took her to church and to the movies and shit like that. The kid fell in love with him so he cut it off very quickly. But after many months he had been able to figure out that what had happened to him was all three things: he wanted to beat the commissioner until she screamed; he wanted to talk to her as an equal so that by listening she was saying to him that he had a mind, that he was a man, and that he should be listened to. But he knew he was also in love with her. He felt toward her the way the kid from 167th Street felt about him. And he couldn't do anything about any of it.

He had been confused when Schrader told him to stand by to go with the commissioner to the CC's office, but when she walked out and nodded to him icily to get into step beside him, he couldn't figure *anything* out because she had fixed herself up and she had dressed herself up and she had put on some stones that had to be worth at least thirty grand wholesale. For what? For a ride to the corporation counsel's office? For just a flash he thought she had fixed herself up for him, but she hardly talked all the way over so he knew she was dolled up for some heavy date later. He had never not known what to do with a woman before. He only wanted one out of the three, like everybody else, but what he wanted he expressed in one way or the other and he got it. His instinct worked for him. He couldn't give any reason, but as she walked up to him when she came out of the CC's office he suddenly realized that she was wearing that jail door pin he had ripped off the whore's dress. It was right on her left tit, just above the nipple, and it was trying to tell him something which he couldn't figure out but which he could feel. Why should a millionaire woman lawyer who had all those stones on, put on a five-dollar pin to go out someplace with some rich guy? She was a libber but she wasn't *that* much of a libber. She was telling him something she didn't even know she was telling him.

So he decided to try the test sentence, because whatever she answered it would tell him everything.

"Hey—was there something you wanted me to do, Commissioner?"

She stopped walking. She turned slowly, placing herself very close to him so that when they were facing each other their pelvises touched and he got an enormous instant erection but it didn't make them move apart. Her spectacular eyes were hot for him—*that* he knew how to read. He couldn't stop breathing shallowly. "I thought you might be free for dinner, Sergeant," she said.

"*Dinner?*"

She let her tongue wet her lips slowly. "Figuratively speaking."

"Yeah."

In the taxi they tried out the hors d'oeuvres. They were all over each other; groaning, moaning, and clutching all the way uptown. They got out in disarray, not having spoken at all, in front of an apartment house at 62nd and Park. The doorman looked at them inquiringly.

"I'm Deputy Commissioner Spano," she said. "Mrs. Cassiman is expecting me."

"Mrs. Cassiman isn't here, madam."

"I know, I know." She held up the keys she had taken from Ames' bureau. "And Senator Cassiman is in Washington." She walked forward to the elevator. The operator took them to the eleventh floor. As Jean let them into the flat she said, "This place belongs to an old college chum of mine. She insisted that we use it while she's in Mississippi."

He *was* covered with hair. He *did* stink. He *was* a rutting, barking, gasping animal. Nothing tired him. He knew things to do to her that a battalion of depraved professionals must have taught him, and she thought poignantly that she was never going to be able to teach these things to Ames, not even if he came to her again, because he would only use them to satiate the Slut. In the darkness she wept silently while Caen used her countless times in degrading, bestial, insatiable and animally analogic ways—frantically, never speaking while he spent himself on her, because whatever else he didn't know about her, he knew this was Caen's Last Stand and the thought of that drove him frantic with alarm and fear and made his body perform so that nothing she might have thought before they touched each other could ever withstand the enormous sensations he was making her feel.

Ravenously, they did have dinner three hours later, and she felt more than just replenished. In total utter control of the male animal as they left, she felt satisfied as well at having left knots of sperm-stained sheets on Alex's bed for her (and Ames) to come home to.

They sat in a corner, upstairs and far to the rear of "21." He had three of the hamburgers; she had chicken hash with a bottle of red wine for him and a half bottle of white wine for her.

He knew he had lost, but he was too exhausted to make any issue of that now. Let her wait a week until she got the hots for him again and she wanted a little more of what he had. He would take it slow and pay it out easy until in a month or so he would have her washing his socks and cooking his meals if that's all he decided he wanted from her.

"I hear you passed the examinations for lieutenant at the top of the list," she said. "Congratulations."

"Where did you hear that?"

She passed him a small smile.

"I'm resigning tomorrow, Caen," she said, "but this morning I told Chief Maguire what a good cop you are."

"Thanks, Commissioner. Thanks very much."

"You're going to get homicide five."

"Wha'?"

"Don't go for captain. You'd hate the paperwork. Stay loose and do your usual job and maybe someday, somebody will be able to set you in Narcotics in the South Bronx."

"We're finished—you and me? Is that what you're tellin' me?"

"We have to be, Caen."

"Why?"

"They are running me for lieutenant governor."

"Holy shit!"

"How's the food?"

He pushed the second empty plate away. "It's okay." He poured more wine and sipped it, staring straight ahead toward the staircase. He had never been dumped by a woman in his life, but this one had no handles. How was he going to get her back just to punish her for thinking she could dump him? That's all I want, he told himself. I want to let this one have it because she doesn't give a shit about me. After eleven months, she locks me in for a couple of hours in the sack and she thinks even that is probably too good for me. But how does a guy who wants to make lieutenant, and who is going to do a job on homicide five, even if she did set it up for him, give her the business? He knew things had a funny way of getting evened out, and whether she was the fucking lieutenant governor or not, his chance was going to come and when it came she was going to get it just as bad as he could figure out to give it to her because he couldn't stand to have to hold still and let a goddamn nothing woman do this to him.

Jean was exultant because of how she had handled the whole situation. She had acted the way any randy man would have acted, she had got what she wanted, and she had neatly disposed of any unpleasant aftermath of it. She was really delighted that she had thought of getting the promotion for the fellow. It would be a whole lot more than the old-fashioned traditional five-dollar bill left on the mantel. If one wanted men, one had to know how to play by their rules. She had kept a tight control over the fellow, and, indeed, over herself. No slobbering sentimentalities and sighing and longing gasps for what might have been mired in love's sweet glue. Mama would have been so *proud* of how she had taken her pleasure, then, with quite a considerable amount of grace, had gotten rid of this sexually exciting oaf.

20

Jean was a model lieutenant governor. She was rich, therefore able to attract rich campaign contributors. She was strikingly photogenic, which improved the PR mix around the State House and added to New York's luster when she was on tour. She was willing to tour, which kept her out of the governor's way, but also, because there had to be a hidden plus for Jean as well, she was able to lock her image in with state committee chairpeople and with the state and key city leaders of the women's movement throughout the country as she moved by careful plan through thirty-one states as the ambassador of the State of New York, selling its industrial opportunities and its beauties as a vacationland. Jean's ascension into that executive office was a wholly reciprocal opportunity all the way.

All states advertised, publicized, and merchandised themselves in all other states of the Union, but Jean did it better, right across the country, for the State of New York.

"New York not only has an eager work force, but it has the big banks—big banks are based there from all over the world," she would tell industrial audiences in her set speech. "What company doesn't have a use for those? And that's just the beginning of our love affair. New York is the hub and center of national and international communications by the most extraordinary combined media force on the face of the earth, and the natural stepping-stone to industrial might and glory."

She operated with a political advance man and a publicity crew which traveled three weeks ahead of her. Susie Orde, hired away from CBS-TV, was her press secretary. She moved into the target city five working days before Jean's arrival to check out all arrangements. The arrangements were built around (a) a luncheon sponsored by the six most prominent women's political and service organizations and chaired by either the mayor's wife of the host city or the wife of the widest industrial or media figure; (b) a cocktail reception at somebody's mansion; (c) a small but elaborate dinner party given by Jean as a party figure, for the state committee members, the fat cats of the party and the powers behind it.

At the luncheon Jean's speech was concerned with all important women's issues: abortion, job equality, child battering, and wife abuse. At the dinners she addressed her guests on the subject of women, the American majority, the aroused constituency, the tremendous army of voters which was, day by day, being welded into a single democratic consciousness that would soon be the ultimate weapon at the polls.

She did business among the most powerful politicians on behalf of Voters' Research, arranging for commitments for the infusion of money where she, as executive director of Voters' Research, could be assured such contributions would do the most good for the women's movement and contribute to Jean's own recognition as a national power within the party. As a crossruff, the party's bosses, state for state, agreed to man the daises of the women's luncheons at every key stop with some very heavy people who could be vital to the ERA when the crunch came—on condition that the response to the crunch were led by Jean Spano. In this way she attracted one ex-president of the United States, eleven senators, fourteen chairmen of key congressional committees, four cabinet officers, and twenty-one state governors to the daises of ERA luncheons given in her honor.

Along the way, to her delight and surprise, she was able to bed a handsome banker; the CEO of one of the country's automakers; one astronaut, and a pleasant and exceptionally good-looking young man who got off at the wrong floor at the Brown Palace Hotel in Denver and rang her doorbell. He was, as it turned out, a Baptist clergyman, and for the six short hours they were together they discovered much in common. His admiration for Ames' operation at St. Grace's and at La Casa was, of course, boundless.

She met Franklin M. Heller for the first time when he was governor of Wisconsin. They sat together at a political dinner party in Milwaukee and spoke German all through the evening. In this instance there was no question of bundling. Heller copulated only with power in the abstract. He was a point-blank man, suggestive of possible, if elusive, opportunities for others. Later, his handyman, Keifetz, would find it necessary to put a makeup man on him every morning and stay at his side whenever Heller was campaigning. But now, as governor, stained teabags still lay like air-turned ostrich eggs under Heller's eyes, giving him an exhausted presence; a cosmetic anomaly because in fact Heller could sleep for three minutes or for ten hours and was always rested. Gordon Manning, in his definitive biography of Heller, *Grist!*, an examination of the president's inner philosophy, wrote that the great man's entire face contributed to a public belief in what he was not and thus lulled all those who would otherwise have been on their guard: his darkened eye bags, his general air of exhaustion, his muscular inability to sustain a smile providing assurances of folk weakness which belied Heller's prodigious energy.

In the sixteen months she was lieutenant governor of the State of New York, before moving up into the federal government, Jean spent a total of three months in Albany, the state capital.

21

When the advance machinery was working at its smoothest, the great Puss-in-Boots show, promoting its Marquise de Carrabas, arrived in Los Angeles, following successful stands in Sacramento and San Francisco where, bravely, Jean spoke on behalf of the wines of her home state.

When Susie Orde arrived at her suite at the Beverly Hills Hotel to check out the readiness, there was a message for her to call Thane Cawdor.

"Thane *Caw*dor? You mean the *superstar*?" Ms. Orde was a young woman who had never been impressed. After all, she'd been a name-broker herself since she left college, but as every American woman knew, this was something else. She called him the instant the assistant manager left her alone in the suite. She knew his voice from the moment he said hello.

"This is Susie Orde. For Governor Spano. Did you call?"

"Ms. Orde. Well, how very kind of you to call me back. You must be the busiest woman in town."

"Oh, no! Not at all! No, no, no!"

"Governor Spano and I knew each other in Switzerland quite some time ago and I thought—well, this is about the first chance we've had to chat in years, so I wondered if you could give her my number—the sealed and private number—and ask her to call me when she gets in—if she has a minute, that is."

"Oh, yes! Definitely. She certainly will. I mean, I'll certainly tell her."

Susie usually left town the day before Jean came in, to move on to the next campaign stop. But this time, because Jean was going back to Albany for eight days for a legislative session—which Susie had planned to be spending in Las Vegas with a certain sapphire miner from Brazil—she stayed over so she could hand the telephone number directly to Jean just to be sure she got it.

"Oh—yes," Jean said.

"Oh, *yes?*"

"I haven't even talked to him since before I was married."

"I don't think in terms of *talking* to him. My God, Jean—do you really *know* him?"

"He was a hire-car chauffeur in Geneva when I was a student. It was—very nice."

"Are you going to call him?"

"Let's go over the schedule for Los Angeles."

They used the next seventy minutes taking the schedule apart, Jean asking endless questions, Susie either giving the answers or getting on the telephone for them. When they were finished, about forty minutes before Jean was to start to work after a bath and a change, they had a drink together.

"You could call him now and you'd be able to see him Sunday night after the big clambake at Malibu."

"Not a chance."

"Yeah. Okay."

"I'm not only a politician, I'm a married politician."

"What about Houston? What about Detroit?"

"They were civilians. There is no way I can be invisible with Thane Cawdor. I have to change now."

When Susie left, Jean ran the tub and unpacked. She got into the tub and relaxed for ten minutes. Then she reached out for the telephone and called the number which she had memorized.

"Thane? Jean."

"We're the star-crossed lovers. I didn't think you'd call, but I've been sitting here and waiting."

"You sound just the same."

"The same as what?"

"As Switzerland."

"Doesn't seem possible. Just the same, you sound even better."

"Are you ever going to open that car shop in Dorset?"

"Oh, yes. A writer said to me out here that he and his wife wanted to make just one more million, then they'd quit. That's about all I want. Three or four more million."

"I hope Dorset will still be there."

"I'll do it. Maybe three or four more years. Will I be able to see you?"

"No."

"Because of that problem we had in New York?"

She laughed. He was the same; she was reacting to him just the same as she had the day he had arrived with that enormous robin's-egg blue Rolls-Royce so long, long ago. "I had forgotten all that," she said. "You still have that old-time whammy on me. I can't see you because I'm grown up now and because I am doing very serious business."

"I think I understand," he said simply.

"Politics is a little like your business, only more so."

"I don't think we can always be apart the way it has been," he told her slowly. "It was too tremendous the other way. I never forgot you. I mean I *never* forgot you."

"I will never forget you, my darling Thane," she said. "And I would never trade the past for what I'm reaching for."

22

Four months before the presidential elections, Keifetz visited Lieutenant-Governor Spano at the state capital. Keifetz was the presidential nominee's eyes, ears, conscience, and feet. He had been Heller's backup man through two terms of office as governor of Wisconsin, and he would be his chief adviser if the voters decided that Heller should settle into the White House.

Keifetz's permanent expression was insulting, as if he knew this could provoke people into blurting out in protest all the truths they had been trying to conceal. He was a strong, compact, dark man with deep cheek dimples, bushy black hair, and eyebrows like military brushes. He was the political caricaturists' ideal and that helped to take the heat away from Heller. Nobody seemed to be sure where he had originated. Some people said they had known him when he had been a tool pusher for an oil company. There were stories that he had been the political adviser to the Dalai Lama in the Tekchen Choeling at Dharamsala in the Dhau lader range of the Outer Himalayas; still others said he had been sales manager for a Pizza Hut chain in Nebraska.

Keifetz was single and a professional pain-in-the-ass whose only positive side was his endless interest in advancing Franklin M. Heller. It was as though he had been created from birth to be an administrative aide or a chief of staff to his leader.

Jean had pulled a report on him as soon as she knew he existed. The

116

bank, Charles Cantwell, Voters' Research, and all resources came up with what looked like very little that was definite or useful. The report said in effect that Keifetz spoke for the candidate—which was all Jean felt anyone needed to know. Also, however, the report turned up one striking peculiarity of Keifetz's which could be seen as a weakness, depending on the circumstances: he was a wild-eyed, trembling-handed secret police buff. He was unable to resist anything or anybody connected with secret-police work. Secretly, he had locked closets filled with paperback novels exposing the inner workings of all of the national secret-police conspiracies of most of the countries of the world. He was able to quote entire pages from the James Bond records, had a clinical knowledge of the advanced masochism of Le Carré's characters, and had taught himself karate from illustrated Japanese manuals.

"Mrs. Spano," Keifetz said expressionlessly, "I knew you were a handsome woman, but this is too much."

She laughed delightedly. "Had you planned to sit around combing the marmalade out of my hair?" she asked, and that got them right down to business.

"The candidate has been talking to the American Bar Association about their nominee for attorney general."

"I had heard that."

"We've also talked to the National Association of Police Chiefs, some media people, and the National Organization for Women. They endorsed you."

"I was there before you, Mr. Keifetz."

"Yeah? Did you cover the civil rights people and labor? Did you check out the capos and the oil companies?"

"It was in my interest."

"You are a direct woman and the candidate likes that."

"But I am a woman. Isn't that where the canker gnaws?"

"That was on *my* mind a little, yes. But not on his mind. Well, good. You answered the question. You'll accept the job if he offers it."

"No, Mr. Keifetz. I'll accept it only if I am guaranteed he will offer it."

"When may I set up a meeting?" he asked her.

"At his convenience."

"Tomorrow evening?"

"Fine. Where?"

"My apartment at the Lombardy in New York."

"Dinner?"

"Just a meeting. The candidate is faking a diet. He kids himself that he can lose weight by willpower. It will be a working night for him. Tell

Mr. Murphy at the desk you want to see me and the Secret Service will bring you up."

Franklin M. Heller was a portly, professionally magisterial man who moved and looked like a clean-shaven Edward VII. He never wore glasses when others were present because his myopia made his gaze more probing. He was not a cordial, nor even a friendly man, but bluff and pseudo-heartily avuncular. The potential genuineness of his smile had an elusive way of concealing itself and, had it been possible to record its thermal temperature, it would have proved lower than the 30 billionths of a degree above absolute zero which is the temperature of outer space, the sort of distancing Heller liked to maintain in order to shatter any jolly-good-fellow myths about politicians, and to prove that he was one politician not coming to power to have his teeth constantly photographed. Heller was the most tireless and effective complainer in American history, mostly about issues which stood in the way of his power.

He greeted Jean with a smile as quick as a camera shutter at F32, bade her be seated where he could watch her, ignored Keifetz, who was seated demurely upon a piano bench, and boomed out with a voice that could have been rented out to play Sir John Falstaff, "We'll announce right after State and Defense, three days after the election."

"Splendid."

"I admire you no less than I want the support of the women of this country, Governor Spano. Beyond the vital work at Justice, you will want to apply yourself to the politics of maintaining that support."

"I'll do that, sir."

"We think it might be a good idea not to make any changes at the FBI. What do you think?"

"I think my own appointment will have to run the FBI."

He chuckled like a ripped oil tanker despoiling a beach resort. "Good. Very good. Precisely the right answer. When I ask anyone to run anything, I expect them to carry the whole load." He unzipped a tiny moment of that awful smile upon her and left the room.

Jean appointed Richard Gallagher, head of the New York State Police and her ardent supporter, as director of the Federal Bureau of Investigation.

23

Within ninety days after Jean had been sworn in as attorney general, and as soon as she had the DJ running in the way she had decided it was intended to run, she took to the road, making fifty-eight appearances in less than a year, addressing the principal women's organizations in key cities, with the enthusiastic approval of the White House and with the support of the party's political apparatus wherever she appeared. She brought the continuing message of insistence about the power of the women's vote as an immense bloc not to be forgotten until the ERA was a part of the Constitution.

Jean produced herself partly as a theatrical show, partly as a female messiah, and partly as a cabinet officer: sort of Harpo Marx crossed with Queen Elizabeth and that puppydog-friendly, pie-baking neighbor next door.

Her appearances were ostensibly based on the administration's advocacy of the still-pending Equal Rights Amendment, but the hard and fast purpose was to raise money for women's organizations for use in that fight. The admission charge to see the superstar was either $50 or $100 a ticket at the box office of the largest auditorium in town—indoors or out, depending on the season. Among other entertainments, she performed on the cello, piano, and harp as a guest of the local symphony orchestra and worked for Musicians Union scale and no share of the gate. In the course of her campaigns for the ERA she was to appear under the auspices of every philharmonic society in the country. She drew capacity audiences of men and women.

When her musical performance was over, Jean went straight to the rostrum and within minutes, using a speech which had been pretested for peaks and valleys known to produce emotional response, and programmed for her by psychologists, sound analysts, pitchmen, and great actresses—at Jean's expense—brought each audience to its feet at her will, cheering and applauding, or weeping and baying, again and again throughout the speech.

She had also programmed the preceding music well, beginning with the awesome sonorities of the cello, playing on an instrument which had been fashioned out of pearwood by Andrea Amati in 1572 and which had once been presented by Pius V to the Emperor Otto IX to become, later on, the glorious possession of Jean Louis Duport. She played Dvorak's B Minor Concerto, op. 104, that complete expression of full-blooded romanticism. With the cello, Jean established emotional logic for her audience.

A piano solo followed because it can be a crashingly assertive instrument, garrulous and dominating and therefore, in the minds of the audience, masculine, expanding strength from strength, rejecting weakness, but it had women's lust in it, a mating call from aeons before there had been human speech.

When she knew they understood each other, Jean moved to the ineffable femininity of the harp, drawing with it all the fabled graces of girlhood, womanhood, and untroubled old age, promising the audience that together they had overcome the darker promises of the cello and the frightening threats of the piano. These sounds from the harp which fell upon Jean's natural constituency were a description of how their fathers had seen them, of how they wanted their sons to remember them, and of what they deeply wished their daughters could be permitted to become. If Berlioz and Meyerbeer could have heard Jean play the harp, they might have dueled to prove who loved her more. Because of the lighting, her emotion, her makeup, and her technique she appeared as the archangel who personified all women as she played.

There was no intermission. That would have vanished Jean's great illusory architecture which was sheltering the psyches of up to forty-two thousand women at each performance. When she took their applause—magnificent in a $2900 dress by Nina Ricci—her enormous storm blue eyes lighted by the diamond fires within them—thanking them with that singular voice which had been trained from six years old, everything she offered bracketed and cherished their great cause that she had journeyed there to serve.

Poetically, she reminded them of their rights. Harshly, she told them their duty to themselves and to all female life to come: that there was no escaping the duty they had assumed when they had been born as women. She left them with more music—everyone standing with crossed-over, joined hands, singing out the ecstasies of "The Battle Hymn of the Republic," that thundering paean to glory written by a woman, then she disappeared into a trick of light and sprinted at the center of six bodyguards to a limousine, then to the airport to fly back to Washington, leaving behind a prodigy of party solidarity and a fusion of steeled wills to hold up any bridge she chose to build to candidacies she would someday assume.

The mail to the White House and to the Department of Justice—plus telegrams and telephone calls—never fell below eight hundred thousand pieces a month during Jean's first three years as attorney general, extolling her.

She appeared on national television, at La Casa with her saintly husband; at Rockrimmon with all national women's leaders, and at the White House with President Heller and Dame Maria Van Slyke, doyenne of the international women's movement. While she did these party things, she conducted, as attorney general, a successful national investigation into organized crime, successfully argued and won before the Supreme Court two milestone decisions affecting civil rights and alleged Defense Department corruption, and was acclaimed as Outstanding Attorney General of the Century by the American Bar Association. She also appeared on *The Muppet Show*.

While Jean marched in the vanguard, Ursula Baggot and Charles Cantwell and the politician-demographers and the press agents at Voters' Research programmed all of the action into computer data and projected the possible combined trends into the political future. The nourishment from her achievements moved Jean onward and upward just as Mama had taught her.

24

After Franklin M. Heller had become president of the United States and appointed Jean Spano as his attorney general, her opportunity for public service and her record of achievement matched the challenge. One afternoon, several years later, Ames Spano, transformed by Urugudine, went to her house in Georgetown and told her he had a substantial statement to make to her.

"Substantial? What an odd choice of a word, Ames."

"It was precise. Jean, what I am about to say, I say without guilt."

"How can you elude guilt? Are you also an auto-shriver, Padre?"

"Mock me not, Jean. My conscience allowed me to step away from you, knowing that you had never been a part of me."

"You look a little nuts to me, Ames. Are you taking something new?"

"I love Alex Cassiman, Jean. And I have loved her carnally as well."

"You and a few hundred others."

"She gave up everything to work with me."

"I knew she was bored to death with her husband and that she didn't fit anywhere in Washington."

"She has washed the feet of the wretched. She has made my work her own life. We see the same horizons."

122

"Ames, if you are asking for a divorce it is out of the question. Oh, *drat!* Why do you always make me say banal things?"

"I must have a divorce."

"No divorce. You know what that means to me politically, so you must have some primitive understanding of what it can mean for you."

"Alex and I will be at work in the Central African Republic by the next election."

"You silly, *silly* man—you still want that."

"I want it," he said nobly, psychotropically far above this battle. "I am needed there. I can ease their burden. I can make their children whole again and I can find Jesus for them. I want that."

"Then you haven't read the charter of the foundation, Ames. I control the foundation. Think about that, then get out of here because your new spirituality makes me gag. Either you wait until after the election or not only won't you ever get to see the Central African Republic but you will find your work in Harlem seriously hampered."

"It is my intention to resign from the foundation at once. As soon as I can get back to New York I will make the announcement."

"An announcement?"

"It is the only honorable thing I can do."

"But what about funding the Central African mission?"

"I never intended to accept your money. We will be funded by the FCMB."

"Who?"

"The Federal Christian Missionary Brotherhood."

She took a deep breath, held it, then expelled it slowly. "Then there was nothing for us to talk about today. You and she had your plans made and this chat is only the release of some vague social obligation."

"You are not blameless, Jean."

"Would you like to go into that in detail?"

"No. It could only hurt both of us and there is nothing to be gained."

"How Christian, Ames. All right. I must accept, I suppose. But I ask you two things."

"Thank you, Jean."

"Please don't make any announcement. Not for my sake. Not for me. For the government. You can harm this government." She had gotten control of herself again. The heat inside her head was cooling.

"Very well, my dear."

"Can you wait until the elections are over before you leave for your mission?"

"Yes. Certainly. We can't have everything ready much before then, Jean. I am the one who is most sorry about this. I loved you but you didn't want me. Alex wants me. The work in the field needs me."

"You'll probably have ample time to examine all that before you die, Ames."

"There is nothing to examine."

"Marriage is bound to the bed, Ames. You left me alone in our bed, then took the Slut into it. It was you who dishonored our marriage."

"I answer you from St. Jerome. 'Matrimony is always a vice, all that can be done is to excuse it and to sanctify it; therefore it was made a religious sacrament.' Marriage has torn me into small pieces or else I should have been whole; serving and saving the Zuni."

25

When Ames had gone Jean went to the piano and played Brahms furiously, pounding at the keys as if they were the teeth of his living body. She drove the speed of the piano's hammers, increasing the volume with increasing amounts of her kinetic energy, swinging her forearms, then her whole arms, not to have to depend on such tiny pounding units as her fingers, sustaining the staccato tones for only half their time value. When she came to the end of it she was flushed and breathing hard but she felt better because she had decided what she had to do. She closed the piano abruptly, stood up at once and walked across the room, picked up her keys and her purse, and went out the side door to the garage where she got into the car and drove it off into the evening.

It took her just about twelve minutes to get where she was going. She left the car, strode up the cement path, and rang the doorbell. A woman answered the door.

"Hello, Madge," Jean said. "Where is Mrs. Cassiman?"

"She's upstairs, Mrs. Spano. In her room. Shall I tell her you're here?"

"Don't bother. She expects me." Jean walked past the woman, crossed the hall and climbed the stairs rapidly. She stopped at the top to call out, "Alex!"

"I'm in here. Who is it?"

Jean walked toward the voice. Halfway there Alex appeared in the doorway. "I can't say why I didn't ever expect to see you again, Jean," she said, "but I didn't."

Jean walked past her, into the bedroom. Alex followed her, closing the door.

"I had to talk to you about this, Slut," Jean said. "How did it happen? How could you let it happen?"

"How could *you* let it happen? He was your husband. You just threw him away so you could get on with your life, and I caught him."

"You and Ames have probably taught yourselves to believe that."

"It is true!"

"Ames saw to it that he was much busier than I ever was. I had the choice of becoming a social worker or what I am. Ames wanted what he has so much that I went out and got it for him. I got him the funding for La Casa, I worked beside him—I *did* become a social worker—then you came into our lives."

"Long before Ames ever noticed that I had come into his life, he knew you had left it," Alex replied. "You were in Albany, or Washington, or other cities across the country—so he noticed me. I didn't lift him on, Jean. Which is to say I didn't *tempt* him, mainly because Ames simply can't be tempted by much of anything except wretched, poor, and hurting people. But he *is* a man. And as a man he turned to me because I was there and—because I am me—the same love-starved me you and I have always known—I responded to him."

"Fair enough under your rules especially crafted for the occasion," Jean said. "But all of that happened for many different reasons—up to the point where he decided he wanted you. Of course, as Ames *now* sees it, and as you so *conveniently* see it—if I had been the wife which men demand as their right, I would have forsaken my silly notions about becoming lieutenant governor of the State of New York and attorney general of the United States to stay at his side, applauding his muddled victories and darning his socks. God knows, every man who knew me would have thought much the better of me for it. Ames, as you observed, is a man. So he expected that much of me, that tiny sacrifice. But isn't it possible that *my* need is as great as his? Isn't it possible that *any* woman's is as great as any man's? Is the responsibility for running the Department of Justice of the United States any less important than washing the feet of the poor? How do you answer that—as a woman?"

"I'm a woman, that nobody can deny," Alex said. "But I'm no ideologue. I don't even think women need liberating, as the quaint phrase goes."

"Liberation? This is *my* marriage and *my* husband that we are talking about. And I'm not saying you took him away from me—because you couldn't do that on the best day of your life if I were only a sock darner and the enemy of the rings men leave around bathtubs when they choose to take baths. That's what it's all about. You don't need to tell me where you stand on women's liberation. You'll wait, buffing your nails. You'll do absolutely nothing to win your rights, but *when we get them for you* you will wallow in them like a hippopotamus in mud. Oh, my dear, I can see that this line annoys you so we will leave it. Well, toots, Ames is your problem now. And, as I am the expert on Ames, I will tell you why you are doomed to failure."

"Not me, Jean. I'm a sock darner, a tub scrubber, and a social worker."

"The more things seem to remain the same, the more they change, Slutsie. Your problem will be money. Ames can't get enough money. Ask him about that. He never lies. He is neurotically fixated on money and luxury for Ames Spano."

"Even if I could give it to him there is no place he could use it in the Central African Republic."

"No, no. Men need money. Money is their medals. Women believe they need men. For millennia men have been *their* medals. One would think the problem could not be solved."

"Your own militant sisterhood would have it that women should need money instead of men, and that men should need women."

"Men *do* need women, but they only concede that when they lift their eyes up from their money. What the militant sisterhood wants is every woman's right to darn socks and scrub bathtubs—if that is what she wants. Or for the right to run after money if *that* is what she wants. Or for the right to take over men's places in the world if men have defaulted—if taking on such work is what the woman wants. We want *you* to have an equal chance with any man in or beyond your life—and, by heaven, Slut, we are going to get it for you."

"Poor Jean."

"Poor Slut."

"What profiteth a woman's soul if another woman can take her man away from her?"

"What profiteth the husband-stealer," Jean said, "if he is all she has in this world?"

Alex made a harsh, bitter laugh. "Life is short," she said.

"Wrong again, my aging friend. Life is long. Life can be interminable."

26

When she returned from Alex's house she called Charles Cantwell to say she had to see him.

"What's wrong, Jean? You sound frightened."

"Frightened? No. But anyway—can you come to Washington tomorrow morning?"

"Of course."

"At the house. Not at Justice. At ten o'clock? Will that be all right?"

"Make it eight-thirty."

"Thank you, Charles."

She had breakfast ready for him. As they began to eat she said, "Ames was here last night to say that he and Alex Cassiman are going to run off to the Central African Republic together to consecrate their holy love for each other and to comfort the oppressed together."

"That girl from Smith? The one you used to call Slut?"

"I wasn't being clairvoyant, Charles."

"Alex *Cassiman*? The *senator's* wife?"

"*Yes!*"

"What kind of a maze is this?"

"Please stop asking rhetorical questions."

"I must talk to Ames."

"Useless. The Jesus mask has hardened on him."

"You've put too many years into making a place for yourself, and if Ames goes through with this, Keifetz will convince the president that you've got to go. Marriages which go publicly on the rocks are poison for American political candidates."

"What will you say to Ames?"

"To *them*, Jean. To Alex, too."

"You'll only get the Reverend Dr. Spano's martyr's look—marked down from $12.95. I don't think anything can reach him. Maybe she can, but Ames doesn't really see women the way other men do. Alex has no money. He needs money to support his inadequacy."

"No money? Who is funding him?"

"The FCMB."

"Who?"

"The Federal Christian Missionary Brotherhood."

"Ah! Good! The Nina Wintringham Foundation is *their* money."

"What's the use? He'll just inhale another forty pounds of press clippings and he'll go to Africa, money or not. Anyway, if we block the FCMB, he'll have other sources we can't reach."

"The bank has quite a reach."

"It's just that Ames isn't balanced anymore. He lusts for the great hosing of attention he'll get when he announces his organized kindness from the top of the Washington Monument or somewhere like that. He feels he has given everything he has to give to the wretched of this continent, the hundreds of thousands of the pantless whom he has succored for his scrapbooks. He's sitting in a darkened room somewhere now, ladling the glories of his righteousness over himself to sweeten his dreams of when he tells the assembled multitudes of media that he is leaving civilization behind to brush bacteria off the eyeballs of children in Central Africa."

27

Ames Spano was found shot to death in his study in the Henstell mansion on Riverside Drive, May 11, a few days after his sixty-fourth birthday, two months before the presidential renominating convention. The police told the press it was burglary and homicide. Dr. Spano had been doing an insurance inventory of his wife's jewelry when he had been killed. The body had been discovered late Sunday evening by the cook and housekeeper when they returned from Canada after a weekend off, and while Mrs. Spano was in a meeting with the president at the White House.

The New York *Globe* had run down a number of the contractors who had rebuilt the mansion for "Dr. Spano's multimillionaire wife, the attorney general of the United States," and the newspaper detailed the electronic impregnability of the house transformed into a bastion of total security which towered above a sea of violence. The newspaper suggested that no one could have broken into that house for a robbery which became a murder, that only someone who lived inside it, who had all the secrets of access to it, could find a way to get into that house to commit a murder under the pretense of robbery. The police were unable to explain how the killer had gained access into the house. The newspaper stated flatly that Dr. Spano and his wife were in the process of separating bitterly when he had been murdered. The newspaper had seemed, for that day's editions, to leave the story there to fester in the public mind.

Monday, May 12, was a dull news day so the space alloted to the murder, which would in any case have been extraordinary, became spectacularly strident. The media stressed the connection of the White House and the office of the attorney general to the murder and promised much professional hysteria to come. A modern saint had been brutally murdered. A leader of the national government could be involved.

On the second day of the babel, the wife of the senior senator from Connecticut, himself a member of the party of the government in power, told the New York *Globe* that "intense pressure" from "unnamed sources" had been put upon Dr. Spano to force him to renounce his intention to bring health, hospitals, and the other benefits of modern science to the Central African Republic, which was to have been only the beginning of his labors on behalf of the poor and diseased throughout the world. Mrs. Cassiman told the *Globe* that Dr. Spano had confided his plans to her as his colleague at La Casa, in New York's Spanish Harlem.

DID US PRESIDENT ORDER
HARLEM PASTOR'S SILENCE?

the screamer on the front page of the *Globe* demanded to know.

28

Lieutenant Caen, in charge of homicide five out of 126th Street, was being worked over (without charge) by two black girls in the Tally Ho Massage Parlor on Broadway and 97th Street when his sergeant, George Fearons, called him at 9:19 P.M. Sunday night, May 11, to report the homicide of Ames Lally Spano. Lieutenant Caen met Sergeant Fearons directly outside the Henstell mansion at 9:47. Even though Dr. Spano might have been the most famous man on the Upper West Side, Caen had not connected him with Commissioner Spano. He always thought of her as Commissioner Spano, so that her enforced authority over him could reduce the humiliation she had dumped on him as if he were a sixty-five-year-old, fifty-cent blowjob working doorways on Eleventh Avenue. He had not stopped thinking about Commissioner Spano since the night she had ordered him to climb her and then had kicked his ass right out into the street and walked away whistling.

He didn't make the connection until Fearons reminded him, when they met in front of the house, that the murder victim was *also* the husband of the attorney general of the United States. He was lucky he had been sitting in his car when Fearons told him, because that news turned his legs into water. Rage filled him like langrel being poured into the mouth of a cannon. Why didn't she stay out of his life? Was she asking for it? What had she dreamed up now to ruin his fucking life? She had taken over his mind. Everything he sweated was tinctured with hatred for her. He had talked to Mom about it. "I mean, I worked with the best in the department. This isn't the first deputy commissioner in my life. They respect me. I got two citations. Jesus, Mom, I'm a proud man, I can't take this."

"Whattayah expect? She's a libber. They're all lady-lovers. And, listen, I know what you're goin' t'rew. Your father was worse than that, believe me."

After ignoring him for month after month after month—and she was a great-looking head, besides the rank—she suddenly leaped on him and proceeded to fuck him blind, then she had dropped him in the garbage. When he had been on the vice squad there had been young quiff who thought they could fuck him around like that and they remembered him to this day, you could bet on that. This one had to get it from him the worst, but she kept going up out of reach and he knew he was just kidding himself even if he did keep it inside his head all the time. There was no way he could touch her, and that was one hundred percent clear until now that her husband had got it through the head right on Caen turf. He got himself together.

"I musta ate a coupla spoiled pizzas last night," he said to Fearons. "All right. I'll go up an' concentrate on the scene an' you get a phone in there and get the medical examiner and the forensic squad over here. Get six men on the job to work over the servants or whoever until they're sure it is straight. Comb the house for everything they can dig out. And listen, George," Caen said harshly, "the most important thing you can do is to find out where the wife was when all this happened." Fearons moved into the house on a run.

Fearons had never seen him like this before; white as a sheet and his voice shaking and shrill. Caen got out of the car slowly, then followed him in, his heart kicking at his rib cage like a stallion, his face as coarse as soda bread.

He stared down at Ames Spano's body, which was stretched full-length on the floor, arms outstretched as if a custom executioner had come in to fit it for a crucifix, eyes staring, mouth open, every wave of silky hair in place, wearing a blue silk dressing gown and pajamas, and shot once through the forehead. On the desk top directly above the body were neat piles of jewelry with separate pieces spread out in rows beside an insurance company inventory. Caen carried a jeweler's loupe after his years on the hotel unit. He put the loupe to his eye and examined the jewels rapidly, while he was still alone, whistling with admiration over some of those. He separated the best pieces from the others on the desk top, then put the five best pieces into his pockets, never changing expression but almost dizzy with the realization of what he was going to be able to do to this rotten broad who had treated him like a nothing whore.

He yelled for Fearons. He had to yell twice before the detective appeared.

"There's an insurance form on the desk," Caen said. "It has the broker's sticker on the upper left hand corner. Go out in the hall somewheres and find a phone. Get the broker and send a squad car for him. Get him over here."

"Right," Fearons said.

"Hey, George!"

Fearons turned back.

"Where's Spano's wife?"

"I'll check it out."

"Ask the housekeeper. Go through every room in the house. If she's not here, put men on finding her. We gotta know where she was when this guy got it."

Fearons left the room on the double.

Caen turned back to the room. A long case clock had been overturned as if there had been a struggle. The hands had stopped at 3:29. A Geochron world map clock screwed into the wall behind the desk had been smashed. The time had stopped at 3:28 P.M. Caen knew it was P.M. because the clock was designed to show day and night and the date.

Expressionless, Caen knelt beside the corpse and pulled the blue silk handkerchief out of the breast pocket of the dressing gown. Mechanically, his hand went into his pocket and came out with a brooch. He pinned the brooch to the handkerchief, then, grimacing, he pulled the two apart and the brooch came away, silk threads from the handkerchief hanging from it. He reached down and picked up the corpse's hand by its wrist. He turned it over and placed the brooch clenched around the frayed silk into the dead hand, then closed the hand tightly over it. He laid the clenched hand on the floor. He stared down at it and very slowly a broad grin spread over his face.

Fearons came back. "The insurance broker is on his way. So is the PC, Chief Maguire, First Deputy Commissioner Mulqueen, and the medical examiner."

"You find the wife?"

"Yeah. She *really* checks out," Fearons said. "The attorney general and the federal attorney caught a shuttle flight to Washington at 2:10 this afternoon, then Mrs. Spano attended a thirty-seven-minute meeting with the president in the White House at half-past three."

"Yeah?" Caen said incredulously.

"Yeah. *Denks Gott*," Fearons answered. "That's all we need is that the attorney general knocked off her husband, the people's saint."

Caen got away from the Spano house after the body had been taken downtown for postmortem, at 1:10 A.M. Fearons had Caen's own car brought to the Spano house at some point among the other two-hundred-odd details he was handling. Caen didn't go home. He garaged the car on 47th Street and checked into a hotel on West 44th Street. He bought a pad and one envelope at an all-night pornography store in Times Square, kicked two hookers in the ankles because they wouldn't leave him alone and, leaving them yelling, flat on their asses, made his way across Broadway and Seventh Avenue back to the hotel.

He hung up his raincoat and his jacket after removing a pint of rye whiskey from one of the pockets and settled down with the bottle and the pad at the battered desk near the window of the room. He printed the words carefully in block letters:

CHECK THIS OUT!!!!!

Spano's murdered body had a brooch clenched in its fist. The pin of that brooch had threads of material hanging from it, plenty of them. That brooch was ripped off a woman's bathrobe the killer was wearing when Spano got it. So who owned the dressing gown and was wearing it when she killed her husband? You guessed it.

But how come the police are concealing this vital evidence? The PC, the chief of detectives, and the deputy first commissioner had a secret meeting at the Spano house at 11:40 last night (Sunday) and they decided that they weren't going to fool around with any case involving the attorney general of the United States.

If you don't do anything about this a high-class murderer will be walking the streets after shooting down a modern American saint.

The NYPD is witholding evidence.

Make them bring this case out in the open.

Is this a democracy or is it Hitler?

The free press has got to save us here.

A FRIEND OF JUSTICE

Caen reread the letter, then sealed it in the envelope. He addressed the envelope to the City Editor, New York *World*, then he got dressed again, walked the letter across town to the newspaper, and handed it to the night watchman and gave him a buck to call for a copy boy to take it up to the city room.

He walked slowly back to the hotel almost feverish in his victory. He locked the room door, took the jewels out of his pockets, and sat down again at the desk, studying each piece through the loupe as he sipped whiskey.

29

On the Sunday evening her husband's body was discovered in New York, Jean Spano was standing in the hall outside the gatekeeper's room before the Oval Office talking to Keifetz about a fine point of organized crime research, when Charles Cantwell telephoned from New York. He had never called her at the White House before. She looked puzzled and alarmed. Keifetz told her to take the call in his office, which was down the corridor to the left at the far corner of the building. Keifetz insisted on going with her. He told the operator to transfer the AG's call to his line and handed the phone to Jean.

"Charles?"

"Jean, I have some bad news."

"What is it?" Keifetz sat across the room near the fireplace.

"Ames was murdered at the mansion sometime this afternoon."

"Charles! No!"

"When can you get back to New York?"

"I can't think—now. Right away."

"I want you to go directly to my house."

"Shouldn't I—see Ames?"

"Not tonight."

"Who *did* it?"

"The police don't know. Henri and Louise found the body."

"Oh, God!"

She hung up and turned to Keifetz. "My husband was murdered in New York this afternoon."

"*Mur*dered?"

"I must go there."

"Of course you must. Sit down; I'll lay on a car and a plane to take you in and a car to pick you up. Now stay right here. Compose yourself." He led her to a chair and sat her down. He patted her on the shoulder and went out of the room. She knew he was going directly to the president.

The limousine brought her to Cantwell's door at the sweet, neat house in Beekman Place. Charles took her into the study, which was warm with books and red leather. He kissed her cheek and held her closely.

"How did it happen?" she asked.

"He was shot. Jewels were stolen. It may have happened at about three o'clock this afternoon."

"I can't *conceive* of anyone wanting to murder Ames! I never knew *any*one who was so loved and so worthy to be loved."

"It happened. He's dead."

"I must *do* something."

"Not tonight, Jean. You need rest. They'll ask you to identify Ames tomorrow."

"Tonight I want to go to Rockrimmon to get the only thing which will let me sleep."

"To get what?"

She knew it couldn't matter anymore if Charles or anyone else knew how much Mama's diaries meant to her. She wanted to go to Rockrimmon to be with Mama. "I want to read my mother's diaries again," she said. "They help me so, Charles."

"Her diaries?"

"I didn't mean that you aren't my own true, true friend," she said softly. "You are my father and my conscience, but tonight I need to be with Mama."

"She is dead, Jean."

"Her diaries bring her to life. Ever since I was twelve years old, everything I've ever done came out of them. I need them now."

"What can a dead woman's diary say to you about the murder of your husband?"

"I can't explain it. But that's how it has always been between Mama and me. Only she can bring me . . . acceptance of what has been done to Ames. People read Bibles, even live by them, don't they, Charles? Mama's diary is my Bible."

30

When she rose the next morning at Rockrimmon, Jean rode a hunter for an hour, had a thoughtful breakfast, then telephoned the police commissioner in New York to ask if he wanted her to make a statement about Ames' murder.

Mitgang said that was very considerate and that if she could be at his office at 11:45 that morning he would have Homicide Five on hand to take the statement.

Mitgang received her in his office. "How do I address you," he asked, "as Governor or General?"

"If you must be formal, I'd prefer Commissioner."

He grinned at her, nodding his pleasure.

"Still a Siamese-food addict?" she asked.

"Well, I eat Swiss occasionally and every now and then I take home a coupla pounds of Chinese, but if I had my way and the missus could cook it, I'd have Thai food for breakfast. I'm shocked about Ames, you know that."

"I can't understand it. I can't make head or tail of it."

"Can you tell us anything?"

She gestured helplessly. "I don't know. I don't think so."

"Your staff at the house made the identification and I corroborated that so we don't need to bother you about ID. The body is downtown now, but your family lawyer has arranged to have it moved uptown to Campbell's."

"Thank you, Commissioner."

"The Homicide man is outside. You know him. The liaison when you were here. Caen? Umberto Caen?"

She looked at him blankly. "Caen? From Legal Matters?"

"He's an all-around cop. He's doing a good job where he is."

She swallowed hard. "I remember him well," she said. She could feel the talons of lust scraping a hole in her stomach, then slithering out and spreading across her loins. She detested the idea of seeing him again, but she wanted to see him.

"Fine."

Mitgang spoke into the intercom and told someone to send Caen in.

Caen looked the same except that he was more sure of himself. He smiled at her the way the wolf had smiled at the little pig whose heart was very gay when he built his house of hay.

"Hello, Commissioner," he said.

"Hello, Caen. This is quite a surprise."

Mitgang said, "The commissioner has been very kind, offering to come in and help us like this. Don't waste her time. She wants to be on a plane to Washington at three o'clock."

"I'll cooperate with the lieutenant in any way and as long as it is necessary," the attorney general said, staring at Caen.

"Thank you, ma'am," Caen replied, "I'll be grateful for anything you can give me."

Caen moved lightly and easily. He looked cleaner, as though success had brought him another shirt. His heavily lidded eyes were framed by hairy ears and thick eyebrows. His mouth—she found it hard to keep her eyes off his mouth—was wet and thick. Everything he could show to her was insolently expressive, while the heavy face and the voice stayed expressionless.

They left the office. He led her through corridors to an empty room, without speaking, then held a chair for her to have her sit opposite him across a small desk in a bare office. There was a police stenographer in the room.

"Just tell us what happened on the day of your husband's murder, Commissioner," he said as thickly as if he had a mouthful of blood. "Your husband's general disposition and outlook on the day of his murder, the positive or negative state of your relationship with him at that time, who might possibly be suspected of the murder, in your mind, if anyone—well, you know—just a statement from a former police lawyer that might help us in any way you know."

She dictated a statement steadily. It took about fourteen minutes. Caen thanked her, saying that the stenographer would type up his notes so she could sign them and that that should be about it. The stenographer left the room, closing the door. Caen looked out the window.

"How have you been, Caen?"

"Okay."

"Taking those examinations for lieutenant made quite a difference."

"Your letter to Chief Maguire made the difference."

"You don't sound happy about it."

He turned to face her. "Happy enough. Happy enough," he said.

"Ah. Good."

"Commissioner, if I were to say to you that it could be a big help to me if you would go uptown with me to your house—to the scene of the crime—what would you think of that?"

"Think?"

"We could work it out up there."

Her cheekbones had taken on a dark color and her eyes glittered. She stared straight into him. "As I said, Lieutenant, I will cooperate with you in any way."

He offered her a cigarette. She shook her head. He walked very stiffly around her. She felt herself trembling under her skin.

"We never—saw each other after that—that meeting at the CC's office," he said hoarsely.

"No."

"I been wondering about that for a long time—about the way you sort of picked me up then dropped me, but I guess you had a long way to go and no time to look back."

"I didn't think it meant anything to either of us."

"Yeah."

They were silent until she said, "What are you thinking about now?"

"The same thing."

"So am I," she said. She had to shut her eyes to try to concentrate on controlling her breathing. "Why don't you send me the statement to Washington," she said. "I'll sign it and have it notarized. Would that be all right?"

"That will be very good," he said, standing slowly. "Let's go uptown."

31

Charles Cantwell was shaken by Jean's statement that since she had been twelve years old, her life had been formed by her mother's diaries. The consequences of such a phenomenon were too much for him. He sat staring out at the East River, drinking whiskey until Stinnett had to put him to bed.

He awoke at 8:20 the next morning and refused breakfast. He asked Stinnett to please clean and brush his shoes in the bedroom so he could be sure something was real.

Stinnett was a masseur. He worked Cantwell over thoroughly on the leather-covered table in the large bathroom, then sat him in the sauna, held him erect under a cold shower, then dressed him for the country. Cantwell refused to eat. He agreed to drink a glass of Guinness instead of a straight whiskey, watching while Stinnett filled a quart silver flask.

Stinnett dressed, then called his master's office to explain that Mr. Cantwell hadn't been feeling well and that everything on his calendar was to be canceled until Monday morning. Stinnett had the Gozzi sent around from the garage. It was one of three bespoke replicas of an open two-seater Mercedes Benz of 1927, turned out like magnificent jewelry by Church Green Engineering in England, with gorgeous floating fenders which made it the most beautiful car Cantwell had ever seen, when he could see. Stinnett got into the driver's seat. Cantwell sat beside him with his head back and his eyes closed. The car oozed itself into the traffic toward Rockrimmon in Connecticut.

Cantwell thought of Charmian. He saw the explosively mined days they had lived together; the living part of his life. The rest of it, on either side of that period, represented a monastery behind the walls of his unending solitude, moated by his loneliness. She had been in his arms in New York, then she was in Europe in Henstell's arms after pleading, screaming, weeping and begging him to go with her or they would both be destroyed as the buildings of the city collapsed upon them, as the earth split open and tidal waves pounded everything under engulfing waters.

He was still bewildered now—decades later—by how she had appeared so suddenly with those wild threats. She had taken it as proof that he did not love her because he had not rushed to pack and to make hoarse arrangements for the transfer of money so they could be safe wherever it was she had planned for them to go.

Everything about that time was unreal except Charmian. The coldness of death came over Cantwell. He took out the long, flat, silver flask and drank from it, staring dully at the traffic ahead. All through each year, almost, he was able to hold the memory of Charmian at bay. After so many years he still fought to keep her out of his mind, becoming a periodical drunk to exorcise her. Whiskey was the holy water and garlic which kept her from feeding at his throat. Love! oh my dear God, he thought, how can I still love her? What has she done to Jean? What craziness has she designed, written into diaries, to be injected like grains of a consciousness-altering drug, word by powerful word, into the plastic mind and hope of a twelve-year-old child?

When they got to Rockrimmon, the old German, Herr Nifleheimer, stumbled out of the gatehouse, muttering in Plattdeutsch, until he saw who was in the car. Then he straightened up, buttoned his fly, and opened the gates. They drove two miles to the main house. It was twenty minutes after three in the afternoon. As he approached the front door it opened and Mr. George said, "Good afternoon, Mr. Cantwell."

Unsteadily, Cantwell moved up the great staircase, then along the wide, portrait-lined corridor to Jean's quarters at the east wing of the house. He entered her room and had no trouble locating the diaries, which were in the unlocked carved camphorwood chest but no longer in their individual boxes. Instead they were piled in a neat stack in the sequence of Volume 1 to Volume 4. With shaking hands he lifted the top volume and placed it on Jean's desk as though it contained nitroglycerin. He sat down and stared at it for a long moment, experiencing terror. He opened the book to the first page, then drank the last of the whiskey in the silver flask. Supporting his head in his hands, the hands by his elbows propped on the desk, he began to read.

> The diaries are for my future daughter's eyes. Should anyone else come upon them let him close the book in shame at having invaded my memory which is now my daughter's sacred possession. As curses were placed upon the invaders of ancient tombs so do I place a curse upon man or woman who on reading these words does not close the book at once and forevermore.

He shuddered and continued to read.

> You will have had a fine education, darling, you may be sure I will have seen to that. You have in your genes the greatness which matches that of any of the great male leaders of your country.
>
> My own people were giants, I have measured their steps across Persian history, and I myself took the marshal's baton away from the men in my chosen field—geology—to the point where men would offer me any price, men who had *no use* for women, if I would counsel them. You have strong people on your father's side, but undoubtedly you know about them.
>
> I am telling you that you will be the equal of any man in the United States, an aristocrat of mind and purse; a vibrant container of vigorous health. I stress this, darling, because you must be told as early on as Alexander was told that you were born to lead. You must study political techniques, hone yourself upon the law, plunge into a mapmaker's understanding of what motivates yourself and everyone of power around you. Highest politics is your certain destination. After you have studied this field of power which fits into higher power which fits into still greater power and you see the significance of your ownership of the stock in the bank and all of the other holdings which will be yours, you will be able to choose the best first step to political power so that it will contrast with, and yet complement, the next.
>
> I say to you that you should cast about in your mind to decide what is the most apparently manly public service you can undertake. I mean you should choose a *symbolic task* with which all the voters—sufficiently advised in the public prints, through your organization of the media—can associate and relate to the obvious hard work and valor shown by the male sex in *their* careers. If, early on for example, you were to arrange to be offered, say, a job as a deputy commissioner in the New York Police Department, by

doing that job exceptionally well and by making sure your efforts were well noted by the media, the voters of this country would associate your capabilities with the talents of the *men* whom they have voted into higher offices. Theodore Roosevelt, remember, began as a New York police commissioner. Every higher post to which you rise after that will be of necessity those which only *men* have held before you, but you will have shown that, with regard to you at least, it is right and intelligent for voters to choose a woman to represent them where only *men* had been chosen before.

YOU MUST WREST POWER AWAY FROM MEN AND USE IT BETTER THAN THEY HAVE EVER DONE!
PROVE WHAT EQUALITY IS!

Cantwell tried to remember the fascinating young woman, Charmian, who had whirled herself away, falling from him as Alice had fallen into the hole, into a world she was determined no one else would be permitted to understand. Anomalously, in the middle of reading this pompous political exhortation, he remembered the night so many years ago when she had invited him to a lecture at the Lotus Club.

"A lecture? What kind?" he had asked.

"Cosmic astronomy, Charles, darling. But I am told that tonight we are going to be told truths. Perhaps your legal mind resists truth."

He had put her off. He had had a hard day and the world was preoccupied with things other than truths about astronomy. She went to the lecture alone.

He was asleep when the doorbell began to ring in long and short bursts, between hammerings on the door. When he got it open Charmian was standing there, ashen and shaken. She had brushed past him into the apartment.

"What happened to you?" he had asked her.

"We must leave the country!" she said, gulping air as if her thoughts were smothering her. "Switzerland will be safe."

He led her into the study and sat her down carefully. He asked her if she wanted tea or a drink of whiskey. She ignored that.

"Tonight is January 27, 1938," she said jaggedly, the words coming from her at an irregular pace to match her panic. "Tonight, just one among an assembly of over eighty distinguished scientists, I listened to Sir Jilmer Rizzo read his paper on the straight line of planets."

"Are you back into astrology again?"

"Not astrology. As*tron*omy. Charles, for God's sake! I am trying to save our lives! Sir Jilmer told us how, in 1939, all nine planets of our solar system would form themselves into one straight line on the same side of the sun, which will bring earthquakes and tidal waves such as haven't happened since the time of Daniel Defoe when two-thirds of London was obliterated. Charles—don't look away! Hear me! That planetary lineup is going to cause an *enormous* increase in magnetic activity when it will be at the peak of its sunspot cycle. Next *year*, Charles! There will be *huge* storms of sunspots and solar flares. The upper part of the earth's atmosphere will be severely affected. It will *greatly* disrupt our weather patterns by *sharply* altering wind directions and, as these terrible winds shift, the frictional effect they will create will brake the pace of the earth's rotation and the whole planet will get such a jolt that earthquakes will be triggered throughout the world!"

"The speaker," he had said as gently as he could because this clearly was going to be one of her more trying, less charming nights, "this man, Rizzo, is he staying at the Lotus Club?"

"How do I know?" she said angrily. "What's the difference? We've got to get out from under these tall buildings which are going to come down on us."

"I'm going to call him," he had said.

"*Charles!*" It was a scream of terrible fear. "He is a *Nobelist!* The whole earth is going to be shifted by great plates of stress and fault. Nine planets will be lined up to disturb the sun!"

"Just let me call him, sweetheart. I'd like to get some straight advice. He's an expert, darling. Let me ask him a few questions."

"How long will it take you to get your affairs in order? Geneva has low buildings. It is on water. It is *not* volcanic. I have all the money we will ever need."

He had tried to calm her and to get her mind off her fright. "We'll sleep on it, honey," he had said. "We'll talk about it tomorrow morning."

"No. You are going to decide this now."

"Charmian, you are ex*haus*ted. You've been driving yourself without reason for weeks and weeks. You've got to get some sleep. Come on, we're going to bed."

"No!"

"Baby, this is big news—right? A Nobel astronomer makes a speech like this, so it should be on the front page of the *Herald-Trib* in the morning, shouldn't it?"

Her eyes had opaqued in a way he had once associated with her instant lust, but this time they had made themselves a curtain between them. "Don't call me baby," she had said. "The news will either take over the entire front page or—more likely—it will be suppressed in the fear that the population would panic."

"Dr. Weiler is your friend, darling. Will you go with me to see him tomorrow morning?"

"*Weiler?*"

"You know how little sleep you've let yourself have in the past month," he had said. "I am dead on my feet myself because of it."

"Are you coming with me to Switzerland? I'm not begging you, Charles. I am a woman. You are a man trying to show superiority, but I love you."

The next day she had persuaded his law partner, Joshua Henstell, to flee with her to Switzerland. They were gone by the end of the week.

He shook his head violently to snap himself across the time warp and back to her diaries on the table in front of him. He began to read them again.

Only *men* have been elected as presidents of the United States. There have always been more American women than American men therefore that is an *illogical* condition. Don't accept its speciousness. Because men earn more money they have this conviction that they have the right to override women's natural plurality. But they have more money because they pay themselves more, because they are *determined* to pay women less, and they *seem* to have more power because from their throats millions of times each day comes the iteration that they have more power—an empty claim when it is considered in the light of women's power over men.

YOUR GOAL MUST BE THE PRESIDENCY!!!

As I write that, I imagine I can hear you gasp, but I would *not* advance such an ambition if I did not know how perfectly possible this goal will be for you. You must take everything in its own time. My advice is that you prepare yourself to implement this life plan:

(1) Beginning *now*, excel at everything you do, far beyond all the others in your peer group, and *above all* control yourself and thereby gain the power to control others.

(2) Graduate with highest honors from a fine *women's* college, then go onward into the study of languages and the law. Win the highest honors at the *best* law schools.

(3) Enter your grandfather's firm *on your merits* and concentrate on dominating it. Charles Coomber Cantwell, my old friend, is senior partner and one of the finest lawyers in the country. He will

be your invaluable aide in achieving these goals and in bringing the
bank's influence behind your political efforts.

(4) Construct a political power base for yourself. The greatest
power base is an inexhaustible money supply. The country is a
patchwork quilt of hatreds and partisanship, each one depending
on political conditioning to provide a basis for her or his "thinking." Organize so that you may appeal to each principal national
partisan group, dress the strength of your ideas with strong names,
then tell them that if they will give you money, you will see that it
is spent to further the aims of their prejudices.

(5) Marry carefully and with *enormous* respectability. I am not
saying that you should not bed and enjoy coarse or low or vulgar
men—I can tell you these are *delicious*—but in the choice of your
marriage partner you must be forever above reproach. You will
know best when the time comes. Remember, I am not asking you to
stifle your natural desires. To make my point I will say that I want
you to encourage your sensuality and to *wallow* in it because the
magnetism that it will reflect back upon you, will project itself
upon the people of the United States who need to be attracted to
you to support you with their votes.

(6) Underwrite the efforts of a highly publicized charity with
whose leadership your name will be forever associated. People
believe in charity by others even if they cannot bring themselves to
support it, and its essence of compassion and humility will help to
hold their loyalty to you if by any happenstance or another's
design, you should find yourself being smeared by your political
enemies.

If you agree with what I have been recommending, you should
then arrange to be offered and to accept work at the NYPD. Then,
using your various organizations and Charles Cantwell and the
bank, you must arrange to be offered the nomination for lieutenant
governor of New York State. Then, planning well and sufficiently
in advance, you and Charles and the bank, with the help of your
record and your political and charitable organizations, must arrange that you be offered the post as attorney general of the United
States by an incoming administration.

From the Department of Justice to the White House, for an
exemplary woman who has shown her superiority over all men who
seek the highest office, in a country where women outnumber men
and where several million intelligent men would support a gifted
proven woman leader, the way is clear, my darling.

*YOU WILL BE ONE OF THE GREAT AMERICAN PRESI-
DENTS!*

Cantwell, gray-faced and trembling, reached for the flask. He tilted it
toward its two-ounce cap. The flask was empty. He turned violently for
help.

"Stinnett!" he screamed.

Cantwell was removed to the Shannon-Philipps Sanatorium west of
Stamford at 1:20 that afternoon, after Stinnett had been able to bathe
him, shave him, and dress him in clean clothing. It was Cantwell's second visit to the sanatorium in the year; the best place of its kind for the
specialities it performed.

The penalties for remembering Charmian Henstell were accelerat-
ing.

32

At 2:07 P.M. on May 18, 1984, Jean Henstell Spano, attorney general of the United States, rose like a plume of smoke from her chair at the center of the stage in the Great Hall of the Department of Justice. She faced opaque professional silence. She moved like the figurehead of a ship to a mooring at the lectern, which was hedged by sixteen microphones. Behind her at her right, seated in an arc facing the auditorium, were the deputy attorney general, the associate attorney general, and the solicitor general. At her left to the rear were the director, FBI; the head of the Criminal Division of the Department of Justice; and the assistant attorney general in charge of the Office of Legal Counsel.

The Great Hall was a rectangle of about 150 by 100 feet on the second floor of the Justice building. There was a surrounding balcony on the third floor. The Great Hall was decorated with "old Roman" statuary as executed by WPA sculptors in the thirties. Its main floor was packed with almost four hundred sweating press, radio, and television people and their equipment, with nearly two hundred more leaning over the balconies and shouting when they felt they had to shout. The air-conditioning system had broken down three hours before—in mid-May, in Washington. It was a bad room for shouting. The noises echoed and reechoed. Every ten minutes or so a sound technician would climb up on the stage and, ignoring the AG, yell out across the assembly, "Will you

150

do everybody a favor, please? Will you try to keep it down, please? Okay?" he would say plaintively, "will you *try* keeping it down?"

This was the fourth time the Great Hall had been used for a press conference. Saxbe had held one there for lottery legislation because a lot of state representatives had wanted to attend. Ramsey Clark had faced down a mob in the Great Hall. Saxbe *and* Clarence Kelly held one for COINTELPRO, and a deputy AG named Civiletti also ran one, but the room had never before been so filled. There were so many agitated working press from so many agencies, magazines, networks, and overseas outlets that the available facilities in the press room on the fifth floor across the hall from the AG's office with its four or five desks and eight or ten phones was useless.

No one in government had ever faced anything like this; there was no precedent for handling it. The media had never expected that the day would come when they would be shouting at and bullying a woman cabinet officer.

A voice from the right aisle called out at the instant the AG reached the lectern, "Has there been a response from the president, General Spano?"

"I spent one hour and twenty minutes with the president this morning," the attorney general said. "We sought a firm basis upon which to deal with the allegations just published in New York. You all know them:—that the New York Police Department was concealing evidence which would implicate me in the murder of my husband last week."

She stared into the lens of the NBC-TV camera on the rolling platform which was eighteen feet at her left in front of her and spoke with slow, bitter emphasis. "The president, the director of the FBI, Dr. Paul Empey, archbishop of the Anglican Church in Washington, and myself sought fruitlessly for reasons why an American newspaper would publish such a shameful unfounded accusation."

Mrs. Spano's voice was steady. She turned to face the ABC-TV camera.

"It was one thing for this newspaper to continue to exist blindly and mindlessly as a reflexive antiadministration reactor. The reason is well known: the grandfather of the present owner of the paper opposed the political party for which the present administration stands. However, it is also a matter of record that this newspaper has developed an impenetrable antifeminist stance. These questionable reasons notwithstanding, its peers—you—the free press—must ask yourselves why would it publish such heinous allegations about the murder of my husband."

She stood impressively, speaking without notes; a tall, light-haired, striking woman with a strong face and enormous deep blue eyes. Her firm voice rang with vindictiveness.

"Because of that viciousness I called this media conference," she said.

"General Spano," the man from the New York *Times* called out, "did the president ask for your resignation?"

"Please call me Mrs. Spano. That title—for this office—is dehumanizing. I brought a signed letter of resignation with me to the meeting at the White House this morning. I delivered it to the president and watched him read it. He refused to accept it."

The Great Hall broke out into rhubarb patches. Inside men murmured into walkie-talkies to outside people. The Washington correspondent for *Vogue* made rapid shorthand notes on the back of a Neiman-Marcus shopping bag.

Stunning. Check age: 37? 39? Hat Van Dongen vermilion. Suit purple-navy 8 button H line. Is she bringing back 1955? Why not? Foamy white scarf. She looks as cool as flowers. No bag. Simple suede shoes. (Spadoni? $110?) Teeth dazzling. (Could set up a v.g. teeth feature: NAME THESE TEETH). Eyes like dyed Easter eggs on *very* white. Voice: steady, clear, *sexy.* Love narrow skirt. V. discreet single-line eye makeup. V. light kisses rouge on sides of face. Call Harry about getting dachshunds to the vet.

The attorney general nodded calmly at the man from The Washington *Post* in the third row.

"Mrs. Spano," he said, "as a former deputy police commissioner of New York, have you been in contact with the New York police about their investigation of Dr. Spano's murder?"

"I was once deputy commissioner for legal matters in that department, Mr. McCarthy," the AG answered, "which hardly qualifies me as a police officer. Nonetheless, I *have* been in touch with the New York police in the sense that I have been questioned by them concerning my husband's murder."

The Great Hall vibrated with sound.

"I went to New York at their request and added my own information to everything else which they have collected."

"You didn't contact them on your own initiative?"

"Yes, I did."

"When was that, Mrs. Spano?"

"I saw the New York police immediately after the newspaper's victimization of myself and my office appeared. Police Commissioner Mitgang immediately arranged for me to talk to Lieutenant Umberto Caen of homicide zone five, in charge of the investigation of my husband's murder. I informed the police of the stated intention of this newspaper, by the publication of that anonymous letter, to charge them and me with being criminally implicated. I also told them that the president concurred in my own decision to order an investigation of the charges, to be undertaken by the Federal Bureau of Investigation."

"Was anything else discussed?" a voice called out.

"Yes. There was one other matter discussed. I told Commissioner Mitgang that the FBI had been instructed to transmit their official report on this case not to me but to the United States attorney in the Southern District of New York so that he could present it as deposed evidence to the grand jury which is now sitting in New York. I told the New York Police Department that when all evidence had been collected by all law-enforcement agencies, if any evidence from any police or any federal agency were to implicate me in any way, I would expect the United States attorney to seek my indictment for murder from the grand jury."

The hall went into an uproar. TV camera operators swung lenses away from Mrs. Spano to cover the crowd. Eleven men and women sprinted like red-assed birds out of the auditorium.

The *Time* man had been able to listen to the attorney general and to arrange his prose options simultaneously. As he watched the action in the hall and weighed what the attorney general had told them, he squirreled away mental notes on the style of his story. ". . . faced a savage press in punishing Washington summer heat which was fired higher by partisan passions flaming out of the most shaming confrontation in American political history." It had to be purple; he knew that. The whole thing called for purple prose. While he made written notes on the turbulence among the transmitting bakpaks, still cameras, Agence France Presse madmen, weekly-piece thinkers, two worriers from the State Department, observers from the women's movement, and a group of twenty-three students who formed the Journalism Club at the James Cerruti Junior High School of Alexandria, Virginia, the *Time* man weighed the matter of what to do with her "blood-red hat and her full, pulpy, blood-red mouth." He worried about veering too far toward Lady Macbeth. He would discard the hat and the lips, but he had to keep the blood-red fingernails to tie them in with the talons of the American eagle—the reason why they were all standing in this river of sweat. Why had he eaten lasagna for lunch in Washington in mid-May? he asked himself. How should he describe the color of those gorgeous eyes? ultramarine? perse? sloe? midnight? As a *Time* reader (as well as a

Time writer) he had the feeling that *Time* persons everywhere would thrill over *perse*.

The woman from the Washington bureau of the grossly offending New York newspaper yelled from the middle of the hall, loudly enough to be shouting from her publisher's office in New York: "I am Engelson from that paper you suddenly don't like!" she shouted. "So if neither the FBI nor the cops find any evidence, what are you gonna do and did you talk about that with Heller at the White House this morning?"

"All right, Engelson," the attorney general said. "That's a good question. If the grand jury refuses to indict me—so that I may bring your paper's allegation to a public trial—I shall drag your paper into court and put the burden of proof of the truth entirely on them. One way or another I am going to get a public trial on this—either criminal or civil—to establish forever that the newspaper you still choose to work for was stupidly wrong, stupidly vindictive, and criminally liable."

The CBS-TV man, MacLeish, cut off his microphone and opened up his great seismic voice to boom like a bedrock implosion along a continental geographic fault. "Holy *shit!*" he said as the media raced up the aisles.

A little more than two miles along Pennsylvania Avenue, the TV network pool was setting up at the White House. The president would appear before the nation at seven o'clock that night.

33

Alex Cassiman was appalled to realize that she found so many men so attractive as she walked from the subway exit, downtown Wall Street, to Charles Cantwell's office building. It was only the day after Ames' funeral. She didn't understand herself. She didn't understand why she should feel ashamed of wanting other men. Ames was gone and, anyway, that had always been her nature. But she wished there could have been a natural moratorium on feelings like these and she wished it weren't all so damned general. Random bodies didn't make any sense. They were unobtainable anyway. She remembered that Ursula Baggot had once informed her that psychoanalysts tell their patients anyone can think whatever they have to think, but the harm is in putting the wrong thoughts into action.

A tall, skinny man got into the elevator with her, and four other people. She wanted to open his fly until she could put both hands into it. *Both* hands? She studied the fire department regulation card and didn't look at him again. There was one thing she was determined not to do: she was not going to remember Ames carnally. That would really be sick. These men who passed by in the streets were at least theoretically available to her, but Ames wasn't available to anything. He had finished his life of service to others—and God knows he had found out somewhere how to service her. She wondered if he had been that complete a lover for Jean. Poor, dopey Jean. She was all mind and stuck with it.

Jean could think okay, but she probably couldn't feel much. It must have been like putting it between two cold rocks for Ames, and she was certain that Ames had been the only man Jean had ever known, because she just didn't project anything but mentality. If Jean was such a terrific piece of ass, Alex reasoned, she would have heard that from Ames.

Ames had been fairly detached himself. He did it the way a great tennis pro plays tennis with his best pupil. It was nice exercise and better than having to volley with some well-meaning duffer. Ames really had been as alive as a burning coal only, she knew, when he was talking beyond La Casa, far into the future, deep into darkest and deprived Africa. He had been a ball of fire in the sack when they had done the Mississippi job together. Then they had come back to La Casa and he had settled into his cool, smooth, tennis-pro game until she had found out that the way to turn him on to enormous action was to talk to him in bed about what they were going to do together to help the people in the Central African Republic. Nothing could turn him off when he heard how badly off those people were and how badly they needed him. She had to spend two hours on the microfilm machines at the New York *Times* taking notes on disaster stories and poverty everywhere to be memorized until she could get Ames back into bed as a tiger in the sheets.

Was everybody kinky? Her own husband used to insist that she get into bed all wet, wearing a green and white shower cap whenever he forgot himself or when he was drunk. Nothing wrong with that. But on the other hand there was *nothing* that could help his case. She had read that people who ejaculated prematurely had trained themselves unconsciously not to be interested in sex. If that were true, her husband had to hate sex and, as a U.S. senator, might be planning legislation against it.

The elevator came to the 53rd floor. She got off. She found the reception room of Henstell, Masters & Cantwell. She told the receptionist who she was and sat down.

In about ten minutes a woman who claimed to be Cantwell's secretary came out to get her. In any other business the people you had to pay would come out and get you, but lawyers used the opposite system because they wanted to tell you that they were very busy and didn't need your business and if you had to come in please make it quick.

But Cantwell actually got up when she came into the room. He certainly was a gorgeous old showboater, she thought. Long, lean. Give me the ectomorph anytime, she remembered, for passing away the years on a desert island. They have the *stamina*. He had one of those faces manufactured by Thomas Jefferson out of Greta Garbo with white hair by Alexandre de Paris. My God, what beautiful clothes! On somebody else they would have to take fifty-two fittings in order to look so rich. He wore them as if there weren't any other kind of clothes, as if he'd had to make do with them. He looked beautiful. She wondered. He was a sane, healthy looking man—how old did a man have to get before he couldn't make out anymore?

"Mrs. Cassiman—I was surprised to hear from you."

"You were kind to agree to see me on such short notice."

"Well, after all, we did graduate from Smith on the same day. How may I help you?"

"My husband and I are estranged."

"I *am* sorry."

"You are Jean's guardian. And her law partner. Well, I was about to go off to Central Africa with her husband—then he was murdered."

"Yes. I knew about that."

"More to the point, Mr. Cantwell, Ames told me you were the executor of his estate."

"Yes."

"The way my husband has arranged things, I am penniless. I have about three hundred dollars to my name. But Ames told me that I would inherit his estate, and although it may be unpleasant for you to have to deal like this with the woman who succeeded your ward with her husband, I have to ask you if it will be possible for something to be worked out so that I can be supported while we wait for his estate to be probated."

"Ames told you that you would inherit his estate?"

"That's right."

"It just isn't true, Mrs. Cassiman."

"Then there must be another lawyer and another will."

"When did Ames tell you this?"

"Last year. At around Christmastime."

"Ames stipulated his final will seven weeks ago and signed it four weeks ago. In it he left you some of his personal jewelry and a bundle of your own letters."

"Personal jewelry?"

"Cufflinks, a ring, and his Japanese digital watch."

"I know you are telling me the truth."

"Oh, yes."

"What am I going to do?"

"You are legally married. I don't handle marital cases, but you may have to ask a lawyer to talk to your husband."

She snorted. "He doesn't give a *damn*, Mr. Cantwell. He says he's too old for politics anyway, and nothing I can say or do can make any impression on him."

"He has to provide for your support."

"I can't wait that long. I have about a week left in my pocketbook."

"There is nothing else I can tell you."

"My husband did leave me with one little jewel, though. He told me he thought Jean might be the next vice president. He thinks the voters are ready for a woman candidate and that she has the best shot at it."

"I'm not really up on that."

"But it would be great, wouldn't it?"

He shrugged. "If she wants it."

"Mr. Cantwell, I don't know how much you knew about Jean's marriage, but whatever it was, it wasn't much compared to what I know. It was a rained-out failure. She tried to destroy a man whose entire reason for living was to serve downtrodden people anywhere because she decided what he wanted to do would interfere with her political ambitions. Well, that was between them. He just got out of her life by staying right where she told him to stay, and that's where the canker gnaws. He threw her out of his bed. He would hardly talk to her. No matter how she begged him to what she called 'normalize' their marriage, he wouldn't go near her. He chose me instead. He took me into his life's work at La Casa. He asked me to live with him there. I was—in effect—his wife. We planned his next missions of service together. Even Jean knew we were going to Africa to fight disease and poverty, and she opposed it—for her usual selfish reasons. She was no wife to him."

"Mrs. Cassiman, this does not concern me."

"Not yet. In a minute. What I am talking about went on for . . . four years. I became a wife in name only to my husband—a United States senator with a lot of clout. Why? I loved Ames. I've never been a moneygrubber. I have to eat and dress and have a place to sleep, but if I had been with Ames it wouldn't have made any difference to me whether it was in Central Africa or the Mississippi Valley. His wife, on the other hand, loved power, or politics, or—anyway, it was something cold and mental. During all those years she had no husband. When he was killed, it was no loss to her because he had already gone and she knew it because she had driven him out."

"Mrs. Cassiman, please . . ."

"Mr. Cantwell, I am going to make you a clear proposition. She is a multimillionaire. She doesn't need any money from Ames. She had eight years with Ames—and I *sweated* for that man—and I had four. I am saying to you that I want to know from her by the end of this week if she is ready to split what*ever* he left—on a six to four basis."

"I have no right to tell you this, Mrs. Cassiman, but if it brings relief or clears the air then it's worth saying. Ames Spano left his entire estate, except for the remembrances to you, to the First Baptist Church of the Central African Republic. His widow has nothing to say about it or to gain from it."

She smiled bitterly. "Then think this over, please. And perhaps talk it over with your partner, Mrs. Spano. She probably thinks—I mean, people's minds work that way—that I stole her husband from her. But that's wrong. She had put him down and counted him out before I ever came into the picture. Therefore, what I want you to talk over with her before the end of the week is that I kept her husband from kicking her career to pieces, maybe. I kept him from walking right out of the United States, from deserting his famous, beautiful wife—and that has to be worth something."

"Worth something?"

"Mr. Cantwell, you've got to believe that I am desperate. I don't know how to do *any*thing. But I have to live. Every cent I have will be gone by next week. I saved her career for Jean. That has to be worth something."

"I'm afraid I can't agree with you."

"That really doesn't matter, does it? What we have to establish here is whether Jean will agree with me. Because you'd better understand this, Mr. Cantwell—if Jean doesn't agree with me, I'm going to have to take her career back. Please! I've thought this through. That's why I keep saying that I have to know what she's going to do by the end of the week. If she decides to ignore me, if she isn't going to do anything for me, I'm going to have to announce that I am writing a book about my secret life with that modern saint, Ames Spano. I am going to have to put down a lot of things he told me about Jean. I can get a $37,000 advance on a book like that, one man told me, and as I say, I need the money."

"I'll talk to Jean," Charles Cantwell said, getting up.

"God, how I hate this," Alex said.

34

At the urgent request of the lawyers for the newspaper, Caen reenacted the crime in the study at the Henstell mansion for John Clohesy, publisher of the New York *World*, and two of his lawyers. He played it as portentously as any expert would.

"The help, Henri and Louise, had flown to Montreal on the Friday night before the Sunday Ames Spano was hit. They returned to the house here at 8:15 P.M. on Sunday night, found the body at 8:50, and immediately notified the bonded security patrol, at that moment checking the house, and the patrol called the police. The security patrol checked the house once in every two hours or thereabouts.

"The victim was alone here," Caen said. "The circumstantial evidence is planted right there to show us that he was murdered at 3:29 P.M. on Sunday while his wife and the U.S. attorney were flying to Washington, where Mrs. Spano attended a meeting with the president at the White House."

"Why are you so sure he was shot at 3:29?" one of the lawyers asked.

"I'm not sure. Everything is just set to *look* that way. And, well, the medical examiner says so, even though he is seldom right. It appears that there was a struggle which knocked over a grandfather clock and stopped it at 3:29. We know it was afternoon because someone had thrown a paperweight which hit the Geochron map clock on the wall. The clock shows day and night."

"Fahcrissake," Clohesy said, "Agatha Christie musta done it."

"Yeah. Anyways, in the struggle the victim grabbed the brooch which was pinned on one of Mrs. Spano's dressing gowns, and he had to have a hold on it when he was shot because when he fell he took it with him, and he took about a square inch of material with him."

"But how did the killer get into the dressing gown?"

"Whoever it was probably sat on a park bench across the Drive and watched the private patrol car roll away, then went in the back door with a key and knew where to look for Mrs. Spano's dressing gown."

"The killer would have to know about the patrol system. The killer would have to have had a key. The killer had to know that the cook and his wife were out of town and how a Geochron clock worked."

"Yeah."

"Then the killer arranged for us all to believe the motive was robbery."

"That's right. Actually, Spano could have been shot in the morning. All the killer would need to do would be to set the two clocks ahead, then smash them, then make sure that he—or she—was outta town at the time the smashed clocks had been set for."

The grand jury refused to indict Jean Spano. It urged a public release of its statement which said, in part, "The grand jury cannot accept that a principal American newspaper, an institution on which its readers depended for true information to the best of that newspaper's ability, could violate such a contract by permitting publication of such shocking allegations concerning a member of the United States government."

At the urging of his lawyers, John Clohesy pleaded with the attorney general's office for a meeting with Mrs. Spano. He was at last successful in arranging this by releasing the president from obligations owed to him by the president, who then interceded with Mrs. Spano to agree to treat with Mr. Clohesy.

The publisher flew to Washington. The AG kept him waiting with his expensive legal counsel for over six hours in the public waiting room before she refused to see him. Mr. Clohesy's basis for bargaining was his offer of public apology and (secret) assurances that the attorney general and the Heller administration could have his newspaper as a powerful ally for life if Mrs. Spano would drop her plans to bring suit.

The attorney general finally agreed to hear his apologies through an eighteen-year-old office boy who listened to Clohesy gravely. Clohesy agreed to publish a full apology on a full page in his daily and Sunday newspapers. The text would be supplied by Mrs. Spano's law firm. In a separate document he agreed to "favor the interests of Mrs. Spano and the Heller administration as a measure of his contrition over any possible damages or embarrassment caused by the offending stories against Mrs. Spano in his newspaper."

Mrs. Spano accepted his apology. As well, she accepted $50,000 from him on behalf of the Citizens Advisory Council on the Status of Women, and $50,000 on behalf of the New York Newspaper Guild.

35

Six days after the settlement with Clohesy, thirteen days after the murder of Ames Spano, Alex Cassiman telephoned Jean. She sounded frightened.

"Jean? Alex." The line she was holding seemed to go dead. "*Jean!* Please!"

"What do you want, Slut?"

"You have to see someone—tonight."

"No."

"*Jean!* Listen to what I'm saying, not to me. You *must* see this woman tonight. Oh God, Jean . . ."

"No."

"Not for me. For you. There is nothing more important than this."

"No."

"I am asking you for the sake of the president and the administration and the future of this country."

"Damn you, you bitch in heat! Who is she?"

"I don't know. I have never seen her before. See her, please! Just say you will see her tonight."

"Tell her to be here at eleven o'clock."

At twenty minutes to twelve that night, Ella Gallagher, wife of the director, FBI, got her husband out of bed. He had eaten an enormous, improvised sandwich at half-past ten and was comatose.

She told him that the attorney general was on the phone and that she sounded upset for the first time Ella could remember. Gallagher said thickly that he couldn't talk until he had a cold shower. Ella went back to the phone and told the AG that her husband would call back as soon as he was awake enough to talk and asked if he should call her at home.

"The hell with it, Ella," Jean said, "I'm going over there." She hung up with a bang. Ella hurried back upstairs to her husband's bathroom to tell him that his boss was on her way over at midnight.

Jean reached Gallagher's at 12:05. Ella stayed upstairs. Dick Gallagher let her in and took her directly to the library on the main floor. Gallagher called it a library because it was where he kept his books on handball. Reflexively, he offered her a drink and to his astonishment she accepted. She was distraught. Her eyes seemed wild and her hair was awry as if she had been unable to stop running her hands through it.

"First drink we've had together in three years," he said.

"Please—give me the drink, then sit down and listen to me."

"Jesus, Jean, you're in a state." He handed her a scotch and sat down.

"Turn on the tape recorder."

"It's on."

"This is Jean Spano," she said at once, "attorney general of the United States. At approximately ten minutes after ten tonight, Alexandra Cassiman, wife of Senator Peter Cassiman of Connecticut, telephoned me. I have known Mrs. Cassiman since college. She said it was vitally important that I see a woman tonight. There was fear in her voice, so I agreed to see the woman, who arrived at my house at eleven o'clock tonight.

"She was a tall woman whose head was wrapped in a silk turban over which she wore a wide, floppy-brimmed hat. She wore a black dress of what I judged to be expensive material and design. The outstanding thing about her, a feature which was skillfully minimized by her headgear, was the fact that the left side of her face was paralyzed. The left eye, cheek, and mouth drooped. A jowl on the left side of her face sagged. The contrast between the right side of her face, which she kept carefully on the darkened side of me, was so startling that I have not been able to put together a clear picture of what her entire face looked like. Nor am I able to estimate the woman's age, because on the left side she appeared much older than she may be, while on the right side, in the glimpse I was able to get of it, she seemed much younger."

Jean saw it vividly in her mind as she told the story of what had happened that night. The servants were in bed. She heard the front doorbell ring at precisely eleven o'clock. She left the chair behind her desk under the James Richard Blake portrait of Ames Spano and crossed the entrance hall. The entrance hall was lined with panels of *papier-peint* which had been designed by Roja-Hunt and block-printed in grisaille relief by Juarez-Jemma. The entrance hall was twenty-six feet high. It was held together for the eye by the panels and by black and gold directoire furniture, and by marble paving laid in diamond patterns under a high-relief ceiling decorated by shallow coffers symmetrically disposed.

"I opened the front door. She was standing there in more than three-quarter profile, looking drugged but not insane—or as if she had deliberately induced paranoia with cocaine. 'Who are you?' I asked her.

" 'Mrs. Cassiman sent me,' she answered.

"I beckoned her to come in, having her pass in front of me. I waved that she was to go down the hall then told her to turn into the study.

" 'Sit down,' I told her. She sat on a high-backed, crimson silk wing-chair which is about eleven feet away from my desk, choosing it carefully, I think, to keep the normal side of her face turned away from me. I sat behind my desk, quite uninterested in where she sat. I asked her what she wanted. . . ."

As Jean spoke to Gallagher and the tape recorder, it was easy to remember everything that had been brutally shocked into her mind: the woman's nerved-up intensity, the wind hitting the shutter above them on the outside of the house, her own impatience to get the woman out of there so she could get on with her own work and get a night's sleep.

"The woman had a relentless voice, neither harsh nor toneless, but onrushing and artificially theatrical.

" 'I was a major in the Marine Corps before I had this stroke—in the 3rd Battalion, 5th Division. I had the stroke when I was on leave, and that was the end of the Corps for me. But, as it turned out, there was more important work to do here.'

"The words came out of the woman in thick bundles because she could only move part of her tongue.

" 'What work?'

" 'I belong to a revolutionary wing of the women's movement.'

" 'This is the first I've heard that a revolutionary wing exists in the women's movement.'

" 'Our outfit is called the Matriots.'

" 'I don't know that group.'

" 'We are going to wipe out the men in power and make things better than equal for the women. No more men dumping on *us.* The women—us, the Matriots—are going to take over.'

" 'Why not let the Constitution do it for you?' I told her.

" 'Don't hand me that shit!' the woman yelled without turning her head. 'You are the attorney-fucking-general and you know better! After giving them blood to get those bastards to ratify, Congress, through the mouths of their rotten men, has sent us back into slavery!'

"It was as though the voice were coming from someone else. She looked away from me across the room as though she were following a billiard match. The side of her face that was turned toward me did not move; could not move. It was all so utterly impersonal that it helped me to hold my temper.

" 'You will lower your voice and change your tone when you speak to me,' I told her, 'or you will be put out of this house and into a police car. What was so important that you had to see me in the middle of the night?'

" 'The Matriots killed your husband.'

"I was sure I could not have heard that correctly; '*What was that?*' I asked her.

" 'We shot him.'

"She opened her purse and took out a black opal pin which Ames had brought back for me from the Eucharistic Congress in Adelaide when he had been the guest of Archbishop Richards. She tossed it. I caught it. 'That was yours,' she said, 'Keep it.'

" 'You killed *Ames?*' I asked her stupidly.

" 'That's right.'

" '*Why?*'

" 'For the rights of women,' she said to me.

" 'That is insane. There was no more determined fighter for women's rights.'

" 'He had to be wasted to bring you into the cause.'

" 'The *cause?* Bring *me* in? You fool—I argued Roe versus Dubé before the Supreme Court and got a landmark decision against anti-abortion laws! I overhauled the antiquated rape laws of New York State and I made every attempt to push through approval of the Equal Rights Amendment. My mother *raised* me on my responsibility to fight for women's rights. The president has put me in charge of the strategy for fullest administration support of the ERA ratification drive. Are you telling me you murdered my husband to interest me in the *cause?*'

" 'The Matriots' cause. To force you to take over the leadership of the Matriots.'

" 'What?' "

"You are going to be the greatest woman leader in American history,' she said. 'We killed him to show you that it is your destiny to lead women to total freedom and equality.'

" 'You actually *believed* that if you murdered *my* husband it would persuade me to comfort you? I *will* comfort you. I am going to have you committed into the hands of good doctors. That is the help you need most.'

" 'Wait! I haven't finished yet. We are going to make you president of the United States.'

" 'Ah, I see.'

" 'First we'll make you vice president, and when you have been sworn in, we will kill the president. You will become president.'

" 'Why do you think I would do that?'

"She laughed. I can still hear it. It was such a grisly sound. 'Because you will be electrocuted if you don't. We can prove at any time that—with premeditation—you shot and killed your husband.'

"I grabbed for the telephone. She stood up. 'Think it through,' she said from the semidarkness beyond the desk lamp. Then she was gone."

Dick Gallagher stared at Jean glassily. When he was able to speak he said, "Where is she now?"

"I don't know."

"Do you know her name?"

"No."

"What about Mrs. Cassiman."

"Alex!" Jean grabbed the phone and dialed. They both could hear the number ringing, but there was no answer.

"She was so frightened."

"I'll handle it," Gallagher said. He dialed the telephone. "This is the director," he said. "Send two agents to meet me outside Senator Cassiman's house inside fifteen minutes."

They drove in the Spano car through the mazes of streets to the Cassiman house in Georgetown. Two men were waiting outside the house. They all went up the front walk to the main door. They rang the doorbell until a woman in oversized pajamas opened the door. It was 1:10 A.M.

"We have to see Mrs. Cassiman, Marge," Jean said, moving past her into the house. "I'll go upstairs to her bedroom. You look around down here."

Gallagher found Alex in her husband's study. She was dead; shot through the center of the forehead.

36

The Department of Justice in Washington, at 10th Street and Constitution Avenue, has no building number. The main entrance is on Pennsylvania Avenue under a stone-carved inscription: THE PLACE OF JUSTICE IS A HALLOWED PLACE.

Jean used the entrance at the 10th Street autogate which led to the parking area. The main entrance had been closed and barred with iron gates since the Nixon era. When Jean was sworn in as attorney general, she had reopened the entrance to emphasize that free access to justice had been returned to the people. She had been forty-two years old when she took office, the first woman attorney general and the second youngest, after Edmund Randolph of Virginia.

The work had expanded since Randolph's time. Jean was the head of the largest law office in the world, but she only had one client: the government of the United States. Her staff throughout the nation comprised thirty-five thousand people. These performed many law enforcement functions in addition to providing legal services to the government.

Jean's responsibility embraced nine offices, six divisions, seven bureaus, and two boards. She controlled the FBI, the Bureau of Prisons, the system of executive pardons, appeals to the Board of Immigration, the U.S. Marshals, and the Drug Enforcement Administration. The jurisdiction of her department covered the Anti-Trust, Civil, Criminal, Civil Rights, Land/Natural Resources, and Tax divisions. Most of the

169

department's more than four thousand lawyers were in those six divisions or in the offices of the ninety-four U.S. attorneys scattered throughout the country and its territories.

The myriad sections within the divisions were: Admiralty & Shipping, Privacy, Patents & Torts, Commercial Litigation, Frauds, Organized Crime and Racketeering, Foreign Litigation, Legislation and Special Projects, Internal Security (treason, sedition, espionage, and munitions control), Fishing Rights, Immigration & Naturalization, and legal advice to the president.

The national media, and the political trade papers which were the local Washington press, keened like musical saws after the Spano murder, the AG's press conference and the president's address to the nation in support of Mrs. Spano. No connection between the murder of Senator Cassiman's wife (by marauders) and Dr. Spano's murder had been made by the police or by the media. It was the administration's intention that it should remain that way until a few moments before such a possibility arose.

Jean sat alone in her office, working on federal prison-reform plans and waiting to be called by the president. She had told Dick Gallagher to take a transcript of her taped report on the visitation by the Matriot and the murder of Alex Cassiman to the White House at the earliest moment the president could see him that morning. She had telephoned the White House switchboard during the night to say it was an emergency matter that the president see Gallagher. She knew the president began work at 7:30 A.M. It was now 8:10. There had been no call from Gallagher so she assumed he had to wait his turn to get into the Oval Office.

She sat at the enormous desk with her back to Constitution Avenue at the short end of the room, which was thirty by twenty feet, with eighteen-foot-high ceilings. There was one large window behind her that overlooked the Smithsonian complex to the south. The windows along the wall on her left faced the Internal Revenue Building and, along one angle, the Mall could be seen. The wall on her right held a large marble fireplace, long unused, and a door which led to the AG's conference room and outer offices. Her desk faced north, where there was an entrance to the "working room." It was here that she stored her overflow of important visitors. Beyond that was the dining room which had been redecorated by Martha Mitchell in a traditional style.

The walls in the office were wood-paneled and painted, covered to a large extent with bookshelves and paintings that were good copies of the valuable *naifs* hanging in her "secure" house in New York.

Flanking her desk to the rear were an American flag and the flag of the Department of Justice bearing the motto QUI PRO DOMINA JUSTITIA SEQUITUR, which asserts that the attorney general prosecutes on behalf of justice.

Four empty chairs were grouped in an arc in front of her desk. An empty chair and a coffee table waited at left near the north side of the office. She waited, staring at the direct telephone from the White House.

Keifetz called her on 555-2001, the routine office number, from a telephone booth in the Lone Star Beef House, a topless bar and strip joint which was operated by the U.S. government and which ran twenty-four hours a day one block north of the FBI building. The government had been forced to take it over because the owner had purchased it with embezzled federal funds. Keifetz asked if he could pick the AG up at the DJ parking lot in ten minutes. She said she would be waiting.

They drove to Andrews Air Force Base where they boarded a White House helicopter and flew to Camp David.

Keifetz said the president wanted her to wait in the Beaver Lodge. "It could be an hour, because we've laid on some routine appointments to make this a dull day for the press. He'll go for a walk while the press is having lunch and find his way here. Dick Gallagher, the DSP, and the chief of Secret Service will get to Beaver before he does."

The three heads of security were waiting in the lodge when Jean got there. She knew Berry James, director of the Secret Police, well enough because he was an all-around party politician, but Moe Michaels, the Secret Service chief, only slightly.

"What's going on, Jean?" the DSP asked. "Gallagher won't tell us anything."

"Judging from the kind of work we all do," Jean said drily, "it might have something to do with security."

"Now why didn't you think of that?" Michaels said to James.

The president came rumbling in at half-past twelve. Anyone who knew him well would have been able to tell that he was agitated because he looked as bland and as unsuspicious as a Carnation cow. He even smiled at them, making him (almost) unrecognizable. Keifetz locked the door, then sat down at the far side of the rustic room, across the pool table where he could watch Berry James work because of his obsessive fascination with any and all Secret Police moves. The president asked Jean to sit beside him. They each had a rocking chair and the president used his with the pleasure of a small boy on a carnival swing. The three cops sat, two in chairs and one on a rustic sofa.

"I spoke to Senator Cassiman in Zurich about the tragedy," the president said. "He's on his way home."

"What tragedy?" Berry James asked.

"Director Gallagher will explain it."

Gallagher summed it up in about forty words. He told them about the AG's visitation the night before, about the Matriots, and about how they found Alex Cassiman.

"You mean the woman *promised* an assassination?" Moe Michaels asked incredulously. "To the attorney general of the United States? She killed the AG's husband, then a United States senator's wife, and now she's ready to do a number on the *president*?"

"Well . . . yes," the president said.

"We are here to stop that threat. And we are also here to try to figure out what we are going to do if we *can't* find this woman," Jean said. "And—just as importantly—what we are going to do if we *do* find her."

"How's that?" Gallagher asked. He was a cop, not a politician.

"If we find her she has to go on trial."

The president nodded.

"If she goes on trial, the sinister proposition she made to me—a presidential assassination plus two murders which indirectly involve members of this administration—has to be made public."

"Well, sure," Gallagher said. "Why not?"

"A campaign is coming up."

"That may be," Michaels said, "but we've got to stop her."

"She may even have to have an accident when we find her," Berry James said.

Keifetz's eyes popped.

"Listen to me," Jean said. "Put that out of your mind."

"Forever," the president added.

"Anyway, let's stop thinking about one woman," Jean told them. "This is a revolutionary organization. That's a big start. Nobody can hide an organization. As for the woman, the Bureau is swarming over Marine Corps files right now. But keep it in your minds that we are looking for an organization committed to assassination—not just one woman."

The three cops were sweating. The president and the attorney general seemed distanced from the problem. Keifetz was attentive.

"Jean," the president said, "lay out the main components of the women's movement for these men. They're going to have to run a couple of hundred agents around those components."

Jean looked gravely at each cop in turn. "As of the night my husband was murdered," she said, "this is how one could look at the main groups fighting for equal rights for women. There is no convenient range, right to left, of violence-preaching to centrist-cautionary positions. There are so many different constituencies within the movement that it is difficult to narrow them down to a few categories. On the other hand, the movement is consolidating more and more into a centrist position— that is, things that were considered radical a few years ago are now being accepted by the mainstream. Furthermore, *no* one within the movement has ever advocated a really cautionary or conservative line. Not that I know of, anyway.

"Three of the four divisions seem to have the most validity. First, the center, the force of the movement which advances under political motivation. Call them the feminists. They are the women who want to have all the rights, options, and privileges that are traditionally enjoyed only by men. The feminists seek change through political action.

"Next we have the radicals—a good designation for them. They are women who want female self-determination. They want policymaking powers as those involve women and women's interests on their own terms. They seek change through overthrow of male domination. The radicals seek control through conflict.

"The third position is held by the right wing of the movement. They are willing to merge with other groups—left, right, and center—to win their objectives, which are the eradication of sexist conditioning and stereotyped sexist roles. They seek change by working together with men to realign our values and our culture. Call them the mergers. They seek change through conversion.

"There most certainly is an active and vocal fourth group within the movement—the lesbians. I don't mean to suggest that there are no lesbians in any other divisions of the movement—why shouldn't there be? But the lesbians say it isn't possible to be a feminist unless a woman is or becomes a lesbian. They stand for the destruction or exile of all men from whatever positions they occupy in society—what*ever* these may be—and that their places must be assumed by lesbians—and I speak now of jobs from the presidency down to the leaders of organized crime. The lesbians are rabid rather than merely violent, hysterical rather than emotional or articulate. They will accept nothing short of their total program."

"Then that's where we look for the Matriots," Moe Michaels said. "And that's where we'll find them."

"I don't think so, Moe," Jean said. "They not only want men out of power, but they want only lesbians in power. That let's me out—and I'm the Matriots' candidate."

"Oh."

"From the drift of what the woman said to me, the Matriots wouldn't waste all this time and two lives to hand the power over to someone who has no connection with or interest in their purpose."

The DSP said, "Except they thought they could blackmail you with manufactured evidence that you had killed your husband."

"Where do *you* think we should look for the Matriots?" Michaels asked Jean.

"I just don't know."

"Try an educated guess."

She smiled faintly. "Well, historically, the organizers of political assassinations have usually been the conservatives of any given country—from Julius Caesar to John F. Kennedy. Why should that change because the conspirators are women? Or maybe we'll find them hidden among the mergers—the compromisers. Political assassination is the most violent form of compromise. This side of war, anyway. I think we'll probably have to rule out the center group. They know they are making progress and they have the patience to wait for the results they are sure will happen. But—we are going to have to rake out every group of them, accepting that the Matriots have to be a fifth group within the women's movement—an entirely new group—the revolutionaries."

"We got a real morning lineup here," Gallagher said. "The entire female population of the United States."

"Thank you, Jean," the president said.

Everyone in the room turned to his basso profundo authority. "I want every intelligence unit of the government to come into this investigation—from the Department of Defense to the National Security Agency—with every technique involved. We'll be leaning heavily on statistical analysis, undercover people, informers, private organizational records and files, Internal Revenue information, and Census Bureau profiles, so all of it must be unified under one command. Beginning at the close of the day tomorrow, to allow us time to advise everyone concerned, the director, FBI, will be in charge of the combined investigation. Every instrument of this government from the Passport Division of the State Department to the Alien Custodian's Office, if and as they become involved in this, will take orders from him. Thank you, gentlemen," he said to the three cops. "We have well over a month to the nominating convention. No need to keep you here."

Gallagher, James, and Michaels left the cottage silently, walking fast, not looking back. Keifetz remained where he was seated.

"Jean," the president said, "a few weeks ago my conscience, seated over there, and I talked about a running mate for the ticket. We have it narrowed down to three names and yours is one of them."

Jean's eyes got wider and her face grew pale.

"The time has come for the nomination of a woman vice-president— and you qualify. Keifetz *agrees* that you qualify, but he's not so hot on the idea of a woman veep. However and nonetheless, since your own tragedy overtook us, the White House has received over three and a half million letters, telegrams, and calls in two short weeks, all supporting you unanimously in what otherwise could have been a scandal which this administration might or might not have ridden out. The support hasn't diminished. It is nothing short of miraculous."

"Mr. President, I—"

He talked right through her attempt to speak. "I can't say yet whether it will happen that way, because a lot of party leaders need to be advised and consulted. So it is too soon for me to commit anything. But about two weeks before the convention—despite your so recent loss— I'll want you to take to the road to address women's groups throughout this country and to meet privately with heavy people in the key states."

"Mr. President, there is a whole gang of women out there who actively oppose the ERA. They will have a field day if I go on the road campaigning while I'm supposed to be in mourning."

"Some women don't want the ERA, or say they don't through some very odd spokeswoman. But if we want the ERA carried, then it is to be either you or some other outstanding woman on the ticket. Congress gave us one more postponement in eighty-two, and we ain't going to get another."

"I cannot run." Her face was haggard and her eyes were pleading. She covered her face with a hand, her elbow on the arm of the chair. She choked back a sob. She slammed her fist down powerfully and said, "Because if that happens, they will kill you."

He put his hand gently on her forearm and patted it softly. "I can't run this country by accommodating terrorists," he answered her. "All these Matriots are doing, in their own way, is dissenting. There will be other dissenters who will object with their ballots. But I think the attorney general knows it is her duty to run, if and when she is called, and to take her chances just the way I am taking mine."

37

The morning after the meeting at Camp David, only twenty minutes before the organizing meeting for the investigation of the Matriots began, Gallagher came into her office, red-faced and unsmiling.

"Anything wrong?" she asked.

"The president personally ordered me to begin an investigation of the murder of your husband and Mrs. Cassiman."

"I thought I had already ordered that," she said mildly.

"Yeah, but I wanted you to know that Keifetz is holding the president's coat while he pushes him into the act."

"A joint investigation? With the NYPD and the DC police?"

"That's what the man wants. He and Keifetz know about the connection between Dr. Spano and—ah—her."

"Thanks for telling me this, Dick."

"He said we've got to be careful that there isn't another Watergate."

"How are you going to run it? Open with the police?"

"We'll move it very carefully."

"Because I'm involved?"

"How are you involved?"

"As a lawyer I'd say I'm involved enough that I can't talk to you about the case after this meeting."

"We won't run open with the police. We'll ask them for whatever they've got but we won't tell them anything."

"Not even about the Matriots?"

"We had to tell them about that."

"I'm glad. Do the DC police want to talk to me?"

"Not right now. Not yet. But they want an Identi-Kit picture from you. On the woman."

"I did that this morning. I needed it for your meeting."

"Keifetz seems to be bugged on one thing. It could be very important."

"That's Keifetz."

"His daughter Mandy is a criminology student at Illinois. She keeps hunching him, he says, that we gotta check out if the same gun was used to kill both people."

"Wouldn't that be routine?"

"No. Not routine. Two separate departments in different cities."

"What if it was the same gun?"

His face was grim. "Well," he shrugged, "that would tighten the circle of suspects, maybe—wouldn't it?"

"But there is a gap here."

"Where?"

"You're about to conduct a meeting with the heads of ten government investigative agencies to find the woman who came to my house and stated that an organization called the Matriots had murdered my husband and expected confidently to assassinate the president. We find the woman—and I don't see how she can escape us—she will provide details on both the organization and the murder. Also, the woman was surely at Alex Cassiman's house when Alex called me, so probably the woman murdered Alex. If yes to both murders, we have both evidence *and* a confession."

"Okay."

"Then why has the president ordered the FBI to undertake a separate investigation?"

"That's how you run a democracy. The more investigations, the bigger the smokescreen."

"This—ah—direction can't be *entirely* because of the intuition of Keifetz's daughter Mandy at the University of Illinois."

"No."

"The president—or Keifetz—must suspect me."

"Not the president. He looked right at me and he said that he not only wanted to find the killer or killers but that he wanted to prove your

innocence in the event that anyone else could want to prove otherwise."

"Who would that be?" she asked harshly.

"You're in politics, lady—you know better than me. The president has
his reasons and maybe you know what they are. I only know that while I
organize the federal investigative community to take off in one direction, the White House has ordered me to take off in the other."

38

Five men sat at one side of a conference table, facing four more on the other side. Gallagher sat at the head. Each member of the meeting had a file folder in front of him which contained a transcript of the AG's statement to the tape recorder, made at Gallagher's house on the night of the Cassiman murder, and six copies of the black and white Identi-Kit picture of the Matriot which the AG and the FBI technicians had composed.

In a line on his right sat Lloyd Deas, director, IRS: Admiral Sissons, head of Naval Intelligence; Brian Perman, chief of the State Department's Bureau of Intelligence & Research, and McHarry Carlos, director of the Defense Intelligence Agency. At his left in the row along the table were Moe Michaels, head of the Secret Service; Berry James, director, SP, and Dr. Harold Hutchinson Harris, legendary leader of the National Security Agency—then Keifetz.

"The files in front of you contain such information as we have to deal with. Moe Michaels, in charge of the protection of the president, will lead off," Gallagher said.

"We got a woman here," Michaels said, "who has admitted to one murder and is probably involved in two—the second being the killing of the wife of a United States senator—who states flatly that her organization, the Matriots, is going to organize the national women's movements to get the nomination for the vice presidency for Mrs. Spano, the

AG, at the next convention, then that they are going to assassinate the president to put Mrs. Spano into the presidency. That scares the living hell out of me and I'm going to stay scared till we nail her. And that's what we're here for—to nail her."

McHarry Carlos, built exactly like the smallest Fiat, stared at Michaels belligerently and said, "Are you telling us that there is a full-fledged assassination plot now operating and the people haven't been apprehended yet?" He was a major general who had been a paint salesman before Vietnam.

"Read the goddamn file," Keifetz said across the table. "We're not here for a discussion, we're here for assignments."

General Carlos shuffled papers, then spoke: "The attorney general said that the FBI will do the legwork on this. We need the NSA for record analysis. All we have is that improvised portrait of the woman. The AG says it's a fairly good likeness, but it isn't the true face of the woman. Still, the paralysis of the left side of the face has to help. We have no name for her but we know that she said she had been a major in the 3rd Battalion of the 5th Division of the Marine Corps until she had the stroke. The Navy is going to have to dig in at the only place we have any information about her. We don't know when she was in the Corps or even if she was lying. But that's nothing—that's easy—it is going to be necessary to break out as many investigators as we can assemble—state by state—to canvass the federal, state, and local membership of every women's organization of record. We'll start with the six biggest cities. The FBI is going to need some additional manpower, so the Defense Intelligence Agency, working out of the military installations across the country, is going to have to supply it.

"If we can get an identification maybe the IRS or the Passport Bureau at State can match that up for us. The Secret Police and the Bureau of I&R will work overseas to find out if there is any foreign guerrilla knowledge of a Matriots organization. Finding the name and whereabouts of the woman and matching it to her face may be impossible, but it is standard routine police work and anyway it must be done. But finding an organization is a different thing. There aren't any other revolutionary women's organizations, as far as we know. When there are members, some of them talk. Our big ace here is the National Security Agency and its special skills and machines which may be able to match up the Identi-Kit picture with every photograph in the Passport Division, in the naval and military and prison records, and in police files across the country. We have a month or so to the nominating convention and five to election day. We are here to keep the president alive and healthy. Any questions?"

The room was limply silent.

Dr. Harris said, "It simply cannot be done."

"It's got to be done," Keifetz snarled. "The director just laid it on the line."

"I speak for the National Security Agency," Harris said simply, "and I repeat it cannot be done."

Moe Michaels pounded his heavy fist heavily on the table. "What the hell is that fucking army of computers for?" he yelled. "It's gotta be done!"

"Come on! Come on!" Gallagher said loudly. "This is a routine investigation, fahcrissake! All it is is bigger than usual. We get out and ask questions and pound the pavements and all Harris has to do is to organize a couple of billion dollars' worth of computers to match one picture against a few million others. We've got the Army, every cop in the country, and the National Guard in fifty states *plus* all those beautiful computers. It's a meat and potatoes proposition. How can she get away?"

"Look at it this way, gentlemen," Keifetz said. "What about the alternative? Where is everybody in this room going to hide if the alternative happens?"

39

The national sensation caused by simultaneous media revelations that the murders of Ames Spano and the wife of Senator Cassiman could be closely linked—as closely as the two victims had been linked in life—lasted for four days of news milking. But the facts were lazy. They revealed that the murdered woman had been Dr. Spano's assistant, with all the innuendos, but no one except Joyce Engelson of the New York *World* took it any further.

There was plenty of art available on Dr. Spano, and a moderate number of pictures of Alex Fowles, several in bikinis, but no photographs of the two people together. However, this was made up for by the wealth of shots of Attorney General Spano with both victims, from campus days forward.

It was Engelson who brought the NYPD ballistics experts together with those of the DC police by urging Lieutenant Umberto Caen of homicide five, NYPD, to find out whether the same weapon had been used to kill both people in widely separated cities, New York and Washington, the line offered by Keifetz's daughter Mandy, which had been expertly stifled. The same weapon had been used and Engelson pegged the story on Caen's great detective work, making him a six-hour wonder across the country.

Engelson still smarted from being dressed down by the attorney general at the monster press conference. John Clohesy, her publisher, had instructed her to file every word of copy on Spano, or the administration's connection with the cases, directly with him in New York. Engelson, who ran the *World*'s Washington bureau, accepted that as a standing order.

The reporter had a sharp hunch about the AG's possible criminal connection with the case, partly perhaps because she was carrying a grudge, but mainly it was wishful thinking about landing such a sensational international newsbeat. She went to work to locate the Spano house servants because they would have inside knowledge of what had gone on at the Spanos'. She tracked Henri and Louise to Paris where they had sublet the apartment of a retired restaurateur in the rue Surcouf in the 7th arrondissement while they conducted bewildering food surveys.

Engelson flew out of Washington on a Friday night after work and was lunching at Henri's groaning table on Saturday at 1:00 P.M. Paris time, interviewing Henri for the *World* on "international food trends." Henri cooked the lunch, which was breakfast for Engelson, and she didn't see how she could possibly eat any of it. Not that she didn't love Henri's kind of food, but she was eight pounds overweight and very much worried about facing her fall wardrobe. Still, she ate everything he put in front of her while she told him she couldn't eat anything because of jet lag, allergies, because of everything except being overweight, because she knew talk about calories was the one thing that food freaks would not countenance. Henri was so transported at being interviewed by a New York newspaper in Paris, France, that he babbled away cheerfully and kept the food and wine coming.

By four o'clock that afternoon Engleson had her story: Spano and the woman had been lovers; they had planned to run away together to the Central African Republic; bitterly, angrily, and even violently the attorney general had opposed them.

Engelson recorded Henri and Louise on one hour and forty minutes of tape, most of it about food, but with solid blocks about the incriminating Spano conflict. They had dates, places, and even two Polaroid shots: Dr. Spano and Mrs. Cassiman being happy together, and a Saturday luncheon picture of Dr. Spano, Mrs. Cassiman, and the AG made in better days.

When she returned to Washington at noon on Sunday she was exhausted, she had gained two pounds, but she had the story. She went home, slept for six hours, then wrote it. She took it into the office on Sunday night and put it on the system for John Clohesy's eyes only, as instructed.

Clohesy called her at 12:45 A.M. at her apartment in Washington.

"Engelson," he said, "this is a serious matter."

"I got that story exclusive, Mr. Clohesy," she said, "and I got tapes to back it up. We'll beat the whole world with it."

"Be in my office at nine-thirty tomorrow morning."

"In New York? Mr. Clohesy, when this story breaks tomorrow morning, I'm gonna have plenty to do—because this town is gonna explode!"

"There isn't going to be any story tomorrow morning—not till you and I check it all out."

She sat across Clohesy's desk with opaqued eyes, not taking the news at all well.

"This newspaper—I, personally—signed an agreement with the attorney general guaranteeing her special handling," Clohesy said. "Listen—don't look at me like that. The woman could have put this paper out of business after what the grand jury had the nerve to say about that letter we ran."

"Clohesy, what are you basically—an accountant?"

"*Mister* Clohesy."

"Clohesy, I'll bet you're not even an accountant basically—you gotta be an advertising man."

"Watch yourself, Engelson."

"You're paying me sixty thousand dollars a year to run the Washington bureau for you, but you never asked me about running that shitty letter. You just ran it. You didn't even ask the office boy or the cleaning women—to name two jobs around here who understand the newspaper business better than you do—you just ran it. Then you signed some agreement. You *have* to be a congenital idiot, Clohesy, because you now have hard news about the biggest story worldwide today and you fixed it up so the *World* can't run it."

"I can understand that you are upset, but—"

"I haven't put in for one cent of expenses on this story, Clohesy."

"What has that got to do with anything? Am I questioning your expenses? Did I ever question your expenses?"

"Also, I got the story on my own time—on my time off—Saturday and Sunday."

"You did a great job! The paper is proud of you. You rate a bonus."

"A bonus for a story you're not going to run? That's not a bonus, Clohesy, that's a bribe. Shove it. All right. I quit as of now."

"You have a contract."

"So sue me and we'll put you on the stand for cross-examination about this story you are trying to kill."

"*Try*ing? It is dead."

"You really are a stupid fella, aren't you? I spent my own money to get the story and I got it on my own time. I just quit. Now I am going to walk uptown to the New York *Times*—or maybe the AP—and I'm going to give them the story because that's the way it has to be."

Clohesy got out of his chair slowly; he walked to the window of his office and stared at the river.

"Engelson, you're pretty heavy on the women's movement, aren't you?"

"I'm out for the ERA if that's what you mean."

"Well, you're right. I *am* basically an accountant—because believe it or not, that's what keeps this paper running. Today's big news is something they wrap fish in tomorrow, but the paper has to keep coming out—if you have any way of understanding what I mean. If that story runs, the AG will sue us for everything we have. So I am not going to run that story. But, believe it or not, I do know what keeps newspapers running and you are one of the important elements. So don't resign. Go back to Washington. Accept the bonus for a great job of newspaper work. Then—and don't forget it was me and nobody else who made you the first woman bureau chief in Washington—I will offer you a national column on women's affairs to run three times a week, with carte blanche to run anything about any side of the women's movement that will lead to the passage of the ERA—or anything else. I'll guarantee you sixty papers for the column to start and the syndicate will be juiced up to add more and more papers—no boilerplate."

He turned to face her. "That's the best I can do, Engelson. What do you say?"

"I'll take it," Engelson said, without a pause. "You really are talking, Mr. Clohesy; and it's maybe just as well that you shredded that story because now that I am a national columnist, I am gonna need big news sources like the attorney general in my work."

40

When Jean had impulsively hired her to run Voters' Research, Ursula was food and beverages manager of a large Hong Kong hotel, buying and importing enormous quantities of fresh food from the San Fernando Valley, New Zealand, Australia, France, and Iran, so she settled into the clearly established management without any lack of confidence. She was a naturally successful woman where the management of other people's businesses or personal problems was concerned, so much so that it was possible she found she had spent the knack where there was a need for successful management of herself. Despite her own Oriental (smashing) good looks, good health, and an instant appearance of prosperity, Ursula was a doormat personality, given her head. She forced herself to serve harder than anyone else. She invented work, which appeared ostentatious to her co-workers. She was first in, last to leave. Nonetheless she was popular at Voters' Research because she was the boss and because she was exotic, therefore mysterious, and likable, in that order.

Jean had installed her in the flat on 35th Street, the flat the Spanos had lived in after they were first married. She let Ursula get settled into the new job, met with her twice a week at first, then once a week to check out results, and invited her to Rockrimmon for one Saturday luncheon in each month.

Ames had liked Ursula, and thought she was a wealthy Chinese refugee, probably of the Soong family, because she had lived in Hong Kong and had gone to Smith. Because he had no interest in putting things into a logical pattern, he could never retain the fact that she was managing the Voters' Research for Jean. Ursula was pretty, Oriental, a Smith girl; she came to the Saturday checkbook luncheons at Rockrimmon, therefore it followed that she was both wealthy and Christian. It never mattered whether Ames was right or wrong because the alternatives were always nearly identical.

Jean was enormously involved in the NYPD and in necessary matters that kept happening at the law firm, then in the cultivation and training of political animals, and finally with her duties as attorney general, so that, business and the one monthly social occasion aside, she gradually saw less and less of Ursula and was uncurious about what her friend did with herself as long as she looked well.

Ursula was a painter. She got back from the office on East 40th Street, which was five blocks away, at about seven o'clock each night. She preferred to cook and eat Chinese food because Western food was barbaric. By eight o'clock she was mixing colors, then working and, after two years, she discovered that finished work had accumulated in the flat, more than she had room for.

One chilly Saturday in January 1984, with two or three canvases under her arm, she toured galleries in Greenwich Village and SoHo, seeking an exhibition; within two weeks she and her paintings had been accepted by a stunning, pugnacious woman who owned a gallery on Bank Street. The woman's name was Gladys. She moved in with Ursula on Sunday, Monday, Tuesday, and Wednesday, then Ursula moved in with her over the gallery on Thursdays, Fridays, and Saturdays. Gladys was an obsessively possessive woman who guarded Ursula from all other people as if she were the Maltese falcon. She bullied Ursula and made her very happy. They exchanged rings, had sickening quarrels, made up with ecstatic tears and keening, and stood off the world. Ursula's one-person show was set for the first Monday in April. She mentioned this happy news to Jean, and Jean's enthusiasm and admiration swept everything before it.

"Urs, we are really going to dress that opening," she said. "Will it help if the governor shows up?"

"I would rather the lieutenant governor," Ursula said shyly.

"You've got her. And the police commissioner, an iron celebrity whom you can take home and cook because he is a walking Doggy Pack of Asiatic food. I'll deliver the mayor. Who else belongs there?"

"Gladys will be glad to see people with money."

"Who's Gladys?"

"She owns the gallery."

"Then we'll have Charles Cantwell deliver a dozen assorted people with money. Who else?"

"Some painters? I mean, the sort of heavy painters who only paint in *People* magazine."

"The bank will handle that. They'll lean on the museum directors. And we ought to have a few actors and a couple of ballerinas—and maybe some pop stars and a couple of musicians. I have a friend who runs a record company and a friend who runs a network."

"Jean—"

"What?"

"Do you mind if I tell Gladys that a friend of my family's—Charles Cantwell—wants to do all this for me?"

"Sure. Why?"

"Gladys and I are—we live together. But she is volcanically jealous. She couldn't stand it if another woman did this for me. She might burn all my paintings."

"For Christ's sake!"

"It isn't as bad as it sounds. She—I—really, she is an extremely wonderful person and a real fighter—I mean a fighter in the women's movement."

"Then how can you be sure she'll take that kind of a guest list from Charles? She probably feels more antagonistic to men than she might to other women."

"Oh, no! Anyway, when I tell her he is an old friend of my family, and how, when I told him about Gladys' generosity in giving me the show, he said he just had to be able to help us, she will be absolutely okay about it if he doesn't take too many bows in front of our friends."

"Your friends?"

"You know, people like us. Like Gladys and me. Gladys is a *leader*, believe me—very, very macho."

The show was a pleasant success. There were flattering reviews in the little magazines even if nothing broke uptown, and *Village Voice* said Ursula would be "the ultimate painter of Chinese food," which Gladys had engraved on a silver bracelet for Ursula after the show closed. They cleared $498. Seven paintings were sold.

Gladys never met either their benefactor, Charles Cantwell, or any of the distinguished guests because she became so overcome with nerves that she got a painful case of shingles and had to be hospitalized at a veterans hospital in Staten Island.

She knew Ursula had to stay at the gallery every night because the rugged elderly woman who agreed to stand in during the days had to be relieved and that Ursula worked during the days. But Gladys became so anxious about who could be trying to get into Ursula's drawers that she tried to kill herself by drinking Dutch Boy Red Lead, then beat up her father because he bawled her out for doing such a stupid goddamn thing. Ursula had her moved by private ambulance to Matsonia. The show closed before Gladys was well again.

After the two murders, Jean told Ursula, almost in a manner of thinking out loud, about the Matriots and how critically important it was that they find anyone who belonged to the organization. Ursula said she was going to ask her friends to go underground and take up the search in places where she doubted the federal security people could ever go.

She had a deplorable time trying to explain this to Gladys, who insisted that Jean was Ursula's lover. But although Ursula never succeeded in quieting those fears, she did get through her meaning, by repeating over and over and over—in bed, at meals, and on the telephone—that it was because Jean had been her housemate at college that Jean had befriended her now. After her sisters had been killed, it was Jean who had made it possible for her to come to New York to work and therefore to meet Gladys. However, mainly because she was so heroically impressed that a woman had made it to become the attorney general of the United States, Gladys said she agreed to organize the hunt for the Matriots throughout the lesbian communities and groups across the country.

But Ursula had fallen out of love with Gladys' violence and had fallen in love with Jean. When it was necessary for Jean to come up to New York, she lived at Matsonia, because she wouldn't go back to the huge house on the Drive. This meant that no matter when Jean was coming to stay, Ursula could not be with Gladys. She knew there was no way to explain this to Gladys. But she had to be free to be wherever Jean was going to be, no matter what chaos it would cause, so she turned herself into Gladys' abject slave, forcing her servility on her, making her accept constant fawning attention, until Gladys lost all interest in her and plunged back into Village life to find another lover. She found a black addict named Peaches and beat her up so constantly and hurled her around their rooms and in restaurants with such abandon that the addict told everyone, "Well, shit, baby, I don't know. Gladys so crazy that people sayin' she a latent heterosexual."

Although Gladys had the initiative in seeming to be the one who had broken up the love affair, she knew intuitively that there was something fishy about the way it had happened, something on which she could not put her finger. So she took it out on Peaches (at first), yelling at her: "I know I got the boot. I *know!* And—oh, shit!—I must still love her because my cooky gets all mushy when I think about her." Or, "Why do I always go for crazy coloreds? Why can't I find a sweet little white broad like me?"

In a desperate attempt to even things with the Fates, Gladys sent a letter filled with "evidence" about the Spano-Cassiman murders to the FBI in New York and named Ursula Baggot as the leader of the Matriots, which had done the killings. The organization's name had been believed to be exclusively police knowledge. The woman named was identified by the informer as being a notorious lesbian. The FBI staged a raid on Matsonia, and, finding Attorney General Spano alone in the apartment in a filmy, long peignoir, they arrested her.

"Are you men drunk?" Jean asked them, outraged by the breach of conduct.

"All right, baby," the skinny dark agent said. "Hustle your ass in there and get some clothes on. You're going to Washington."

"Give me your shields," she barked at them. "You are either drunk or drugged in the performance of your duty." She went to the telephone and dialed Justice in Washington; connected, she asked for the director, FBI.

The men guffawed like vaudeville comics. The tall one dug the short one in the ribs with his elbow as if it were stage routine.

"Put him on," Jean said. "This is the attorney-general."

The men gaped at each other, and to complete the comic vaudeville effect, ran out of the room.

Nonetheless it was recorded in the attorney general's own FBI dossier that she maintained an apartment in New York, separate from her own house in New York, her second house in Washington, and her third house in Connecticut, for the year-round use of a known lesbian who had been named as leader of an organization which police and federal law enforcement authorities had straightforward evidence to believe had murdered the attorney general's husband.

This file would be used as an indictment of Jean Spano when the White House decided to move into action.

41

Jean flew to Houston on the day following the aborted raid on Matsonia to address the 89,000-strong National Women's Conference, which was described over and over as "a rainbow of women" who had assembled to call for the passage of the Equal Rights Amendment; free choice of government-paid abortion; a national health insurance plan; the extension of Social Security benefits to housewives; Medicare for single women; the elimination of job, housing, and credit discrimination against all women and all lesbians, as well as the lesbian right to custody of their children; an expansion of bilingual education for minority women; a federal campaign to educate women on their right to credit; federal and state-funded programs for victims of child abuse and for education in rape prevention; state-supported shelters for wives physically abused by their husbands; and a federal rural program to overcome isolation, poverty, and underemployment. Five wives of former presidents were guests of the convention.

Jean was met at the airport by Susie Orde, her public information officer, two network camera crews, seven still photographers, and a national committeewoman who interrupted conversation all the way into the city with wails that she had runs in her pantyhose and that they were going to have to stop someplace and do something about it.

"We can't stop, Mrs. Zendt," Susie said, "we are running twenty minutes late."

"I don't give a goddamn about that. I'm not going to sit up on that platform with ruined legs. Just stop at Sakowitz's. I won't be five minutes."

"About ninety thousand women are waiting, Mrs. Zendt."

"Goddammit, Mrs. Spano, would you sit up there with three gigantic runs in your hose?"

"Never," Jean said. "I'd take them off."

"Oh, damn! All right," Mrs. Zendt said and scuffed her shoes off.

Jean was introduced to the convention by the legendary Dame Maria Van Slyke, honorary chairperson. She was 107 years old, yet refused to wear elastic stockings. She neither stood nor spoke for the introduction of the attorney general; she merely waved her hand and Jean came forward to the assembled microphones while 89,826 women rose to their feet, cheering.

"Sisters—and gentlemen wherever you are," Jean began, "I stand here today straighter than I have ever stood, taller with pride as I look out at the representatives of all American women—that not inconsiderable unit of our population, representing 51.8 percent of all of the people in all of the states of our Union."

There was wild cheering.

"No previous gathering could begin to match your diversity of age, income, race, occupation, and opinion. It was a huge accomplishment to achieve this assembly: 130,000 women gave up a part of their lives to participate in the long delegate-selection process leading to this conference. Today, 1442 official delegates, representing 120,000,000 American women, who were elected at fifty-one state and territorial meetings open to the public, are here to participate in American history, while four hundred more of you were appointed at large by an overseeing national commission."

She wondered about the women who had been against attending this meeting; the antilib women, the women who had been brainwashed by the right-to-lifers, by churlish husbands, and by the organized propaganda pounding of Phyllis Schlafly's right wing and the bitter antagonism of the men who controlled important media and who had the money to buy their way into confused women's minds. She had to find the power from somewhere within her, from Mama, from the whole meaning of her life to turn the timid women of America toward the passion to achieve equal rights for *all* women.

"You are black, white, yellow, and brown—Chicano, Nisei, Indian, and WASP—and four of you are Eskimo. You are rich, poor, radical, conservative, Democratic, Republican, Communist, and politically uninvolved. You are straight and you are gay. You are all bound together with the single determination which we all share—to demand the ratification, thus far refused us, of the Equal Rights Amendment."

She thought of Ames and the Slut, murdered. She thought of Caen and shuddered as she stood at the rostrum, inundated by the roar of the crowd. She smothered the preying thought that if American women really wanted the ERA, they would have it. The bands played "Over the Rainbow." Women wept and sang and pounded rhythmically on the backs of the seats in front of them. Jean held her arms high over her head, palms outward, and gradually the uproar subsided.

"As attorney general of the United States, I am here as the representative of your president—as well as of my own convictions—to call upon this country for the swift passage of the ERA. Other plans and programs will be discussed at this convention which are yet to be considered by you, and which therefore are not yet the concern of the government. You will have big political issues to act upon at this meeting.

"You will have the usual divisions of opinion on these issues, but whatever they are, there are certain things that women of the right, left, and center ardently support. Even those who do not consider themselves feminists are unwilling to accept unequal treatment under the law, and more and *more* and MORE will join with us to fight all discrimination against them. In the most obvious sense, anyone could wonder why it was ever necessary to convene this meeting at all. We are assured into permanent numbness that we are living in the world's greatest democracy, and we sell the words human rights until they run out of other nations' ears."

She saw the thousands of faces, each one with a different inner yearning, none thinking that all of them together was truly a statistical political force because every one of them who had made the effort to be in that auditorium had a different longing reason for being there, cherished separate reasons which she, somehow, had to shape into one universal reason with her words.

"The implacable existence of real and living democracy is the entire *basis* of the Equal Rights Amendment. Even the old die-hard enemies of the ERA—even those fight-unto-death enemies—would agree that the human species is divisible into only two parts—women and men.

"The men demonstrate forcibly for all the rest of us, by their actions suppressing our equal rights, that there is, to them, admissibly only *one* unit within their species. The other apparently cretinous claimant—demanding title to belong—is evidently vaguely related to some species of cow."

Her eyes flashed indignantly as her voice rose to shake them. Then, with the skill of a great performing artist, she switched emotions. She became compassionate, ready to take the hopes of men, and their right to an equal life, into her bosom along with her faith in the equality of women with men.

"BUT . . . WE . . . FORGIVE . . . THEM . . . THEIR . . . IG-NORANCE!"

She pounded each separate word into the lectern before her, and her punctuation resounded out of the sound system and throughout the arena. "Since there are more women than men in this one-person-one-vote democracy, how can it be that only *one* of these life forms has full rights under American law, while the *essential,* truly *vital* form—for the concern of life itself, this other half, responsible for the continuation of the species—does NOT have equal rights under the law?"

The enormous cheering and applause shook the building. The ovation lasted for seven minutes, then gradually Jean brought the almost ninety thousand women back to quiet attention.

"The past ten years and more have seen every nonsensical objection treated and have placed these for all Americans to see in relation to the truth. And the truth concerns the simple matter of legal equality between the only two thinking, communicating animals that exist—the only two partners in humanity—women and men, men and women."

A loud, happy, deep voice shouted from somewhere in the auditorium, *"Vive la différence!"*

Jean stood calmly at the lectern, smiling her pleasure. When the assembly finished applauding that fine sentiment, she began again.

"I am speaking as a woman first. But I am speaking as your attorney general and for your president—the ninth consecutive president of the United States beginning with Franklin Roosevelt who has whole-heartedly endorsed the ERA and urged that it be welded into the Constitution.

"In that framework of American history—and not so much for you in this auditorium who have given so many of your days and years to fighting on behalf of the ratification of the Equal Rights Amendment, but for the millions of people at home who are watching what we are accomplishing through the many network television cameras in this arena, through radio, and by the constant support of American news-papers on whom we depend so much to bring the truth to all of us—men and women—I want to recount briefly the history of the ERA so that perspectives on it may be measured.

"On August 26, 1920, Secretary of State Bainbridge Colby announced that the 19th Amendment, which granted the vote to women, had become part of the Constitution. He signed the proclamation at his residence, but, being macho—that expressive word which instantly describes all of the child-men all of us have known—he made sure no one from the National Women's Party or any of the suffrage leaders were there to share in the glory of his signature. As he said at that moment, 'Effectuating suffrage through proclamation of its ratification is more important than feeding movie cameras.'

"Nonetheless, he did take time before his breakfast to congratulate women—whoever they were or wherever they might be—on the successful culmination of their efforts in the face of discouragement, and declared that the day marked the opening of a great and new era in the political life of the nation.

"That was in 1920, and we have been fighting for equal rights for women under the law ever since.

"The ERA was introduced to the Congress in 1923—*as it has been reintroduced to the Congress every year since then.* There was a sort of flurry of interest in it after World War II as a gesture toward women's war efforts. The Senate passed the ERA twice—in 1950 and in 1953. The House Judiciary Committee, led by the neanderthal Emanuel Celler of Brooklyn, New York, buried it deep in 1947 and sat guard over the grave which he had cemented over.

"Then came the sixties and the resurgence of the entire women's rights movement—the new rights organizations, the consciousness-raising groups, and the lawsuits charging discrimination under the Equal Pay and Civil Rights acts. All this brought about a renewal of interest in the Congress.

"In February 1970, Senator Birch Bayh, chairman of the Senate Judiciary Subcommittee on Constitutional Amendments, sponsored an ERA, with eighty-one of the 100 senators cosigning it. Senator Bayh announced hearings to be held that May, forcing the issue over the head of Senator Erwin, the Judiciary Committee chairman, who had kept it bottled up for years.

"Meanwhile, in the House, Representative Martha Griffiths, a Democrat of Michigan, a member of Celler's trussed-up Judiciary Committee, successfully filed a petition for the discharge of the bill from the committee and got it out on the House floor under Celler's nose. It was debated for less than an hour—twenty-three years after moldering in Celler's committee—and was passed by a vote of 350 to fifteen on August 10, 1970. The full Senate didn't pass the ERA until March 22, 1972, by a vote of eighty-four to eight. In October 1971, after further extensive hearings, the House passed it *again* by a vote of 354 to twenty-three.

"The ERA has to be an overwhelmingly popular legislative notion, because the Senate has passed it twice, the House has passed it twice, and nine presidents of the United States have supported it!"

She was pounding her points home like nails going into a board. She could feel the audience ceasing to wonder where she got her clothes, silently criticizing her hat. She was filling the entire frame.

"In March 1972, the amendment went out to the country for ratification by thirty-eight out of fifty states by March 22, 1979. By January 1977, thirty-five states had ratified the ERA, although four of the states announced that they wanted to rescind their votes—a proposal of doubtful legal value.

"On August 15, 1978, the House voted 233 to 189 to extend the deadline for ratification until June 30, 1982, and defeated a key amendment in the bill to give any state the right to rescind approval; another extension was needed in 1982."

"So what that thumbnail outline of the history of 51.8 percent of the population of this country means is that 136 years after the first convention for women's rights was held in Seneca Falls, New York, and sixty-four years after Secretary of State Colby proclaimed the successful culmination of women's efforts and the beginning of a thrilling new era for American women—and men—and sixty-one years after the ERA was introduced into the Congress, we are *still* fighting a battle to be recognized as equal citizens under the law.

"The ERA is still in limbo, but we are gathered here to face that denial of our rights and to persuade, convince, and overcome all of the opposition in government that denies our rights.

"God speed you!"

The president watched the extraordinary ovation given the attorney general by the eighty-nine thousand exultant women at the Astrodome as it came into his small study on three television sets.

He looked across at Keifetz. "We can multiply that eighty-nine thousand by the number of all the women who are watching her across this country," he said flatly.

Keifetz grunted.

"Spano is a vote-catcher, kid. They don't come along like that except once in a generation. If she was a man she'd be Franklin Roosevelt. She's really got what they think they've gotta have."

"That isn't all she's got," Keifetz said.

"What are you talking about? You've seen the analyses of the mail she's been drawing. She's getting nearly three million pieces a week, and every one of them on the subject you're worried about. The voters don't see any scandal. They see the personal tragedy of an admirable woman who has lost a husband whom they revered and they see it as a crying injustice that that newspaper tried to maul her."

"I wish I could be so sure."

"What the hell do you need to be sure—*five* million letters a week?"

"Frank, listen. That Cassiman killing is still playing out there. Fahcrissake, think about it! The revered husband and the Cassiman woman were making it together. And she wasn't just any senator's wife, but Iron-Ass Cassiman's wife! And they were also cheating on the attorney general of the United States, and *both* injured parties are very much a part of your administration. Let one reporter—like that Engelson woman—put the whole thing together and there'll be nothing left but the biggest and messiest illicit-love-nest-leading-straight-to-unsolvedmurders and much juicier stories than were ever generated by Watergate. Whammo!—there goes the election."

"Horseshit! That isn't the way it would play," the president snarled. "What do we have here? We have an absolutely *brilliant* leader of fifty million American women, who is also the beautiful, magnificently behaved widow of a modern saint at whose side she sweated in the kind of poverty in the South Bronx which *nobody* can paint over. Try beating *that*, my friend."

"Yeah, yeah."

"Her entire record is *positive*, which is even better than being spotless—which it also is. Are you going to tell me that the media are going to take sides against a woman like *that*? Do you believe the people of this country would turn on a woman like *that*? She can deliver *car*loads of votes. She's the greatest goddamn vote-catcher we've ever had, and that's why I need her on that ticket!"

Keifetz took out a big white handkerchief and wiped his forehead. "Frank, please," he said. "We have five weeks until the convention. Promise me you'll keep an open mind on your choice for veep until"—he took a deep breath—"two days before the convention. Once you throw her name into that hall, that's the point of no return, and a lot of things *could* happen between now and two days before the convention. What do you say, Frank?"

The president stared at him from behind the puffed and stained halfcircles of orbital fat under his eyes, then continued with the needlepoint he was working on.

"All right," he said. "I'll wait."

42

The handshaking, autographing, and embracing seemed interminable before she could give the sign to Susie Orde to have the car waiting. She made it to the stage door, then the car, told Susie she would see her in Washington the next morning, and the car rolled away to the Houston airport and the Braniff flight to New York.

She was trembling with excitement; not only the excitement of her triumph but because she knew what she was going to do and could do nothing to stop herself. Caen was in New York.

She was going to have time in the afternoon because she couldn't see Caen until night anyway, so she would be able to carry out a happy family duty. She had had a short note from Charles saying that Dr. Weiler's ninety-fifth birthday was approaching and remarking on how much pleasure it would give the old man if she were to call on him, particularly if she were to bring along a bottle of Southern Comfort. She telephoned Weiler's residence from the Justice limousine as it left LaGuardia and was told he would be delighted to receive her.

The Weiler mansion was "one of the last of the great houses in New York," as M. Gäbel had written in his New-York Historical Society monograph. It had been designed by Hastings (of Carrère & Hastings), decorated by Sir Charles Allom, who had received his knighthood for harmonizing interiors for George V, and furnished by Lord Duveen with such objects as the marble fireplace that had once graced the

Bagatelle, as well as two Vermeers. It was Dr. Weiler's pride that he had built the house entirely with cash, all with the tax-free cash fees from patients. In his sixty-seven years of medical practice in New York, he had made exactly five house calls. Retired, he was the same kindly prototype of the great healer. "A peer of Hippocrates," the late Morgan minor had called him. Dr. Weiler had told Charles Cantwell that had dermatology reached the vogue it later came to enjoy, and if he had had the sense to specialize in it, "I could have made double, maybe triple."

He was delighted to receive the attorney general, whom he had delivered into the world. He cackled over the booze Jean brought him. "My doctor took me off it," he said. "Now the old son-of-a-bitch can *really* worry."

"If I had known that, I would have brought you Poland Water," Jean told him.

"Don't worry." Weiler grinned slyly. "I'm my own doctor. Who else would come out when I needed one?" They toasted each other. Dr. Weiler said fondly, "I not only delivered you, I delivered your mother."

"I know."

"I was the family doctor to everybody on every side of your family, but especially on your mother's side."

"What was it like, being doctor to a Persian family?" Jean asked eagerly. "Did they have special customs? Were there certain restrictions you were made to observe?"

"*Per*sian?"

"My mother's family."

"Persians? They were Episcopalians! Your grandfather came from Illinois and his wife was from Maine. They were both blond, with blue eyes like yours and your mother's. They were so American, I can't tell you. What's this about Persians?"

Jean was bone-tired as a reaction to the strains of the morning in Houston, but she loved the old man even if he had at last gone round the bend, so she humored him. "I suppose because of all Mama's success in the Middle East that I just leaped to that conclusion."

"I can't even follow this conversation." He put his glass down, and Jean could see that the drink had been too much for him.

"Jean—what successes in the Middle East?" he asked.

"As a geologist."

"Your mother? Charmian Goddard? She was a débutante, then she married Henstell and they moved to Switzerland, then she— When could she suddenly become a geologist?"

"I—I don't understand."

"Who said that? Some servant at Rockrimmon, I bet. It's funny what sticks in our mind from when we were little kids. I had a brother who told me that the great Admiral Dewey was our uncle, and to this day—about eighty-five years later—I still can't get it through my head that it isn't so."

She stared at him blankly.

"Hozzabot another dring?" the old doctor said and fell asleep in his chair.

Jean stared down at him, confused and shaken. Then she remembered how old he was and in what formidable disarray the past must appear to him. She left the room quietly and encountered a plump uniformed nurse in the outer hall. "We had a birthday drink and he is sleeping," Jean said. "It's sad to see a mind like his get old."

"Old? His body sure is old, but if anything that mind gets younger and younger."

Jean told the Justice driver to take her to the Murray Hill apartment. She called Caen as soon as she got there. All the way downtown through the traffic she tried to sort out Dr. Weiler's memories of her mother, but Caen kept crowding into her mind and she could feel wetness on her thighs as she thought of him. She knew that his brutishness was the aphrodisiac; he was the underside of desire.

The second time they had been alone together he had taken her to a garish motel in New Jersey which showed disgusting pornographic movies on television sets in tiny rooms which were all bed, and what they watched had aroused her wildly.

The films just might have been weak on story and characterization, but they transformed Caen into a frenzy of lust. One showed a Kanaka seaman screwing a still-living female shark as it hung upside down from a heavy hook suspended from the yardarm. Recovering from each other after the first movie, Caen ordered up another, in glorious color, showing a Chinese seated on a plain chair while two women laved his penis from tall, yellowed jars of chicken fat, then split a live chicken in half by impaling it on the man, its bloody death struggles agitating the man into glassy-eyed release and sending Caen into another sexual delirium.

Seated in the Justice limousine, she could feel herself bathing in Caen's pollution. The teeth-baring, grimacing distaste she felt for him as an individual had nothing to do with her omnivorous need to possess him, to feel him inside her, grunting and bleating in every feral position around her, then, thank God, after an hour of it, she would race the car back to New York and unload him wordlessly at the first hack stand.

43

Jean was on the 8:00 A.M. shuttle to Washington the next morning. She had alarmed herself by spending almost forty minutes in the shower that morning, soaping and resoaping herself, thinking of Caen as the trained donkey in the mythical sexual circus sideshow of a woman and a donkey making love, as she and Urs and the Slut had often laughed about it on Paradise Hill. She felt as if his thick sweat had come off on her like a decalcomania peels off on plastic, the sharp, acrid stench of his label clinging to her. She closed her eyes as she sat in the airplane, as if that would shut out the vision in her mind of the lumpy, stained pile of his underclothing beside the bed. When her body was moving away from Caen's she deplored her rutting desire for it, but when she was approaching Caen's spoor, where she knew he should be even if he wasn't there, her lust became low, animal noises deep in her throat until she could telephone him, hear his coarse breathing, and have him tell her on which rented bed they would meet, instantly if possible.

She went directly to Justice and absorbed the first fruitless set of no-progress reports from the divisional heads conducting the search for the Matriot. She worked consecutively with the Anti-Trust, Tax, and Organized Crime divisions until a quarter to six in the evening. Then, as she was about to pack the files for study of her federal prison-reform project, Keifetz telephoned from the Lone Star Beef House and asked if he could stop in to see her or would she rather go out for a drink. She asked him to come to her office.

His smoked-ivory face was expressionless, his eyes neither kind nor unkind. He wore an execrable orange, black, and yellow tie and a blue star-sapphire ring. Jean had figured out some time before that Keifetz dressed the way he dressed in order to keep people from staring into his eyes. He relied on his eyes not to signal anything, but he felt the work he was doing was so important that it would be better if he took no chances on revealing anything. People wore baffled expressions wondering how the man who had the ear of such a stylish president could wear such haberdashery, jewelry, and, frequently, orange shoes.

He refused a drink.

"What brings you here?"

"The president saw your speech. It was a good speech and a tremendous effect."

"Thank you."

"I knew you'd like to know that."

"What else do you figure I'd like to know?"

"Senator Cassiman was first man in to see the president this morning. The president didn't want you to have to find out about it in some newspaper or on TV."

"Hear what?"

"The senator found a large number of letters from your husband to Mrs. Cassiman. Love letters. Very passionate letters."

Jean shrugged.

"The president turned them over to me. I made requisite copies, then passed the originals to the FBI."

She kept control and hung tough. "What can I say?"

"You don't object, I hope?"

"No. Not to my late husband having written the letters to a woman who is now dead, nor to your copying the letters, nor to your passing them to the FBI."

"You have an analytical mind, Mrs. Spano. You went right to the nexus."

"The nexus, Keifetz?"

"The complicating thing here is not that Dr. Spano sent the letters to Mrs. Cassiman. Not at all. But that they are violently dead."

"I would guess that is for the FBI to sort out."

"We are fortunate in one sense. It's an ill wind, et cetera. The FBI is a part of your house. Gallagher is your man, so he'll make sure the letters aren't published."

"Is the president worried that they might be published?"

"Wouldn't you be if you wanted your attorney general to be accepted by the nominating convention and this came up?"

"Keifetz, I'm not quite sure why you are here. We know the president will do whatever he has to do to protect himself, on the one hand, and we know that Gallagher and I are going to take those letters wherever our duty demands, on the other. How else am I involved? Is there something else you wanted to say to me?"

"Where is Gallagher going to take the letters?"

"The correspondents were *mur*dered, Keifetz. The FBI has no jurisdiction—as you probably knew when you dropped the problem on Gallagher. The FBI is a conduit of information to local police, so Gallagher will see that the letters go to the New York and DC police in charge of those cases."

"You're aware that that kind of a decision could cause trouble or embarrassment for you?"

"That doesn't even remotely come into this. I told the president while you sat there that I did not want the vice presidency on the terms offered by the Matriots. I am the principal law enforcement officer of the United States. My husband's killer—and Mrs. Cassiman's—must be apprehended. Therefore I will instruct the director, FBI, to pass the letters along to the NY and DC police."

"I certainly didn't think you'd do a thing like that, Mrs. Spano. Suppose some lucky newshawk gets his hands on them?"

"What would you have advised? A cover-up? Transfer the radiation-hot evidence to my department, then look the other way until some fine day when you decided it was necessary to lower the boom? Not me, Keifetz. And if the president sent you to lay all this out for me, you'd better explain to him what kind of an AG he is toying with."

"The president didn't send me. I'm here because it's my job to protect him from the political future. All the president wants to know—and then only in the sense of wrapping this thing up—is whether your husband had letters from Mrs. Cassiman similar to his to her?"

"I don't have the answer to that, but it is a good, political question and we'll find out about it."

"And he wants an expression from the NYPD homicide people about what directions they are going to take with the case."

"What directions did he have uppermost in mind?"

"I want you to get the nuances here, Mrs. Spano. If a married man and a married woman exchange this particular kind of love letters, then—let's face it—a jealousy motive springs up."

"That Senator Cassiman or I or both of us were homicidally jealous?"

"Right. Now, you were with the president in the White House when your husband was killed and there is every reason to believe you were with the director, FBI, when Mrs. Cassiman was killed. Senator Cassiman was in Switzerland when both of them were killed. All clear?"

"To me it is quite clear."

"Mrs. Spano—please keep remembering that I am trying to think like a homicide cop to protect the president from any possible scandal in his administration or in the party."

"Of course."

"The next police assumption would be to find out whether you or Senator Cassiman—say both of you or separately—paid someone to kill those two people."

"There is just one thing which I find odd here, Keifetz."

"Tell me, by all means."

"Since this is your scenario, perhaps you won't mind if I ask you why you haven't mentioned the one condition of both murders that has been accepted by the NYPD, the DC police, and the FBI from the beginning."

"What's that, Mrs. Spano?"

"The Matriots."

"Because of this new *evidence*—these *letters*. They have to be accounted for from a motive standpoint. They are the kind of fodder that the public is willing to eat by the ton. Until we are given the official judgment by the homicide police experts involved that those letters do not offset the previous basis of these two murder cases—the so-called Matriots—a tremendous political consequence will be in jeopardy."

She leaned back in her chair and closed her eyes. "I agree with you as a politician, so I have to agree with you as a suspect," the attorney general said.

"Besides," Keifetz said, "with all respect, we only have your word for it that the Matriots exist—that there is such a thing as the Matriots."

When Keifetz left, Jean shut off all calls for ten minutes, went into the washroom, and ran cold water over her wrists. She felt as though she could never open one of Mama's diaries again. She felt like a traitor who had cost Mama the vice presidency. Even if it hadn't been her fault that the Slut had dragged Ames into her bed, then rendered him silly enough to send her letters when Jean was in Washington, it had all led to death and now to exposure which, if Heller made his mind up, would remove any chance of her ever reaching the top. She wanted to weep, but even more she wanted to scream and scream and to keep screaming. If she were chosen as vice president, the party, as well as her own fluidly oiled machinery, would make her the indispensable presidential candidate the next time around. The problem of Ames and the Slut had been reasonably safely tucked away, but now *this* had to come out of the ground like a deadly snake. It could mean the end of the line for her.

She bathed her temples with cologne. She returned to her office and asked Gallagher if he could come in before he closed up for the day.

The first thing he said was, "They told you about the letters?"

She nodded.

"Keifetz, in front of the president, told me not to mention the letters to you until tomorrow, so I supposed he wanted to tell you himself."

"Yes, he did. What have you done with them?"

"I wanted to talk it through with you before I did anything."

"Thanks. I know that was hard to do. But we both know what has to be done. Copies have to go to the NYPD and to the DC police. I'm not saying we can't ask them to keep them under lock and key, but they have to have them."

"My turn to thank you. That's exactly what has to be done."

"The president wants us to find out if there are any other letters— from Mrs. Cassiman to my husband. If there are, they'll be in Ames' safe at the house on Riverside Drive. I want you to send an agent you can trust up there to look for them."

"I'm the agent I can trust."

"You'll need keys to the house and the combination to the safe. Henri and Louise are taking a leave of absence in Paris. He's taking a cooking course at La Varenne. Can you go to New York tonight?"

"Daylight is better. It looks better anyhow."

"That will be fine."

"Strictly speaking, I should put the NYPD on notice. If they want to send a man with me, they got a right."

"I would agree if it weren't my own house. If you do find such letters, you'll give them to me and I'll hand them to the president to be handed back to you, just the way Peter Cassiman handed over Ames' letters."

"Okay. I'll see you in the morning."

"But call me from my house if you find the letters."

"Will do. Did Keifetz try to get rough with you?"

"Well—he did his best. But it's his job to look for trouble before it happens. Only the president can give me a hard time."

By the time Gallagher got back to his office he had reconsidered everything. Through the intercom on his desk, he asked who was handling the Spano homicide at the NYPD. When he was told it was a Lieutenant Umberto Caen, he told the voice to get Caen on the phone.

The operator said Caen wasn't at 126th Street and that he wouldn't be back until the following morning. Gallagher told his secretary to put the call as first thing on the agenda for the next day.

44

After Gallagher left her office and while she was packing her briefcase with the federal prisons data she wanted to work with at home,
Jean remembered that Charles Cantwell and Ursula were coming to
dinner at eight o'clock to talk about the statement for the end of the
fiscal year at Voters' Research and what they should do with year-end
surplus capital.

She locked the briefcase in her desk, called for a car, and went
home.

After dinner, while she poured coffee in the study, Cantwell said he
thought she looked distraught.

"Do I? Perhaps I'm getting a cold."

"Something *is* on your mind, dear," Ursula said. "You haven't made
much sense all evening."

Jean burst into tears.

They were so astonished at this inconceivable phenomenon that for a
moment both were speechless and motionless. Then Ursula sprang
across the room and took Jean in her arms while Charles went for the
brandy. It was a few minutes before Jean could stop sobbing. But, all at
once, she was entirely composed again.

"Good *God*, Jean," Charles exclaimed. "What has happened? You
haven't done that since—you haven't *ever* done that."

She told them what had happened and how the nomination for the vice presidency was at stake. "I've been working very hard to get it, then . . . the murders . . . I thought everything was over, that every possible chance of it had been destroyed. Then—miraculously—millions of people took my side and wrote to the White House and it turned the president right around. He actually brought the subject of the nomination up to me, and he gave me better than a best hope that I was going to get it. Now these letters from Ames to Alex have turned up. Oh, Jesus! Keifetz says the voters will *wallow* in stuff that is in those letters, and now the White House thinks letters from Alex to Ames may turn up in Ames' files in New York."

"Oh, Jean!"

"Theoretically, as Keifetz put it, the letters supply a motive which could have so many people suspecting me of killing both of them that there couldn't be the ghost of a chance that the president would let them run me."

"Oh, darling . . . Jean!"

"What are you going to do now?" Cantwell asked grimly.

"I have asked Mr. Gallagher to search the New York house personally to see if he can find such letters from Alex to Ames. He will be there first thing tomorrow morning."

"If I may say so, Jean, I think I should be the one to get those letters. I can be at the house tonight," Cantwell said stiffly.

"No, Charles, thank you. This has to be an official FBI operation, undertaken directly at my request. There can't be the remotest *shad*ow of even a hint of any attempt at cover-up."

Ursula sat beside Jean and held her hand. Cantwell drank his brandy broodingly. Ten minutes later, Ursula and Charles left together for New York.

45

Gallagher talked to Caen from Washington the next morning. "There's something we want to look for in a private place in New York and we don't want to have to ask for a search warrant."

"Well, I don't need to tell you that you would be outta line. You know how the commissioner wants interdepartmental harmony with the feds."

"Listen—I agree. That's why I'm calling. It is strictly your jurisdiction, particularly involving a case like this."

"What case?"

"The Spano."

"That's my case."

"Correct. Hence this call."

"What are you looking for?"

"Some of the people here think there is a possibility that a woman name of Cassiman may have sent love letters to Dr. Spano. If she did, they would be in his study. Did your people find anything like that?"

"No."

"But they weren't looking for letters, so I'd appreciate it if you'd take another look."

"Gladda do it."

"You know about the safe?"

"I don't think so."

"The safe is inside a—they call it a reliquary. You know what a reliquary is?"

"No."

"Well, this reliquary is a box with four sides and a top, each one a different holy picture. A reliquary is to hold sacred objects."

"I got you."

"It is between some religious books on the bookshelf on the left wall if you were sitting at the desk."

"What kinda lock?"

"A simple combination—3, right—1, left—8, right. Okay?"

"Absolutely."

"Can you make it over there this morning?"

"Absolutely."

"If you find the letters call the agent-in-charge in New York. He'll have them picked up."

Caen wasn't sure what God had handed him, but he knew whatever it was he was going to be able to beat the cold bitch to death with it if he could find those letters. Jesus, any DA would see those letters as jealous-wife evidence. Cassiman! Holy *shit*, the broad who had been shot in Washington with the same gun that shot the bitch's husband! Hot letters from her could tack baby right in a cold cell in Sing Sing. Finally things were happening right. He was going to shove it all the way up her ass and break it off in her if he could only find those letters. He put on the hat to keep the bald spot at the back of his head out of the sun and left the building on 126th Street. He got into his car and started across town and down Broadway to the Henstell mansion on the Drive.

Caen let himself into the house as if he were a tenant. He locked the door behind him and sauntered toward the back of the house to the study where he had found Spano's body. When he reached the room the door was ajar. He could hear someone moving inside. A woman wearing a floppy hat was opening a box on top of Spano's desk. Caen could see the holy pictures paneled on two of its sides and the underside of the opened top. He waited, watching her hand dip into the box, then pull out a bundle of square yellow envelopes held together with two rubber bands.

He eased his service revolver out of its holster and said, "Okay, lady. Drop it."

Unconcerned, she turned to look toward the sound of his voice, but he couldn't make out her face in the half light above the heavy desk lamp.

She put the letters down carefully next to the side of the box visible to him, then casually picked up something from the invisible side, blocked from his view by the box. The bullet hit the door beside his head. He fired his revolver and the impact of the hit knocked her off her feet. He found a wall switch and turned on the bright lights in the room. He walked to the body while putting his weapon back into its holster. He went down on one knee beside her. The bullet had gone up under her jawbone and had come out at the top of her head.

Caen stared at the face, but he had never seen her before: a funny-looking, old-young broad with the left side of her face paralyzed. He got to his feet, retrieved the packet of letters, and pocketed them, then called George Fearons at homicide five. He had to get Fearons over there with some detectives and the forensic people while he got away for twenty minutes or so and stashed the letters.

46

While she waited, aching with worry, for Gallagher's report on his search for the letters in New York, Jean went through the desperation of wondering what she could do with her life if she were forced out of politics by scandal. She wouldn't be able to return to the practice of law. Mercifully, she remembered her recent meeting with Thane in her own office at Justice, and she realized that she had always been meant to be with him. Keifetz had telephoned one morning in early spring to tell her that a film company wanted to make a movie in which their star would play a modern-day attorney general of the United States, and that the president said he thought it could be a good idea politically, and that he was ready to agree to give Paramount all facilities and permissions if all of it met with Mrs. Spano's approval.

Jean reacted immediately.

"A *woman* attorney general?" she asked.

"A man. Hollywood is old-fashioned."

"Is there a script I can look at?"

"Sure—I'll send it over."

"What actor will play the AG?"

"Fella named Thane Cawdor. My secretary says he's very big."

A ringing started in her ears.

"Oh."

"Any objections?"

"When must you know?"

"The sooner they make the movie, the sooner it will be in the theaters next year."

"I'll read the script over the weekend."

When she read it, she decided that they must have had the life of Tom Dewey in mind, except set in Washington and the Supreme Court. It was full of brave battles with organized crime, and corrupt unions, and race riots, all of which the hero quelled nicely. She had no objection to it and she told Keifetz so, returning to work, greatly impressed by how Thane's life and hers were entwined.

Then one day, after elaborate telephoning by his staff and hers, Thane appeared across the desk from her asking if she would be willing to help him to understand the workings of Justice as very necessary background for the part.

"You'd have to be a lawyer to be able to follow it," she said. "Anyway, they have a script, because I read part of it. So all you have to do is to follow that."

"You don't understand," he said. "I have to *know* what I'm doing as an actor and why I'm doing it."

"Why you are doing it is all in the script, and you have also played Hamlet at Stratford, and its a pretty fair chance that you've never been in Denmark."

He grinned and she felt herself melting. "I didn't mean we had to talk about your department all the time," he said. "What I had in mind was that it would be a reason anybody would have to accept for my being invited here and to your house."

She blushed.

"I must have been imprinted on you," he said somberly, "the way those ducklings were imprinted on Konrad Lorenz and followed him wherever he swam. You are the only woman I have ever thought was beautiful. Maybe we both gave away too much time to the things we thought we had to do, but I've been in love with you for twenty-six years, Jean, and I want us to do something about that."

"Please, Thane—not here, anyway."

He grinned again and everything which was resisting him seemed to fall from her. "It's the Department of Justice, isn't it?" he asked softly. "We deserve a little justice."

He got up, moving in her direction. She held up her hand weakly. "Tonight?" she said.

"Yes." He stopped moving and stood looking down at her gravely.

"Everything has changed in my life," she said.

"I'm going back to England."

"To rebuild old cars?"

"Yes. And if you were only an ordinary woman I would ask you to come with me. But it doesn't seem likely that you could run the Department of Justice from Dorset."

"We've waited twenty-six years. I won't always be attorney general. The future will have to sort all of this out for us."

"You are a glorious woman."

"We fit together," she said huskily.

"Your house? Eight o'clock tonight?"

"Please, Thane."

It was as though the twenty-six years hadn't happened, as though she had walked up the hill from the university to the old town and had climbed the stairs to the flat where they had lived together for a year, and when she had opened the door, no farewell note was there, he was there. They were perfect again in the indefinable way she had tried so many times to take apart and examine, each delicate part of what they felt and what they did with each other. They were perfect again. Wherever they were, no matter what the year or what the century, they were perfect.

47

Caen took the letters to his room at Mom's and locked them in his strongbox. Mom was on a boatride to Bear Mountain with the Kilkenny Women's Sodality. He didn't rush anything, but he got back to the precinct house as soon as he could and called Gallagher in Washington.

"There were no letters, Mr. Director," he said respectfully. "But when I got there a woman was raiding the box with the holy pictures on it, and when I called her on it she shot at me so I shot back and she's dead."

"A woman? Who? What kind of a woman?"

"No ID. White. Maybe mid-fifties. It's hard to say, because the left side of her face was paralyzed."

"*What?* Where's the body now . . . We'll want pictures . . . Okay? Just stand by. Okay?"

Within seventy minutes Caen was bewildered by reports that the city morgue was swarming with people from four federal agencies, packing in around the woman with the dropped face as though she had a dice game going, and they all brought photographers. The NYPD had printed the woman, but the FBI printed her all over again. Caen was ready to blow his cork: Gallagher had treated him like he was some little fucking office boy. Caen got into his car, opened the siren, and skidded downtown. The whole fucking mob of them was still there. He found the FBI agent and flashed his buzzer. "This woman was my collar," he said. "What the hell is goin' on? Is anybody left in Washington?"

The agent shrugged.

"Listen," Caen said, "you guys get pretty good cooperation from us. We help you, you help us. It's Gallagher who wants it that way, so we try to be nice."

"So ask Gallagher."

"I'll tell you what I'm gonna do, J. Edgar. You are on city property. Both the building and the body. You are loitering and you are tampering. We are gonna confiscate the cameras and the print layouts and I am gonna take every one of you pricks in and book you. And the commissioner is gonna back me up, because cooperation is a two-way street."

The agent was only six weeks out of New Orleans. He said, "What I'll tell you is off the record, I never said it. But this woman is the prime suspect in a big murder case."

"Yeah? Is that so? What case?"

"Spano the saint and Mrs. Cassiman, the senator's wife."

"Well, hodda you like that? The Spano case is my case."

"That's all I know. Now we gotta get this woman's body measurements and photograph her all over."

To Caen there were suspects and suspects. He didn't want anyone hogging the spotlight as *the* suspect until he could set it up that the real suspect was his own Ice Queen. The NYPD hadn't been able to make any identification on the dead woman, so the feds were obviously going on something they had held out on the NYPD, which was a fairly shitty way to think they could do business. Caen was going to take the holdout right to the commissioner through Chief Maguire if Gallagher refused to share the wealth.

Caen telephoned Gallagher from the morgue office. He laid it on the line. The morgue, which was city property, was crawling with four different kinds of feds and they were handing out a lot of bullshit. If the woman was involved in the Spano killing then it was local police business and the FBI belonged the fuck out of it. "Either you open up and tell me everything you got on this case," Caen said, "or I am gonna confiscate everything you got here today and bar all your people from the morgue."

"Caen?" It was a plaintive, helpless sound.

"What?"

"Go fuck yourself." Gallagher hung up on him.

* * *

Caen didn't exactly stick his neck out by confiscating cameras and running in feds, but he drove directly to the office of the chief of detectives and got them to send word to Maguire that his business was urgent. Maguire called him in. Caen told him the story, loading it as far as he thought he could go against the FBI.

"Fahcrissake!" Maguire said. "Have they resurrected Hoover?"

Maguire picked up the phone and got the police commissioner. He explained the situation. He listened. Then he hung up.

"The PC just had a call from the White House about this, Caen," he said. "I hope that answers your questions."

When Caen got back to 126th Street there was a message to call the director of the FBI in Washington.

"The attorney general wants to make an official identification of that body in the morgue," Gallagher said. "She's flying to New York late this afternoon and we'll appreciate it if you'll meet her at the morgue at half-past six today."

"Certainly, Mr. Director," Caen said. He held the phone away from himself and grinned at it broadly.

48

Caen took Attorney General Spano into the morgue at 6:20 P.M. The attendant rolled out the drawer holding the sheet-covered, refrigerated body. They stared as the attendant pulled the sheet away.

If one side of her face had been turned away from them, Jean thought, she would have been a beautiful woman. But if only the other side of her face were shown, she would have been a sagging, bloated, wasted hag.

"It's the woman we've been searching for," she said to Caen and the attendant. "God—look at her."

"This was no bum," Caen said. "You should see the clothes she had on her; and six hundred and twenty dollars in an alligator purse worth eighteen hundred and about two grand wortha jewelry."

"What else was in the purse?"

"Nothing. And no labels. No laundry marks; the fingerprints are just ten blanks so far. Nothing."

Jean turned away from the body. "She is an awful-looking woman, so she must have been awful because we make our own faces."

He stared at her sullenly.

By half-past seven they were stripped and on a bed together in a motel for unrestrained, unfaithful dentists just off Queens Boulevard.

218

By a quarter to ten, while they lay like landed mackerel, gasping, he slid an 8×10 brown envelope across the bed and dropped it on her heaving chest.

"What?" she panted.

"Take a look," he said. "You'll get a kick out of it."

Three or four minutes went by before she found the energy to open the envelope and to slide out some white sheets of paper. When she turned them over, they were photographs.

They were hideous color photographs of herself and Caen making what was despairingly called love. They were the sickest, most sickening things she had ever looked at. She saw that all this time she had lived with the illusion that it was Caen who had begged for indignities to be committed upon him, using every degrading sewer route to his disgusting needs, but the photographs would show forever that it was she who was degenerate, hungering to be transformed into depraved dirt by the magic of his wand. She screamed out her horror, flinging the things from her while he barked with laughter.

"*What are they?*" she exclaimed with loathing. "Where did you get them?"

"A frenna mine . . ." But he couldn't get the words out because of his choking laughter. This was paying off like he never thought anything so dopey could pay off—and they were only at the beginning. "A . . . frenna . . . mine took them. At the Jolly Times Motel in Bryson, New Jersey. He said you were the hottest piece he ever watched."

"He *watched* me?"

"Baby, he took the pictures. He offered me two hundred bucks for the negatives. He could make a fortune direct-by-mail witchew."

She began to dress, staring at him as if he had turned into a perched pterodactyl. At last she spoke. "Caen?"

"What, sugar-ass?"

"Did you also send that letter to the New York *World?*"

He glared at her because she had spoiled part of his fun. He had just been ready to tell her about that. "Yeah. I set you up."

"*Why?*"

"I hadda find out if you could feel anything outside that snatch you got."

"What are you *talking* about?"

"I am talking about I am a man and you treat me like I was some lace-curtain whore getting her ticket punched at the head of a mineshaft on payday. I am some kind of slime from the lower depths to you.

But you figure what the hell—he's just a dirty animal but I'll use him to get my jollies because I am a libber, right? And what is a man to a libber? A man is nothing, right?"

He stood hugely in front of her, a hairy, sweating, white-on-white lump, blubbering at her with self-pity.

"Don't let them tell you you're insane, Caen. *I'm* insane."

"Sure, maybe you are. But you are also a whore—and a degenerate whore. And if I knew how I could get a dose of clap with safety I'd pass it on to you."

Jean began to shake like the branch of an aspen tree in the wind. She ran into the shabby toilet and vomited loudly. When she emerged she stood unsteadily in the doorway, white and haggard, and said, "Give me the negatives, please."

"Wha'?"

"Please, Caen. So much is at stake. I am begging you. Please give me the negatives."

"Ho, ho, ho, Lady Whore. Do I hear you say I should *give* you the negatives?"

"Do you want to *sell* them to me?"

"Not the way you think."

"How?"

"We are only just beginning on this route."

"Caen, what do you *want?*"

He slipped on his shoes but not the clocked socks and walked to the closet. He took up his raincoat and burrowed into the pockets, removing pieces of jewelry from them. He tossed the pieces onto the bed. "Recognize these?"

"You killed Ames!"

He shook his head, grinning. "Never. I was in charge of the case and I got there in time to liberate these. This is the deal. You can have the negatives as a present from me if you buy these pieces back from me."

"I have to get used to how *much* you hate me."

"Forget it. This is business. You know what the jewelry is worth and I know a little about stones myself. They're worth three hundred thousand dollars, which has a nice sound to me, and I'm gonna let you have them for a hunnert and fifty."

"How can I do that? Keep the jewelry and I'll pay you the money for the negatives."

"How come?"

"If I have possession of the jewelry which has been missing since my husband was killed while doing its inventory, then a case could be made that I killed my husband."

"Yeah. You're a very wise broad, aren't you? But you gotta take that chance or no negatives. And when I get finished arranging to have the prints from those negatives handed around Washington, you ain't even gonna be able to get a job in your own law firm, Commissioner. You know what I mean?"

"Caen, please . . ."

"You are gonna tell me that I got it all wrong, that we rilly had a tender relationship here, and that you are my woman come rain or come shine—right? Well, last year I woulda loved to hear that. Maybe, you know how it is, I wouldna bought it—I mean we *know*, right? But a year ago you hadn't really sunk the harpoon in me yet. I just imagine that you think I am dirt—right? But after a while I couldn't even kid myself anymore, so I looked around for a harpoon to sink into you and I come up with the pictures which are gonna gorrontee you are through as a politician *and* a lawyer—or the jewelry where you are gonna have to take the chance of facing a murder rap on really sure-shot evidence I have put together against you—before you can get rid of it. So whatta you say, Commissioner? How you gonna call it?"

"I must have twenty-four hours to think."

"Sure," he said. "Why not? So be here at nine o'clock tomorrow night."

"I am so *sick!*" she sobbed. "We are covered with filth, you and I."

49

She found a cruising cab on Queens Boulevard and told the driver to take her to the apartment on Murray Hill. She was stiffened by fear. Shame and self-loathing burrowed into her and consumed her. She could not stop thinking of those photographs and of the people in her life she would have to face after they had seen what she was. She would have to face Charles because she could not dispose of the horror and this threat by herself. She would need to smash his regard for her to save herself. But there was nowhere else to turn.

She had thought of Mama looking at those pictures and she moaned and bent double, hiding her face in her hands. Mama's dreams had been stained and spoiled. In the mythology which must have sprung out of the American western movie, women were graded as having fitter feelings. Their capacity for lust was proclaimed as being almost deficient; as long as there was a Mother's Day, the mothers of our children were pure. Water solidified into ice in her stomach, spreading out across her body. She couldn't weep and she couldn't die. She thought of the president staring with disgust after the pictures had been passed up to him through the hands of senators and congressmen and she knew there was no chance of her survival.

She had no plan except to be with Mama. She had to go to the diary she had brought to Matsonia from Rockrimmon so that she could find some calm again. Then she would have to transfer part of the weight from herself to Charles, who had spent his life preparing solutions for other peoples' problems. But first she had to be with Mama.

She fled out of the taxi, into the building at Matsonia, and ran up the stairs. She unlocked the heavy teak cabinet in her study and drew Volume 4 of the diaries under the reading light on the Florentine desk. She flipped through the pages until she found the passage she wanted:

When one loses a husband to death, it is one more injustice to be borne, because God is a man and He giveth and taketh away from women according to his own rules. I did not love Joshua Henstell and I caused his death. But had he tried to seek any equality between us, had he seen that if he had respected me as his wife he could not have caused the death of my father in Iran, he would not have brought upon me the indignity of his murder.

But each time a man dies there is one enemy less. We lose many men in our lives and death is so final. When the break is made, it cannot be repaired again any more than can death.

As you grow you will know many men and you will lose most of them and, if you are lucky, you will lose only those who bring you pain. I tell you that you will be saner and happier if you go on to the next man and if the man you have lost, through life or through death, is someone who had betrayed you or brought you humiliation, then even though death has taken him, I ask you to rejoice and to go onward into your life, your strong back turned upon his weak memory.

Go forward into life and fight for the equality of women and men, for true and complete equality so that even when a man whom you love dies, you may wear the dignity of mourning him.

But, if this man who has departed in life or in death has wronged you, if even the bald fact of his death is by circumstance misunderstood, then you must rise up as an example to yourself and to other women and resist inconvenience, social oppression, and calumny because you *know* that he wronged you in life and you will not *permit* him to wrong you in death. By demanding justice, you will enforce respect for women and further the meaning of the equality of all women under the law and in the very souls of men.

Men must be reeducated! Their entire reflex systems must be reconditioned! They are *exactly* as we are with the exception that for eight millennia they have been told, taught, and titillated into belief in their superiority over women. But these things can be changed no matter how longstanding. Women were once as deluded. When there were only goddesses as rulers of the universe men were downcast.

We have tried both ways. Women have ruled men and men have ruled women, each superior to the other in their ascendancies. You have been trained to seek solutions and to redress the balance between the sexes. You must gird yourself to be one of the women who lead the way to eternal equality for, when that is done, what cannot the world achieve in harmony?

My father killed my mother, causing her death by oppressing her with unending injustice, by mauling her with his shouting, by battering her with his unfounded accusations until she could hardly withstand his assaults. And, to escape them, she climbed out upon that windowsill in protest against his ways and, slipping, fell to her death before my eyes. Did he care? No. He glanced at the empty window frame and left the room. She had offended him and now she had been punished for it. My mother could be alive today if *strong and intelligent* women such as you had spent their lives reeducating women to reeducate and recondition the static reflexes of men. My father and mother would have recognized each other as *equals*. They would have *discussed* their differences as equals. They would have discussed their differences as men discuss them among each other. My mother would have been freed from having to revenge herself upon his snarling, the only recourse she had against this heinous inequality. Harmony, mutual benefit to both, would have resulted instead of the mounting fury of the one and the decomposition of the character of the other. But instead, like all of the world excepting you, my darling, you the savior-to-be not only of women, but of men, they wallowed in the continuing pain, to die under the illusion that one of the two kinds within the species whom God had given the power to think, believed it was superior to the other.

If you are wronged in any way, then you are being wronged as a woman! If you are wronged then stand up and display this delusion of man to the world and say to them that you will not accept it under the conditions of inequality with which it was offered. Justly defiant, exemplar to the more timid and stupider members of both sexes, you will be reeducating and reconditioning men to associate injustices against women as having sprung from the insane conclusion that males are superior because they sweat more, stink higher, and are *demonstrably* poor hunters who have had to learn to smite harder.

Man is woman's salvation! Woman is man's salvation! Their souls are knit by links of steel into one immortal soul which encloses this world.

She was staring at the page of the diary when Ursula came into the room.

"Jean! I didn't hear you come in."

Jean didn't look up.

"Are you all right? No, of course you're not all right." She went to Jean and, kneeling beside her, took her in her arms. "My sweetest love, what have they done to you?"

Without reflecting, clinging to Ursula in need, she told her what had happened and how it was the same as being the end of her life.

"I won't let him do it," Ursula said.

"He can't be stopped."

"Charles can stop him," Ursula said. "Charles knows about handling these things and if he and the law firm and the bank can't stop him then something else must be done. When do you have to give him an answer?"

"I have until tomorrow night at nine."

"Where?"

"At—at the same place. Where we were tonight."

"You've got to see Charles now."

It was twenty minutes before one in the morning when she arrived at Charles' house in Beekman Place. Stinnett answered the doorbell, fully dressed. He said Miss Baggot had telephoned and that Mr. Cantwell was expecting her. He led her to the study where Charles, with an expression of concern on his face, silently drew her into the room and closed the door.

"This is a surprise, Jean."

"Charles—I am in *terrible* trouble."

He put his arm around her shoulders and led her to the sofa set at right angles to the fireplace, then sat on the facing sofa.

"What has happened?" he asked.

She tossed her hands helplessly. "I don't know where to begin, but I have to begin."

She took a deep breath. "When I was deputy commissioner, Ames decided to transform himself into an active holy man and he decided that this must include a rejection of sex. Between *us*, that is. He was hurt because I had told him that he could not transfer his mission to Central Africa. I explained my own political plans. I will not deny being selfish any more than I will deny anything else tonight. I had carnal relations with another man while Ames was still alive." She turned away from Cantwell out of revulsion at what she had to say, then made herself turn back to face him again. "A terrible man, a gross sexual pig of a man—and I wallowed in the slime with him, wrapping myself around him."

"Who?"

"A cop named Umberto Caen. I met him when I was deputy PC. I saw him and I lusted for him and I took him and I thought, you know—a woman telling herself that she is only thinking like a man?—that Caen wanted the same thing I wanted out of it, just rutting sex. But—well—it was different with him. Maybe he was telling himself he was only trying to think like a woman—he got bad feelings about me because I reached out and took him because he saw that as a kind of emasculation of himself. He began to hate me. He is a primitive—and I know now—a dangerous man who has been feeding on his hatred of me. It has turned into a horror story. I didn't think things like this happened to people."

"A horror story?"

"By the insane happenstance of Ames' murder, Caen has found a way to pay me back for what he thinks I did to his self-esteem."

"How is he connected with Ames' murder?"

"He is the homicide lieutenant in charge of the murder investigation."

"He didn't force you into sex?"

"No."

"Has he ever confronted you with what he considered to be the insult to his manhood?"

"No. He was—he was just a mindless animal."

"You had no idea of how he really felt?"

"No. And he was very much on my mind. I couldn't get him out of my mind. After a while—after about two weeks—I lusted to see him and I flew to New York straight from the women's convention in Houston. I am sorry that this is all so sordid, Charles. We went to New Jersey, to an amazing place called the Jolly Times Motel in a grubby little town called Bryson. We spent the night there, then I went back to Washington the next morning. I have seen him three times since Ames was—since Ames died."

"Don't turn away from me, Jean. Look at me. It will be better—later—if you look at me now."

She turned to face him, made herself look at him. "The thing is, I don't love him. I don't even like him. And, as humiliating as it is to have to tell you this, I have never liked him. He is . . . lower on the evolutionary scale. But I had to have him again. We drove to a motel. Fluorescent lighting in the rooms, metal mirrors on the ceiling, plastic furniture which could hardly fit in the room, and the offer from the room clerk to supply another woman or another man if we wanted to have a real party. It was almost as sordid and dingy and cheap as the present attorney general of the United States."

"Self-pity is something new for you," Cantwell said. "Just tell me what happened."

"Gallagher didn't do what he said he would do. Instead of going to the New York house to look for Alex's letters, for political reasons of cooperation between the FBI and the NYPD, he called the man in charge of Ames' murder case to ask him to make the search—and that is the man who was my lover. My lover who told me he had the letters."

"A tangled web, isn't it?" Cantwell remarked lightly.

"When this police lieutenant went to my house on the Drive, he found the woman we call the Matriot—the weird woman with the half-paralyzed face—rifling Ames' safe. She fired a gun at him so he shot her. He killed her."

"My God!"

"Her body was taken to the morgue. We had mounted a national manhunt to find her, but I was the only one who had seen her—except Alex, poor Alex—and had heard her confess to Ames' murder and to an intention to assassinate the president."

Cantwell's head was shaking in tiny, spastic movements. "This is terrible," he kept saying. "Terrible."

Jean took the glass out of his trembling hand and poured whiskey into it. He knocked the glass back.

"I went to New York to identify the body, which is still in the morgue. As soon as I established that the old wreck was the woman who had confessed to me and threatened the president, I telephoned Gallagher, then the White House. After that Caen and I went on to our grotty tryst in Queens."

"What happened there?"

"Oh, we went at it like boar and sow. Then—afterwards—he tossed me a large envelope. It contained about eight *color* photographs of Caen and me doing what we did to each other."

Cantwell stifled a sound in his throat.

"Caen had had a friend take the pictures at the Jolly Times place in Bryson. He said the friend had offered him two hundred dollars for the negatives."

"And now he is blackmailing you."

"Not anything as simple as blackmail, Charles. Hobson's Choice."
Her voice broke. "He said he would give me the negatives if I bought
back—from him—my jewels which he had stolen at the very outset of
the investigation of Ames' murder. If I don't regain the negatives in
that way, he will circulate prints throughout Washington. He all but
admits that when I buy back the jewels, which were missing from the
insurance inventory, to get the negatives . . . that he will arrest me
for Ames' murder. I simply don't know what to do."

"What did you tell him?"

"I said I needed time to think. He agreed to let me have twenty-four
hours. I am to bring my answer to him at that—at the same place
tomorrow night at nine o'clock."

"I want you to stay here tonight, Jean."

"Thank you, but I mustn't. Ursie is waiting up for me."

"Please allow me to have Stinnett drive you home."

"I would be grateful if he would get a taxi for me."

"No, no. I must be sure you are safely home."

"Thank you, Charles."

"I am your lawyer. You will stay well out of this and I will deal with
this man."

"You won't bring in the police!"

"No. I will talk with him. We will negotiate this thing."

"Oh, Charles—I am so ashamed!"

"Lust is an everyday matter," he told her and left the room. After ten
minutes Stinnett came in, dressed in a light-gray topcoat and carrying
a cap in his hand. He announced that it was time to leave. Jean said she
wanted to wait to say goodnight to Mr. Cantwell, but Stinnett explained
that Mr. Cantwell wasn't feeling at all well and had decided to rest.

Cantwell finished the half bottle of whiskey in his room, put on a hat,
and left the house, feeling clearheaded but remote from everything still
living on the planet. He shambled across Beekman Place to 49th Street
and, without thinking that it could be otherwise at 2:20 in the morning,
immediately flagged down a taxi. He told the driver to take him to the
city morgue. As the cab rolled downtown, Cantwell broke the seal on a
pint of scotch and took one long belt.

At the morgue he told the desk that Lieutenant Caen of homicide five
had asked him to provide secondary identification of the woman who
had been brought in that morning, having been shot to death at a house
on Riverside Drive. The desk found the bin number and an attendant
took Cantwell through the corridors of the morgue to the bin. He rolled
open the drawer. Before he exposed the face, Cantwell took him by the

elbow, gave him a twenty-dollar bill, and asked if he could be alone with the body for ten minutes.

"Why not?" the man said.

When the attendant was gone, Cantwell pulled the sheet down and stared at the ruined face. He took the half bottle of whiskey slowly out of his pocket as he stared down, brought it to his mouth, and drank steadily, still staring. He screwed the top of the bottle into place and dropped the bottle into his jacket pocket.

"Goodbye," he said and pulled the sheet up over the face, covering it. He turned away and walked along the same corridors until he found the desk. He thanked two men, said he could not identify the body, and went out into the night.

50

On the night of Jean's appointed rendezvous with Caen, Charles Cantwell laboriously got out of a taxi in front of the Friendship Motel on Zimmerman Avenue in Queens. Absentmindedly he handed the driver a ten-dollar bill and moved on into the building, carrying an ostrich-skin attaché case.

There was no one at the desk as he came in. He got into the elevator and pressed the button to take him to the third floor. As the car rose, he looked at his wristwatch. It was ten seconds to nine o'clock. He knocked sharply on the door of 318. A bleared voice called out, "Who is it?"

"Charles Cantwell."

"Who?"

"Mrs. Spano's attorney."

There was a shocked grunt, then the door opened.

Cantwell hadn't known what to expect, but he felt nauseated as he stared at the semidrunken, huge and hairy figure who was grinning at him like a sweated hyena. Caen was grinning because Cantwell's appearance reassured him: class with a capital C-L-A-S-S. "Whatta you doon here?" Caen said thickly, needing to adjust his gears because he had been expecting Jean.

"I stand here so that I may go into that room to discuss the business which you wish to complete," Cantwell said without any effort to deemphasize his distaste for Caen.

"Okay, Pop. Come right in." Caen stood aside and Cantwell swam through the whiskey fumes to a chair at the far side of the tiny garish room with the metal mirror on the ceiling, the round double bed, the television set, and a bright red table which held a bottle of whiskey, a paper bucket of ice, and two paper cups.

"You wanna drink?"

"Certainly not."

The window curtains were drawn closed. Caen sat on the bed. Cantwell faced him on a red chair.

"You bring money?"

"Yes."

"Lemme see it."

"After we have come to an agreement."

"Show it to me. If you can't show it, no meeting."

Cantwell lifted the attaché case to his lap and undid the clasp. He reached in and took out a bank-wrapped packet of fifty $100 bills. He held it up wordlessly, staring at Caen. Caen nodded. The money went back into the case. He half-sprawled back against the pillows of the bed. He was wearing a pigskin shoulder holster that Mom had given him for Christmas, from which the butt of his service revolver showed.

"Whatta you wanna tell me?" Caen asked. "There's nothing to negotiate. One price, that's it."

"Please turn on the radio and the television set to high volume," Cantwell said. "Neither of us wants this conversation recorded."

"Yeah. Right. You do it."

Cantwell turned on both sets, getting loud music. He turned to Caen. "I am here to buy the negatives."

"And the stones."

"Perhaps."

"No perhaps. You can't have one without the other."

"All right."

"If I was you I'd be very careful walkin' around with that jewelry. It is very hot."

"So I was told."

"I don't give a shit if she doesn't come herself to get it. If you are her lawyer on a thing like this then you always been her lawyer. So either you'll be carrying them as her agent or you'll have them because you are the one who killed the husband."

"The negatives, please."

Caen slid a small envelope out from under the bedpillows. He opened it and took out a small metal can of film. He held it up. "You wanna look at them? Terrific stuff."

"What is my insurance on copies?"

"Prints and dupe negatives don't innarest me, my friend. All this roll of negative is to me is that you are gonna pay me, then walk outta here with the jewelry."

"Where is the jewelry?"

"You hand me the money and I hand you the negatives and the jewelry."

"Okay."

"Now."

"I must see the jewelry in hand, please."

Caen pulled a paper bag out from behind the bedpillows and dumped its contents onto the bed. The jewels looked as gaudy as the room. "All yours for the money," Caen said.

Cantwell lifted the flap of the attaché case, reached in for the money, and brought out a .38 caliber revolver which he fired into Caen only once, through the blaring music. The bullet hit Caen in the center of his forehead.

Cantwell replaced the revolver, stood up stiffly, and poured himself a drink of Caen's whiskey into a paper cup. As he drank it, he turned off the television and modulated the radio. He dropped the can of film into his case, then wiped the whiskey bottle and the knobs on the TV set and radio carefully with his handkerchief. He slid the paper cup into the case. He stood for a moment staring down at Caen's astonished dead face, and, leaning over slightly, spat on it. He stared at the jewelry, leaving it where it lay.

Caen's body was discovered by the maid on Friday morning. Chief of Detectives Joseph Maguire told the press Caen had been killed instantaneously during a high-risk stakeout and in the line of duty. His funeral was given full department honors at Calvary Cemetery, Queens, and was attended by senior police officials.

Riding back from the funeral in the car with the PC, Maguire said, "I still don't get it. Caen recovered the Spano jewels on that stakeout—or whatever the hell he was doing in that crummy hotel—so how come he still had them out on the bed beside him after he was knocked off?"

"It is very fishy," Mitgang said.

"I agree it could be fishy. I agree it sounds fishy. But it doesn't have to be fishy. Did you look at the FBI report?"

"Not yet."

"It adds up. I mean, about why Caen's killer didn't take the jewels. The FBI thinks that Caen was killed by a buncha political revolutionaries called the Matriots."

"Why would they want to kill Caen?"

"They were tied into the Spano killing, weren't they?"

"They took the jewels that time."

"If it was them, if they took the jewels then."

"That is what is so fishy," Commissioner Mitgang said.

51

When Jean had left Caen at the Friendship Motel on that terrible night, she had taken the envelope with its eight disgusting photographs with her.

She knew she couldn't carry them around with her, but she didn't know what to do with them, deciding that not even her wall safe would be secure enough. In the end she decided on her steel filing cabinet as the safest hiding place for the envelope. She placed it among papers in a file marked ADMIRALTY (PENDING), then deliberately did not lock the drawer.

Just before 6:00 P.M. the next day in Washington, she knew she wouldn't have the courage to wait for Charles' call. She ordered a car to take her to the airport, flew to New York, and took a taxi directly to her apartment in Murray Hill. She let herself in and went into the living room. Ursula was sitting beside a bottle of gin and a bowl of ice. She was half-drunk, the first time Jean had seen her that way.

"I saw the pictures of you and Caen," she said dully.

"Urs!" It was a cry of pain and shame.

"I had to!"

"I want to die."

"How can any normal person want to *keep* vile pictures like that?"

"Where are the pictures?"

"I burned them."

"I am sorry, Urs."

"What are you going to *do*?"

"Charles will see Caen at about nine o'clock tonight at that same Queens motel on Zimmerman Avenue."

"But all Charles can do is to pay money for some negatives."

"That's all I want."

"No! A scavenger like that will have duplicates. The higher you move up in government the more he will threaten you."

"Charles will think of some failsafe way," Jean answered dully.

"I've wanted to die every time I knew you were with him," Ursula spoke into her drink. "But you always say I have no claim on you. You have done everything for me. You made a second life possible for me. You knew how I loved you, how much I have always loved you, and you allowed me to have that without question because, in your own way, you love me and because I will never be able to stop loving you."

"I don't want to talk about these things tonight."

"Those pictures are *not* you!" Ursula began to weep. Her hair fell stringily around her oval Oriental face. She dropped ice cubes into a glass and slopped gin over them. Jean said, "Drink up, Urs. It's time for a nap."

"No!"

Ursula raced out of the room to her own quarters. Jean made herself a whiskey and water very slowly, then dialed Charles' number.

Stinnett answered. Jean greeted him, then asked for Mr. Cantwell.

"Mr. Cantwell is dressing to go out, Mrs. Spano," Stinnett said. "He asked me to tell you if you called that he intends to telephone you directly on his return."

"I'll be at the New York apartment. He must call no matter what time it is."

"You may count on that, Mrs. Spano."

Jean looked at her watch. It was three minutes until eight. She sat at the harp and played, suspending herself in the tranquillity of the music. After a while she heard the front door slam. Reluctantly she went into Ursula's room, but Ursula was gone and her clothing and luggage had gone with her.

Charles still had not called at 1:10 A.M., so she telephoned to the house on Beekman Place.

"Has he come in yet, Stinnett?"

"No, madam."

Stinnett was sick with fear. He wanted to pull down the curtain between himself and the world and to lie down until he could be sure of order among the things he respected. He peered into his troubled affection and watched Charles Cantwell move that evening within his mind. He had refused dinner. He drank steadily. He was not morose; he was in despair. But he had dressed carefully and had permitted himself to be shaved. And, although Stinnett prided himself that no one else could detect it, Mr. Cantwell had been drunk when he left the house to get into the waiting taxi.

At 2:40 A.M., after Mrs. Spano had called for the third time, Stinnett telephoned to an old-time private arrangement, a detective named Francis Manning Winikus, whom he had known for thirty-five years, from when, as a cabin steward on the old *Queen Mary*, he had been able to do a few favors for Mr. Winikus (in those days sometimes Mr. Parkhurst or sometimes Mr. Israel), a frequent passenger and high-stakes cardplayer during the high seasons.

Francis Winikus claimed he had not slept for eleven years. He lived at a West Side hotel called the Bosworth on 53rd between Seventh and Eighth. He wasn't nearly as busy as he used to be.

"Mr. Winikus? Castor Stinnett here."

"It is grand to hear your voice, Stinnett."

"Thank you, sir."

"How may I help you?" Behind the voice Stinnett could hear the endless traffic noise from Eighth Avenue.

"Mr. Cantwell has disappeared, sir. He's been gone for over a day, sir, but he went on urgent business and people important to him were depending on his earliest return."

"Foul play, d'ye think?"

"There was reason for that, sir. But Mr. Cantwell had begun to drink when he left. He's been deeply troubled by something. Ate very little. Pulled the windowshades down in his bedroom. Stopped reading the poetry entirely, and has taken down all the pictures from the walls of his room which had hung there for years."

"What sort of pictures?"

"They were pictures of a lady, sir. The same lady. Nineteen framed photographs."

"Then do you think that, in a kind of desperate melancholy, he may have done away with himself?"

"Oh, no sir. Not Mr. Cantwell. At least not straight out like that. What I think is that he is locked in somewhere, drinking his life slowly away. I have called you, Mr. Winikus, to ask you to scour this city until you find him."

52

The FBI had the news of Caen's murder in Washington first. Gallagher took it personally to the AG to be sure she wouldn't be surprised and because he was a very delicate fellow.

Jean passed the word to Keifetz for the president. "That only makes everything more complicated," Keifetz told her. "The Matriot who contacted you was dead for two days when Caen caught it."

"Obviously, then, one part of our theory is being proved out. There are more active Matriots. There is a revolutionary women's organization."

"Yes. Sure. If they did it. If somebody else entirely didn't shoot Caen," Keifetz said.

Jean slowly hung up the phone, alone for the first time since Gallagher had brought her the news. Almost despairing with anxiety about Charles, she forced herself to move slowly and to think carefully. After a few moments, she asked her secretary to get her Commissioner Mitgang in New York.

"Commissioner? This is Jean Spano. Director Gallagher just told me about Lieutenant Caen."

"Yeah. Very bad. He recovered your jewels, though."

"My jewels?"

"The jewels which were taken when your husband was murdered."

"How could that be?"

"Whoever took the jewels killed Caen."

"You don't know yet who killed him?"

"We will, Commissioner. Bet on it. Somebody killed a cop."

She replaced the phone and stared at the far wall. She shuddered, then ordered a car to take her to the airport to catch a shuttle to New York. She had to find Charles.

She went directly to Charles' house in Beekman Place. Stinnett opened the door.

"Good afternoon, Stinnett," she said as calmly as she could. "Mr. Cantwell, please."

Stinnett stood aside as she entered the house.

"Mr. Cantwell isn't here, madam."

"Stinnett, for some time you and I have been pretending to each other that we didn't know that Mr. Cantwell, in occasional fits of depression, drank."

"Yes, madam."

"It is necessary that I see Mr. Cantwell. So—please take me to his room."

"Certainly, madam."

They climbed the stairs to the large bedroom overlooking the river, but one glance inside told Jean that he wasn't there.

"Is he at the office?" she asked unbelievingly.

"The fact is, madam," Stinnett said as they retraced their way down the stairs, "he left this house well over twenty-four hours ago and has not returned. Nor has he telephoned, which is most unlike him unless he was—"

"Drinking?"

"Yes, madam. But even if he were drinking, he would have got word to me to come to fetch him. He always has, madam."

"Have you called the office?"

"Yes, madam."

"Have you called his club?"

"Yes, madam. To be sure. But when the time to drink comes on Mr. Cantwell, he never drinks at his club."

"What are we to do? I hesitate to call the police yet."

"Best not to call the police, madam. The newspapers would get hold of it. It will be best if we wait just awhile longer. When Mr. Cantwell—ah—recovers, he will telephone."

53

Keifetz placed the FBI report on the Spano-Cassiman murder investigation at the center of the president's desk.

"I don't want the whole goddamn thing," Heller said. "Just the part about Mrs. Spano."

Keifetz neatly cut the 420-page typescript with two hands as if it were a deck of cards. Then he separated one neat clutch of pages from the secondary body and, with two moves, put the whole thing together again except for a thirty-page section. He moved the main block of the report out of the way and pushed the thin sheaf under the president's nose.

"We don't have time for this," Heller growled. "Summarize it for me."

"Although Mrs. Cassiman was a schooldays' chum of Mrs. Spano, she and Dr. Spano were lovers. This caused a physical separation between the Spanos. Dr. Spano and Mrs. Cassiman intended to leave the United States to settle in the Central African Republic as missionaries. They were going to leave before the elections, even though Mrs. Spano threatened to withdraw all funds from him if they did that. Mrs. Spano knew that Cassiman's life was in danger when Cassiman telephoned her, but she allowed well over an hour before she remembered to do anything about that. Mrs. Spano lives with a lesbian in New York."

"A lesbian? Who?"

"Ursula Baggot. She shared the house at the college with Mrs. Spano and Cassiman."

"Oh, *that* kind of a lesbian! I roomed with a fairy once at Carnegie Tech, but I didn't know it and maybe he didn't know it until about ten years later."

"Mrs. Spano has lived with this woman and no one else for the past three years. The FBI has compiled a very thorough report on this, Frank. There is no doubt about this, and it would never get past the voters. But, at the same time, Mrs. Spano was deep into an affair with Umberto Caen, the homicide lieutenant on the NYPD who was just murdered."

"A love affair with a cop?"

"With the cop who was in charge of the investigation of her husband's murder," Keifetz snapped. "And now he's dead. That is, now he's been murdered."

"Where was Mrs. Spano when he was murdered?"

"She says she was at home in Washington. Caen had Mrs. Spano's jewels on him when he was found."

"What does that prove?"

"It could have been his fee for killing Dr. Spano and Cassiman while Mrs. Spano stayed far from the scene of the crimes."

"What the hell happened to the big Matriots theory you people were so hot on?" Heller asked.

"The woman who started the whole government on the trail of the Matriots is dead in the New York morgue, and two thousand investigators can't find one shred of evidence which will link her to *any* organization, much less one small women's organization. *The Matriots never existed.*"

"Never existed? What the fuck—? All right, what conclusions do all you hawkshaws draw from that, and don't try telling me that you haven't arrived at a very unhealthy conclusion for Mrs. Spano."

"Frank—you'd better hear this out. The supposition is, *if* the woman in the morgue had no Matriot connections, then there are no Matriots. And if there are no Matriots, it seems pretty evident that Mrs. Spano invented them. And if Mrs. Spano invented the Matriots, that had to be because of a very elaborate cover-up."

"Cover-up of what?"

"If all those other things are provable, then Mrs. Spano murdered her husband and Mrs. Cassiman—the motive for that already exists—then she had her lover, Caen, kill the woman in the morgue, then she, Mrs. Spano, killed Caen to silence all the witnesses."

"Caen killed the paralyzed woman?"

"Yes. But wait! The New York Police say that in the shoot-out between Caen and the paralyzed woman, she used the same gun on Caen that was used to murder Dr. Spano and Mrs. Cassiman."

Heller glared at his counsel sourly.

"Spell out the police significance of that for me."

"Well, fahcrissake, Frank! If Caen, who is now dead, switched guns with the dead woman now in the morgue *after* he shot her, the woman had already taken the credit for shooting Spano—according to Mrs. Spano, anyway—the heat would have been off Caen, wouldn't it? And Mrs. Spano would be forever cool, *if there had even been a Matriot organization.*"

"I'm not just kidding you, Keef. I think you'd like to railroad Mrs. Spano."

"That is plain nonsense. Just stay with me for a little while, Frank. We have maybe two thousand agents out there combing every group of three or more in this country, with more experts and more coordinated machinery than has ever been put together for a manhunt before. They can't find anything remotely like the Matriots. So I am asking you to believe—for a minute or so anyway—that maybe Mrs. Spano and that stiff in the New York morgue were the entire Matriots organization. All right? I am saying that the stiff was the red herring for Spano's lover, the dead cop. That he killed the husband and Cassiman, but the woman on the slab in the morgue said she did it. Or Spano tells Gallagher and everybody else that she *said* she did it. Which *nobody* can prove. Who sent the tipoff letter to the New York *World? Some*body knows something—or knew something—and it almost scared Spano bald. Then, by a freaky chain from me to Gallagher to Spano, Spano sets up the dead woman with those letters she says they have to get—or else. Then she sends her lover to make a kill for her, because she knows the FBI has to buck it to the NYPD, and that they have to route it through the lover because he is in charge of the case. There is only one little patch she has to clean up herself—that's the lover. She gets him to hang by his crotch in that crummy Queens hotel and she knocks him off—leaving all her own jewels behind, because it tends to make the cops wonder about the cop and she knows the police have to give them back to her anyway. Okay, two people are out of the way because they thought they could run off together and make a fool of her, and two more are dead because *they*—with the whole cockamamie story about the Matriots—are what made Spano a public heroine in this country, what drew those millions of letters in her defense, and what has you ready to hand her the vice presidency." Keifetz held out his hand and fluttered it frantically. "Just a *mi*nute, Frank, just a *mi*nute! You think I would give a damn if that's all she did? I'm not a homicide guy. I'm not the NYPD. But she told us that the woman had told her that once Spano was vice president you were going to be *murdered*—inevitably, with ice-water logic—because Spano has more ambition than everyone in both parties put together." Keifetz stood across the desk from the president, glaring, nodding his head like a punchdrunk fighter. Then he turned away weakly, found a chair, and sat in it.

"I have a couple of things to say, Keef," the president said gently. "First, I am—as always—grateful for the way you look out for me. But you have to get this absolutely straight. As far as I am concerned, all that is a fairy tale. Because if it weren't, there isn't anyone who could stop Gallagher, an honest cop down to his toes, from taking your whole case to the NYPD and the DC police. Wait a minute, wait a minute! I'll even say that if you can get an indictment based on what you told me— sometime after election day—that I will buy everything you say one hundred percent. But what have you got? First, no connection between that woman lying in the morgue and Spano. None. And you *certainly* can't connect the dead cop with the murder of the husband and Cassiman. No way. And listen, Keef, do you think I would object to this woman having a lesbian on one side of the bed and a hoteyed homicide cop on the other, considering that she is the biggest vote-pulling star in politics since Ike? We still get three hundred thousand letters a day, worried about her. Is she all right? Is the president doing everything he can to help her over this bad time? Am I crazy? I can have a vote machine like that on my ticket, and you want me to dump her because you *might* suspect her of murder—and I don't think you do suspect her, I think you are just trying to deep-freeze her in *case* somebody could say she did something. Well, I'm not worried. If she can stay out of jail just a little longer, she is going to get the nomination for vice president. I want this report destroyed and I want to see Gallagher's copy in my hands so that you can destroy that. I like it here, Keef. I'm real keen on serving a second term. I'm not absolutely sure I could do that on my own right now, but with Jean Spano on my ticket this November—Keef, we can't miss."

"Frank?"

"What?"

"Will you let me show her this report, then ask her if she'll submit to cross-examination strapped to a lie detector?"

The president got up and walked to a window on the far side and stared out at the rose garden. "Suppose I were the best attorney general this country has seen in this century. Suppose I had just lost my wife violently but I had carried on like a soldier. Then suppose you came to me with that pile of—of infor*ma*tion and asked me to take a lie detector test. What would I do? I'd resign after I had asked the president straight out if he knew about that request. Well, that's why you can't do it. But I appreciate your sentiments, Keef. You want to protect me. So do everything you can in the short time you have left before that nominating convention to pin *real* evidence on Spano. If you can do it, I'll take over from there. If you can't, then she's the next vice president of the United States of America."

54

Keifetz's smoked-ivory face, as stylized as a temple carving, smiled promise at Berry James, director of the Secret Police, in a White House car-pool Chevrolet whose radio was playing Sinatra/Count Basie rather loudly to discourage effective recording of what they might have to say to each other. Berry James of course was Keifetz's secret hero, as director of the Secret Police Agency of the United States of America. Berry James was a Michigan politician who had been secretary of the interior and ambassador to Cambodia, then a party chairman before becoming DSP. He was a lanky, dark man who may have had a quart or so of Huron blood in his veins, a recipe mixture of one-third Huron to two-thirds ice water. The wild range of his ambition was a joke in Washington. He was the original of the slogan, "Promise him anything but you'd better deliver the Arpège." James was short on ability but long on revenge. He had to be. He had gotten where he had gotten because, while he wasn't especially inventive or bright, he was a bad man to have for an enemy, and he knew well that in an open election he couldn't be elected senior class president at a barbers' college.

Keifetz knew that James felt the DSP assignment had taken him as far as he could go; and that he had squirreled away all the information from SP files for his own future uses, which was why he had gone after the job in the first place, and that he wanted to cap his career by being named as Heller's secretary of defense in the upcoming administration.

"You're a man who knows his friends down to the last payoff, Berry," Keifetz said. "Which is why I would rather talk to you about my problems than anyone in Washington."

"You've always delivered for me, Keef. In my book there can't be greater praise for any man."

"I'm glad," Keifetz said, "because I need some help. Delicate, understanding help."

"Name it and claim it."

"The nominating convention is around the corner, Berry. The president feels that the time has come to run a woman on the ticket with him."

"That's good thinking."

The outstanding woman—anywhere in the country—is Jean Spano. Not only because of her record and her grasp, but because—and I tell you this confidentially—she has drawn over four million letters to the White House alone since the tragedy of her husband's murder."

"She is the right choice, Keef."

"But—and here we come to the delicate part already—the FBI ran up a report on the various ramifications of the AG's position, and frankly, Berry, it just plain scares me silly."

"Scares you?"

"You've been a professional politician operating on the national level for most of your life, Berry. You know better than I know that where there's smoke there's fire. Well, that FBI report is filled to the rim with smoke."

"Jean *Spano*?"

"I'm going to ask you to take along the only copy of the FBI report. I knew you are going to respect its almost sacred confidentiality. I know you'll return it to me intact and uncopied not later than six o'clock this evening, and I am doing this to demonstrate my trust in you."

"That's purely fine of you, Keef."

"Now—when you read this report I want you to read it with that one terrible worry of mine at the very forefront of your mind. The agony of my anxiety for the president, for the ticket in November, and for your appointment as secretary of defense is contained in that threatening phrase: where there is smoke there is fire."

"You are saying that we—the president, that is—can't take the chance that some possibly dangerous statements in the FBI report—in terms of hard evidence, that is—might one day return to plague all of us?"

"That is correct, Berry. That is my grief in a nutshell. All right—the report had to be thrown together by the FBI overnight and may contain a bulk of raw material—gossip, hearsay, and the sort of quasi-evidence that I couldn't possibly take to the president and hope to persuade him to choose a different name to run with him on the ticket. It's only the vice presidency. There are a half dozen women or more who could fill that job. But suppose, just suppose, between now and election day the opposition could lay it on the line and prove that this raw material in the FBI report was actual, factual fact? Well! We damned well *know* what would happen. The president would be defeated at the polls and some goddamn *lay*man would be moved in to take over Defense. Now, that's your job, Berry. You said yourself without any prompting that I deliver what I say I am going to deliver. But you're going to have to deliver, too, because a lot is going to depend on you."

"Like what, Keef?"

"If the SP reopened the Spano investigation and checked out that raw material in a really thorough pro*fess*ional manner, it could very well turn out that there really *is* evidence concerning the attorney general— evidence based on actual, undeniable, and irrevocable hard facts."

"No doubt about it. Where there's smoke there's fire."

"Then I can leave it with you?"

"It's my job now, Keef."

"You don't have much time."

"We'll be over this like a circus tent in the next six hours."

Jean was rigid with anxiety. In her mind she recited, again and again, her mother's admonitions that control was the most important strength she could possess. Stinnett would tell her nothing when she telephoned. She had called three times the night before and although it was only ten minutes after eight the following morning in Washington, she had called twice, once from home, once from her office, only to hear Stinnett's bland and impenetrable voice tell her. "There are no new developments, Miss Jean."

When she came out of her chilled reverie of foreboding, Gallagher was leaning across her desk, supporting his torso on his two arms and saying softly, "We want to come in here and sweep this place, Jean. Will you work in the conference room for a half an hour?"

"A bug? In *here?*"

He nodded grimly.

She swept up the sheaf of papers in front of her, a yellow pad and a jar of sharpened pencils, and strode out of the room. Gallagher nodded at the two men who were waiting near the main door behind him and they began to assemble electronic equipment. In twelve minutes they found two bugs. In seventeen minutes they found three of them.

"It's clean now, sir," the taller man said.

"Thanks," Gallagher said. "Have those checked out in the lab. Anything they can get."

The two men left with their cases of equipment. Gallagher opened the door to the conference room and said, "Okay, Jean."

She came back into her office with the papers, pencils, and pad and sat behind her desk. "Find anything?"

"Three."

"Whose are they?"

"The SP. We'll have to sweep your house twice a day—and anywhere else you'll be meeting or talking on the phone."

"Who turned the SP loose?"

"Our people tell us that Berry James has put a high-powered team on you, trying to prove out the report we made on you to the president. Our people in the White House tell us that the president refused to buy what Keifetz tried to prove out of that report, but that Keifetz is afraid that if anything in there is hard fact it could be bad news in the campaign. He wants to knock you out of a chance at the nomination to reduce what he sees as an election risk. Nothing personal."

"They can't build any case against me because there isn't any."

"It depends on how badly they want to build a case against you. If Heller wants you out—they'll do it."

55

Francis Manning Winikus said into the telephone, "I found him."

"How is he?" Stinnett asked fearfully.

"Pretty bad. Pneumonia. I found him in a hotel on 37th Street, and when I saw the shape he was in, I had him admitted to the Polyclinic Hospital."

"Thank you."

"They are pumping a lotta stuff into him now. If there is anybody who ought to see him, I think this is the time."

"That bad?"

"Well, maybe not. But he isn't conscious and he wasn't conscious when I found him. If this had been wintertime, he'd be dead."

"I will call his friends now," Stinnett said and hung up the phone. He was amazed to discover that he was weeping.

He called Dr. Weiler. The old man came on the line at once and listened carefully.

"He was drinking heavily?"

"Yes, sir. If you have friends on the staff of the Polyclinic—"

"I have friends. Also, I'll go myself. Have you called Mrs. Spano?"

"Not yet, sir."

"All right. I'll tell them who she is and that she must be allowed to see him."

248

Stinnett found Charles Cantwell's address book and carefully wrote down the private number at Justice. He dialed it and waited. Mrs. Spano came on the line.

"This is Stinnett, Mrs. Spano."

"He's home! Oh, thank God!"

"Mr. Cantwell is in the Polyclinic Hospital at 345 West 50th Street, Mrs. Spano. He may have pneumonia. Dr. Weiler is on his way to the hospital now and he will tell them that they must expect you."

"Pneu*monia*? But—"

"Best to be on your way, Mrs. Spano. That was the advice I was given." He put the telephone down softly in its cradle.

He went to the front door, wearing a street jacket and a floppy Panama hat. "If we only knew who we were," he murmured to himself. "He thought he was a young lover waiting to be called back to all that time ago." He locked the door carefully, then set out for the crosstown bus.

Jean had been sad and depressed all through the day before Stinnett had called her about Charles. She had had a letter that morning postmarked San Francisco. It was from Ursula Baggot and said that she was on her way "home to Hong Kong where I belong." Jean knew she would never see her again. Even if she went looking for her she would find a different woman, changed by their lives. She tried to remember the first time she had seen such a different girl come into a room at Paradise Hill, grinning and saying, "Who are you?" Thinking of that Ursie made her remember the elegant loveliness of the Slut. Ames was gone, too. Thane and Charles were the only trees still standing upon the landscape of her so distant past, and if Charles— She could not bear to think about ever losing Charles.

It was 6:10 P.M. when Jean got to the Polyclinic, gnawed by fear and anxiety. She asked for Charles Cantwell. A tall, dark man in a white coat came out to see her. His face told her nothing.

"I am Dr. Arias," he said. "My first practice was on your late husband's staff at La Casa."

"I remember you, Doctor. How is Mr. Cantwell?"

Dr. Arias produced an envelope. "Dr. Weiler was here. He honored us."

"I want a report on Mr. Cantwell, please." Her voice was harsh.

He handed her the envelope. "Here is Dr. Weiler's report. He wishes you to read it, then I will take you to Mr. Cantwell."

She took the envelope and opened it with slow dread. "He was in such perfect health when I saw him last," she said helplessly to Arias. The doctor nodded noncommittally.

The brief letter was in Dr. Weiler's careful, vivid handwriting.

Dear Jean:

Your intelligence is my comfort because you know there is an end for all of us. Charles will die sometime tonight, Dr. Arias and I are in agreement on that. He will die because he must have decided he had finished with living. Everything else was in order. He got to the hospital in time, everything available which was indicated was done for him, but he decided against allowing these things to save him. He asked for you twice while he was conscious and there is the possibility that he will be conscious when you get here. Accept his death as he does.

> With my love,
> ABE WEILER

She began to sob, then seemed to remember that there was no time for that. She ran a handkerchief over her eyes and asked Arias to take her to Charles Cantwell.

She sat beside the bed, holding his hand, listening to the silence in the room and the uproar of the city outside. She stared at his mask and thought instantly of the first time she ever remembered knowing he was there. She was four, sitting on a large white rocking horse while he moved it back and forth carefully as he sang, "Come, little leaves, said the wind one day/Come o'er the meadow and we will play/Put on your dresses of red and gold/For the summer is gone and the days grow cold." Since that instant he had always been there between her and misunderstanding; then, at the end, in his house the night of Caen's blackmail attempt, between her and mortal danger, always caring that the world remain a single, unfragmented piece for her, because she could be sure of his love and always assured by him of who she was.

When he died tonight whom would she become? Would she stay intact without his wisdom and the storehouse of his strength? She tried to think of the world without him. She wanted to plead with him to tell her if it could be true that he had decided to die. She had to know why because to her it was the ultimate weakness and therefore utterly alien to him.

His eyes did not flicker, they opened wide. He looked directly and deeply into her and smiled with a beauty which touched her and imprinted itself upon her the way life from primordial seas imprinted itself upon two-billion-year-old rock.

"I killed Caen," he said.

It was as if a bolt of lightning had passed through her, as the worst suspicion of her life came true. She had dreaded facing what she knew was true. Charles had gone to that evil little motel and had shot Caen in cold blood.

"Killed? *You?* You killed Caen?"

He stared at her sadly. "He killed your mother."

"My *mother?* Charles, what are you saying?"

"Your mother was the world's only Matriot," he answered hoarsely.

"That woman with the twisted face was Mama?"

He stared at her.

"How can you know such a thing?" She felt ripped in half, torn away from her sanity. "She died when I was a baby. How could she—"

"She didn't die, but she was very ill. Too ill to be allowed out in the world. She was mine, just the same. I took care of her in a small house on Long Island." He stopped to reassemble strength to speak. "I have spent every Monday night for over forty years visiting with her. I brought her news of you. News of you was all she wanted to hear. No detail was too small for her. Over the years I was trained by her—I can see that now—not to withhold from her one instance of what I had been able to glean about your life. I couldn't stop myself. Every Monday night in that uncarpeted house in Port Washington, in that locked bedroom, lined with books on Egyptology, I sat with her and I told her the minutes of your life."

Tears ran down Jean's cheeks. Pale and dazed, she stared at this man she had never known.

"God help me," he said weakly, "I told her about Ames Spano and Mrs. Cassiman and how this would wreck your career in politics, but I didn't understand what I had done until it was too late. When she came to you that night and told you she was the Matriot and you described that woman to me, I knew it was your mother and I searched for her frantically, but she would not be found. Then, on the following Monday night, when I went to the Port Washington house, she was there and demanded all news of you. She had convinced her nurse—with her for twenty-seven years—as she could convince anyone of anything under the inexorable pressure of her belief and intensity, that what she must do was what *had to be done*—and the nurse let her out into the world."

Cantwell went into rapid, shallow, desperately raled breathing. His eyes were perplexed as he looked at her, uncertain whether she had understood the relentless logic of his life.

"I loved you, too," he said. The gentle smile came back, but the unseeing eyes stayed open. She knew he had gone to find Mama.

She sat holding his hand. The summer twilight fell and Dr. Arias came into the room.

"Does he know you are here?" he asked in the normally loud voice used by technicians in hospitals.

"Not anymore," Jean said.

The doctor felt for Cantwell's pulse, then he closed the dead man's eyes and gently disengaged his hand from Jean's. "Mr. Cantwell's friend, Mr. Stinnett, is waiting," Arias said. "He will take you home, Mrs. Spano."

56

They crossed the city in a taxi, moving as slowly as time seems to move for children. Stinnett said, "Before he left the house on the night he disappeared, Mr. Cantwell gave me something to give to you, Mrs. Spano. It is a letter to be delivered, he said, in the event that he could not tell you himself. I have it safely at Beekman Place."

"Thank you."

"Not at all, madam."

"How did you meet him, Stinnett?"

"He always crossed on the old *Mary*, Mrs. Spano. He traveled in my cabin when I was a steward then, when I was promoted to smoking room steward and put in charge of the ship's pools, we began to talk to each other, particularly on the winter crossings when the weather kept most passengers below and when there weren't so many passengers anyway. He won the big pool, the auction pool, twice. Once it was twenty-seven hundred pounds and once it was eleven thousand-odd. Each time he asked for an envelope, put the money into it, wrote FOR THE SEAMEN'S BENEVOLENT FUND across the front of it, then handed it to me. The first time I said to him, 'Well, that is very generous, Mr. Cantwell, but I know how much money is in this envelope, so you can't be sure the seamen will ever get it.'

" 'It's your problem now, isn't it, Stinnett?' he said to me.

253

" 'Best to hand it over to the purser and get a proper receipt, sir,' I said.

" 'If I did that it would diminish you,' he told me. 'If you accept it from me the way it is, then you will confirm the world the way it should be—for both of us, that is.' Then he went back to his newspaper and his cigar and we didn't speak of it again.

"Now, the first time he handed me the envelope, I kept the money. I put it in a bank in Shaftesbury and I went about my business. I knew he was going to follow me up with Cunard to make sure that I handed in the money. I knew they would threaten me—and fire me—but they couldn't prove anything and I had the four thousand-odd quid for my old age and that was a lot of money. I served him again in the smoking room on three crossings during the next twenty months. Nobody did anything to me. Nothing changed so I knew he hadn't spoken to anyone at Cunard. I didn't know how he knew, but he knew. I could tell by the way he looked at me that he *knew* I hadn't turned that money into the fund, but he never said anything about it. Then the night came when he won the eleven thousand quid. We always settled up with the winners the next day, and before lunch, while he was enjoying a half bottle of Krug, I brought the bundles of cash on a silver tray over to his table, covered with a napkin. He didn't count it. He asked for three large envelopes, and when I brought them he wrote, straight out, across the face of each, FOR THE SEAMEN'S BENEVOLENT FUND, put them back on the tray, and pushed the tray toward me.

"We must have stayed there in silence for minutes, not moving. He was seated like a block of marble, staring at the tray. I stood beside him, thinking. He would not speak first. I could not pick up the tray. I said, 'The fact is, sir,' I said finally, 'I did not turn in that last lot you gave me.'

"He wouldn't answer me. At any rate, he didn't answer me.

"I said, 'I banked that money, in Shaftesbury, in my own name.'

" 'At interest?' he said.

" 'Yes, sir.'

"All the more for the seamen then,' he said.

" 'Yes, sir,' I answered him. I took up the tray with the three stuffed envelopes and walked across the smoking room to the purser's office. I told them I had to see the purser personally. I brought the tray into the room and I said, 'Gentleman who won the ship's pool last night just donated all of it to the Seamen's Fund.'

" 'Eleven thousand pounds?' the purser said, his mouth like an open porthole.

" 'Yes, sir,' I answered, 'and I suppose he would like a proper receipt.'

" 'He shall have one!' the purser said, and began to open and close drawers and to search for some receipt form.

" 'That isn't all, sir,' " I said. " 'He tells me he's going to hand me more of the same when we get to Southampton, which I will bring straight back to you, sir.'

" 'Who the devil *is* this lunatic?' the purser asked me.

" 'Mr. Charles Cantwell, sir—402, A deck.'

" 'Ah,' said the purser, 'that explains it. Mr. Cantwell is the legal counsel for the Seamen's Fund at the North American end, and he knows how we can use the money.' "

Jean sat silently, staring out at New York as it crawled past. "What a thrilling story, Stinnett, because . . . Mr. Cantwell was . . ." She began to weep uncontrollably, holding her face in her hands. Stinnett stared straight ahead, looking far, far ahead of the city and into the past.

57

An amethyst-colored Rolls-Royce limousine was waiting directly outside the Beekman Place house when Jean and Stinnett arrived. As Jean
got out of the cab, Thane Cawdor got out of the Rolls. She went to him
and put her arms around him.

"You've been crying," he said gently. "How can I help?"

"Just being here helps. Come in, Thane."

Stinnett had gotten into his white jacket when they came into the
house. "Will you have tea, madam?" he asked.

"Yes, please, Stinnett. In the study."

She closed the study door behind them. "The greatest friend I've ever
had died about an hour ago."

"I'm sorry, Jean."

"Now that I'm able to get a little used to it, I am merely amazed to see
you here. Why were you sitting in that enormous car out there?"

"Your office said you'd be here—and there was something I had to
tell you. I finished my last film three days ago. I'm on my way back to
England. Over twenty years ago I told you what I wanted to do, and now
I'm going to do it."

"I am so proud of you!"

"And I think it finally happened because I had once sworn to you that
this was the way it was going to be."

"I wish I had sworn such an oath before you. Then I would know, right now, where I am going."

"That is why I was waiting outside." He moved across the room and sat beside her. He took her long, almost porcelain hand in both of his and kissed it. "I'm going home. I want you to follow me when you can. I want to live with you for the rest of our lives, however you choose. Someday you'll be able to extricate yourself from politics, or you may wish there were a way out. I am the way out. I love you, Jean."

She leaned across and kissed him gently on the mouth. "I love you, Thane. I feel how I felt when I raced up the stairs every night in Geneva, wondering if you had got home before I did, breathless and dizzy at the thought of seeing you again after six whole hours. I never stopped thinking about you when I was married, when I was happy or unhappy. A politician and an actor are what we became, not what we are."

"We are what we need to be. You are all I have ever wanted, all I need now."

"You go," she said. "I'll follow—someday. Too many people and plans are dependent on me right now. But that can't last."

"I will fly out to London at ten o'clock tonight, and in my wildest hopes I never thought that what we want could happen instantly. Nothing could be more worth waiting for."

"How will I find you?"

"Grove House, Malmesbury, Wiltshire, will reach me."

"It may never happen."

"I know. But I also know it *will* happen."

She twisted a ring off her finger. "This is the ring Chai gave me the day he went back to Thailand. He was the bridge for us. Carry it with you, darling."

Stinnett knocked on the door, then, after a moment, came in silently with the tea table.

Thane got to his feet. "I wish I could stay," he said, "but I must get back to the hotel to pack and get out to the airport."

Jean rose. They shook hands formally. Stinnett saw him to the front door. Jean turned to the tea table. On it, propped up against the Georgian silver teapot was a large buff envelope. She stared at it as if it were foreign currency, but on its lower lefthand corner she read the familiar printing: HENSTELL, MASTERS, CANTWELL & SPANO.

Across its front, in Charles' bold black handwriting, it said: *To be handed to my ward, Mrs. Jean Spano, on the event of my death.*

The flap and each seam of the envelope had been sealed with bright-green wax. She broke the seals and slid out the letter, which had been typed in single space.

She began to read it as a lawyer should read any postmortem document, but her objectivity vanished with the first paragraph of the letter.

DEAREST JEAN,

This letter will be about your mother.

I must be frank and direct about everything I know about your mother as she has entwined herself around your life and my own. This letter would not have been written except that, by accident and because of fatigue, you told me about her influence upon you through her diaries. Just thirty-three years later than I needed to be told, thirty-three years after your twelfth birthday, when the diaries came into your life to haunt you. If I had known earlier, I could have given you the truth before the things she had ordained for you had hardened forever in your mind.

Your mother became my mistress when she was eighteen years old. To this very moment I do not know how this came about. I was introduced to her at a football game at New Haven in 1937; that night I found her in my bed in New York.

We had been introduced. We nodded and smiled and went on our way. I drove back to New York with friends, and, while not having forgotten your mother—she was unforgettable in her beauty and in the vigor of her attack upon every minute of her life—I was enjoying myself, so she went out of my mind. Nor did I have any intention of seeking her out or of telephoning her. I was ten years older than she was. I had my work to attend to, and intense young women, however beautiful, were the furthest thing from my plans for myself.

I returned to my apartment, which was on Madison Avenue at 63rd Street at just after eleven o'clock that night after a good dinner at the Stork Club. Not more than five minutes after I returned home—she must have been waiting in a taxicab across the street—the doorbell rang. It was your mother. She was wearing a sable coat. Her blonde hair and her extraordinarily deep blue eyes, like your own eyes, the wonderful natural palette of her face as she stood, unsmiling, almost as tall as me, is as I write this to you still like a carved jewel in my memory.

"I love you," she said and shrugged the coat off her body to make a pool of fur on the floor. She was naked. She held out her arms, her eyes glittering dangerously. I can write that word dangerously now, but I did not think that then. She was only glorious then. I lifted her into my arms, kissed her while she clung with both hands to my head, and carried her to the bedroom.

From that instant forward—perhaps from the instant of the introduction at New Haven—it was established and understood forever that I was hers. So was it to be. She did not remain mine, but I belonged to her. That has never changed nor have I ever wanted to change it.

Your mother was a brilliant, erratic, and haunted woman. She was never a girl and only for a very short time a child. She was tortured by a memory of her father and her mother. She would be wildly happy, then the terror bequeathed to her by her parents would return to her and almost break her. She could not stand knowing how and what her parents had been. She invented a family so exotically foreign to her true parents' Middle Western and New England background as to be alarming. She gave herself Persian parents, as the diaries told us. They must have been very real to her. How she boasted of the centuries of their lineage going back to Aryan conquerors out of India! She gave herself a position in the world, not only constantly within her own imagination and belief but also confirmed as she informed me with stunning retrospective falsifications which were utter truth to her. She made herself a famous geologist. The powerful *men* in the world (to your mother there could never be any powerful women) came to her and she became their counsellor on matters concerning the world's riches in oil and therefore in power, she fantasized.

It was not something which began as a playful attitude between lovers. She could not tolerate her true background because it had caused all of the principals involved in it so much pain. She broke down the walls of reality to escape its tyranny. She rejected her past as a falsehood and so had to invent her own truths.

I loved her helplessly. I knew she had crossed over into insanity out of pleading necessity, but how could that change how I loved her?

Her family's physician, Abraham Weiler, was the only fixture of her past which remained intact. He had been her family's doctor—in a sense like having Hippocrates crossed with Schweitzer as one's family doctor—and he had defended and comforted her mother during the fearful years before her violent death. I fixed an appointment with Dr. Weiler at his formidable house. I explained in the gravest detail I could summon what was happening to your mother, how she was evolving from being just an erratic woman into a psychotic. He was silent for a long time before he answered me. "What can I say?" he told me. "I knew her mother. Perhaps it was inevitable."

I asked him what could be done. He said, "Nothing." I asked him what I was to do. He said, "Has she shown any need to do anything harmful to herself or to you?" I said she had not.

"Is there anything else I should know?"

"She thinks she is pregnant."

"By you?"

"Yes."

"Will you marry her?"

"When I talk to her about marrying is the only time she becomes violent. She will not hear of it. She says marriage is a disease, it killed her mother, that she will never marry, that marriage is unnatural; animals do not marry and yet they are capable of being both compatible and faithful. She cries out that she will not marry, does not need to marry, and that the only thing which could ever stop her loving me would be any more talk about marriage."

Jean was seated unnaturally, rigidly erect. Her face was as jaggedly planed and faceted in the sculputre of horror as a nightmare by Edvard Munch. Her eyes stared out at the letter like the multicolored marble eyes of a Cuban cemetery statue. Her mouth was held to her face like a slash of pain. Her life, which she had thought of always as a strong, swift river had flowed over a mile-high cliff and had become the trillion particles of a crashing waterfall. There was nothing left. She could not believe any single moment of her entire life, a three-dimensional sham staged by a madwoman.

Your mother and I knew a young lawyer named Joshua Henstell. He was hopelessly in love with her but her only acknowledgment that he existed was to make fun of him, in mime, to amuse me. He was a chunky man, with very red cheeks and a wild brush of black hair, whose idea of conversation was to explain forever and to anyone how ill he was. I had known him since childhood, going back to the Knickerbocker Grays, Squadron A, and Harvard. It was his friendship which brought me into his family's law firm.

I must repeat how beautiful your mother was, but even more than that she had irresistible intensity which drove her to total possession of what she wanted and complete rejection of what did not interest her. She never concealed how she felt, and this caprice was an endless and punishing fixation. This encompassed me (and other people), ideas, fads—everything either institutionalized or transient. She was so dazzlingly wealthy that this capriciousness was seen mostly as the reflex of a badly spoiled child. But this was not so. She was paranoiac even then. She saw everything as either inferior to herself or as commanding her. There was no such thing as equality with anyone or anything for your mother. What her beauty, wealth, and magical magnetism did for her was to render almost everything inferior to herself. Insofar as I could see, the only beings (no institutions) she felt to be superior were the very few men who spoke to her in a certain way. For some reason I seemed to possess that extraordinary quirk.

Dr. Weiler said the reason was that my voice projection was somewhat, somehow, like the projection used by her father as she remembered him in the plastic years.

Consequent to feeling herself superior to everyone (most certainly to all women), she felt that she was required to worship herself as a goddess and, as time went on, time about which you have no knowledge, this is where she rested her life.

She *willed* things to be right. If in some of these, one or two might seem to have been wrong, she applied her godhead retroactively to make them right again. Not that she was safe, for as the millennia show, even the gods are not safe. She felt herself persecuted by all of the men on the planet who had not been singled out to receive her love—as had Dr. Weiler, the butler Herbert George, and myself. She feared the apparent power of men and so wished to look no further to examine it. She despised women because to her they suffered supinely under this male power and therefore deserved all they reaped from men. The gods were male, therefore she felt persecuted—until the inevitable happened. One night, heaven knows how it happened, she arrived at my flat with two invitations to a dinner at the Lotus Club where Sir Jilmer Rizzo, the Nobel astronomer, was going to speak. I told her I had work to do against a deadline. She pouted and coaxed and wooed but in the end she went off to hear the great man speak, alone.

I should have known that she had to go. Rizzo was not just a man, he was an authority on the heavens, and in her tilted mind he was more than just a passing acquaintance of the gods.

When she came back that night, she was in a frenzy of panic. She said we must pack at once to get away from what was about to happen. It took me much time to make her explain coherently what was frightening her so badly. At last she got the panic out of herself. She told me that the Nobel Prize-winner had just warned them all that in 1939 all planets would be in alignment and—but you have read all of this in the diaries.

When I refused to take her seriously, perhaps for the moment I became like her father, forcing her, within her mind, out upon the high, icy ledge of that building. She panicked. She stared at me in frightened horror and ran away from me.

On the second day I was quite worried because I could not find her anywhere. She was not at the small flat she kept, mainly to hold her clothes, on East 57th Street. I had the office staff at the firm call fifty or sixty hotels. She wasn't at any of them and she had no women friends in whose houses she could be hiding.

On the eighth day, when I was haggard and despairing because she could not be found, Joshua Henstell asked me to go into his office where he told me that your mother was on the high seas on her way to Switzerland; that he was about to follow her so that they could be married there.

"Marry *you?*" I shouted at him. "She thinks you're a clown."

"No matter about that," he said coolly. "I love her; I have always loved her."

"She loves me!"

He shrugged helplessly.

"Josh—she's pregnant."

"She told me."

I was about to prove to him that she was also clinically insane, but he hadn't ever had very much out of life. Hypochondriasis extends to attitude. If you need to believe your body is sick then you need to believe that your soul is sick and still people do not sympathize.

She had left me. But to her I was unique. I was the positive side of her father, a side for which, although she denied its existence, she had an urgent need. She loved me for the wrong reasons, but she loved me. She had spoken so much about sex and violent love, of lust and more lust; but that was the way she whistled into the hurricane of her loss, of never being allowed to understand who she was. In all her life, from girlhood on she had never slept with or made love with or as much as viewed carnally anyone but me. She came to me a virgin. She returned to a virginal state while she lived with Henstell and she never married him.

How I have been tortured since I read those diaries! I can only just barely measure the lunacies she has been pouring into your soul since you were twelve, horrors which *I* made possible but which I was never aware that either of you were thinking.

* * *

As she read the truth about her mother, the thousand shapes of Thane Cawdor, her one continuous year of him, swarmed across Jean's mind. He had made her happier than Mama had ever been able to be. Then, like sixty-foot sharks in a black sea, moving in with open mouths, she felt Caen's presence again and the starchy grease of his body and his stink upon her. She had celebrated wantonly as Mama had demanded that she do, because Mama had not been able to dare to celebrate herself. Jean felt herself to be a centrifuge spinning through garbage, hacking its way out into clean air. Mama had been unable to cling to any belief but her love for herself. Jean felt the special disgrace of the dupe. Mama, her great teacher, her hope above all hopes, ascending and soaring, had been a timid maniac, a colossal and ridiculous stage mother with a ruinous hunger for the vicarious.

She read on.

They stayed in Switzerland until ten days before you were born, then she came home because she said she had had a dream which threatened her with terrible vengeance (by some male god) unless you were born at Rockrimmon.

You were born. With that arrival there were two departures. Joshua Henstell died in Cologny and your mother left the rational world altogether. When you were born she had a stroke which paralyzed the left side of her beautiful face, but, with the powers of one who was her own goddess, she was able to ignore that completely. She could stare into the mirror during those long visits she had with herself and not see what her face had become.

With everything, she was paranoiacally logical—and logically correct. She started writing those diaries when we became lovers—but not before she had gone mad.

I cannot write to you about the diaries. We both know what they contain. All that went into the diaries affected so much of your life—perhaps some of it even for the better—but, to your mother's shame, changed much that should never have been changed. You will be feeling mangled by the truth. It will take time for you to get well from this battering. But you will get well. You will become stronger and truer to yourself, the terminal point of all advice from all parents. You loved me. You admired me. Therefore you must pledge to say to yourself with me, over and over again, that you are a fine woman.

Jean felt herself being strangled by the entwining ropes of words;

thousands of long-forgotten strands of words, hundreds of thousands of meaningless words giving mock-counsel. She was swinging in the wind on the entwining, bitter, empty words of her mother and on the gallows cord spun out of the desperation of a man who had found the courage to tell her he was her father after he had died and who could no longer explain anything about either of them.

Stinnett knocked on the door. He waited. There was no answer. He knocked again, then opened the door. Mrs. Spano looked up for a moment, seemed to stare right through him, then looked back to the letter on the desk in front of her.

"Forgive me for entering without permission, Mrs. Spano," he said, "but the White House telephone operators have called here twice since we've been back. I haven't told them anything without your instructions." He waited. She didn't seem to hear him. He withdrew, closing the door.

You know now that there are no Matriots and that the president's life was never in danger. You know that your mother shot and killed Ames Spano and Mrs. Cassiman because they had flouted the respect due to the daughter of a goddess. Your mother saw all of that as being clearly right and necessary. She knew she must search the house on Riverside Drive for those letters. Respect for a goddess was at stake.

Trust yourself, dearest Jean. Be true to that. The pain will depart and you will live again.

With all my love,

CHARLES

58

She folded the letter and returned it to the envelope. She got up slowly and uncertainly and wandered, looking for her purse. When she found it, she put the envelope into it carefully, then crossed the room, opened the door, and walked across the main hall to the coatrack.

Stinnett appeared instantly from a doorway. He got to her light raincoat before she did and helped her into it. "Your office at the Department of Justice *and* the White House have been calling, Mrs. Spano."

"They must have told you where to call them back. They always do," she said colorlessly.

"Yes, Mrs. Spano."

"Call them, please. Tell them you spoke to me and that I am making funeral arrangements."

"Yes, Mrs. Spano."

She left the house. "Shall I expect you for dinner, madam?" Stinnett called after her, but she moved away from him, crossing the street, staring at nothing.

As she drifted away from Charles' house, away from her mother, and away from everything she had believed in, she tried to imagine what she could do with her life. Charles wrote that she would survive. But the wound was still clean upon her. It hadn't begun to fester yet. The pain of the loss of the great companion of her life, Mama, had not really begun yet. Mama! Poor victimized deluded Mama, who had been calling out her demented advice from behind every tree, warning her with lunatic thoroughness at every step against all those things on which all other people built their lives.

She felt twelve years old again; back at the day when Charles had brought her the diaries, but this time around, without Charles to help her understand what she was doing. She would have to start out all over again at where she had found Mama—so far back, so long ago—and like everyone else teach herself how to grow up with rules she would have to write for herself; trying, failing, then starting again the way everyone else who had not been reared and trained by a psychotic mother, had had to do.

Mama had ordered her to hold fast to the control of herself and all events, but Jean did not know how to do that anymore. Mama had ordered her to hate men. She knew that she would be safe if she followed Thane Cawdor to England and built her new mind there. Mama had commanded her to lead the people of the world. But to where? She was so confused. And her past, Mama's twisted gift, was strewn with shame and sorrow. Where did a confused woman with the obligations of two funerals, a murdered husband and lover, an immediate past which was strewn with shame and horror, lead which people? She could no longer lead women, she knew, because she had taken the places of men in politics, in sex, and in her insatiable ambitions. She didn't want to be a lawyer anymore. She didn't want to be a politician—leave that to the men. She had never troubled to find out about God, so she couldn't turn there either—and Charles was gone.

*

There were four months left until election day. Heller had been kind to her, so she couldn't just resign at Justice and walk away from him because that would make trouble for him and perhaps cost him the women's votes. So she would have to go to Abe Weiler and tell him part of what had happened to her, then he would need to draw his heavy cloak of medical invisibility over her, seal her in some famous hospital. Then, when the point about her dire illness had been made again and again and again she could be withdrawn invisibly behind the gates of Rockrimmon where she could recuperate until the election returns were in. Then she would find Thane. She would disappear into England and teach herself to trust her life again.

She walked home thinking through the decisions which were so opposite to what she had been that morning. Everything was changed forever. Everything she had desired so militantly or feverishly was as dead

as Mama, chilled blue in that drawer at the city morgue. To every meaning of life, she had died. She was forty-five years old when she had
awakened that morning. Now, at twenty minutes to seven in the evening, she was twelve years old again—but the slate was not as clean as it
had been then.

She let herself into the apartment at Matsonia, didn't remember to
take her raincoat off, and walked to the safe where she kept Mama's
diaries. As she opened the safe door, the telephone began to ring. It
rang twenty-six times.

She carried the four volumes to her desk. She opened Volume 1 and
tore out as many pages of her own life as her strength would let her
take. She opened her purse and took out the envelope from Charles. She
separated page one of his letter from the other pages and laid it on top
of Mama's ripped-out pages, then fed these into the shredder beside her
desk.

This is my funeral, she thought. Theirs will happen soon. They are
together at my graveside—as normal and whole and sane and healthy
as they ever were while they wrote my life and my death separately.
Requiescat in pace all of us.

It took her twenty minutes to destroy the diaries; the pages of the
letters were gone almost at once. With each destroyed sheaf of pages
her mind became clearer and the weight she believed she would carry
wherever she went for the rest of her life grew lighter and lighter. She
had killed the wicked Mama but the good Mama lived on.

She left the apartment while the phone began to ring again for the
third time since she had started on her work.

She found a taxi and gave him the address of the city morgue. The
same white-coated men were in the same conspiratorial conversation at
the desk. The fat one greeted her as General Spano and, without her
asking, led her through the corridors to Mama's refrigerated drawer,
slid it open, and left her.

She soaked in the silence of death and shivered in the cold of it. She
reached over and drew aside the sheet so she could see Mama's ruined
face.

I wish I could be sure it would ever be over for you, Mama, she
thought as she stared down at the grotesque face through the silence.
You believed everything you believed, so fiercely. You loved me. You
were protecting me from everything you thought was wrong or harmful
and you wanted those things for me which *you* thought were golden and
desirable. You couldn't live *for* me, because that is impossible, so you
assumed command of my life, because what did you know of how wrong
that could be? Now, finally, it is all sorted out. We understand ourselves

at last. We know what we have done to each other and we have forgiven that. Goodbye, Mama.

She pulled the sheet over the dead face and rolled the drawer shut. She made her way out to where the two men were having their perpetual conversation, and, released, she went out into the summer night.

She decided she wanted the dinner Stinnett had offered her. And he could handle the funeral arrangements while she saw Dr. Weiler in the morning. She would like to have them buried side by side at Rockrimmon. While she was still in the United States playing out the last months of the drama of her political illness, they would be near her. Her plans were to go to whatever hospital it would be that Weiler would choose, as soon as she could terminate her commitments in Washington.

She telephoned Stinnett from a phone booth on First Avenue in the Thirties. He was delighted that she would be there for dinner. "It will be a half hour before I get there," she said. "I'm going to walk home."

When she went into the study at the house in Beekman Place, Dick Gallagher was sitting there smoking one of Charles' Cuban cigars.

"Jesus, where have *you* been?" he said.

59

She stared at him. She knew him well, she liked everything about him, but the connection was different than before. He hadn't changed but she had. "Is something wrong?" she asked.

"Heller has done everything but call out the troops to find you."

"Why?"

"He just fired Berry James."

"*Fired* him?" The shoptalk was reviving her the way it always had. Great gossip was better than the opening night of *My Fair Lady*.

"He turned in the cooked SP report on you. The report proved nothing, but the boys had framed it beautifully and it made a tremendous case against you. Anybody but Heller woulda figured why take a chance with stuff like this that might explode in the papers."

"How could it make a case against me?"

"Whatsa difference? They did it. Print it on the front page of the Washington *Post* and bye-bye election for Heller. But he knows like in a fraction of a second that if he doesn't fire James and announce you, that James can blackmail him with that report for the rest of his time in office. But if he tells James that he is a blackmailing son-of-a-bitch to try to smear the leader of the women's movement in this country who is going to be the next vice president of the United States, that James is a lucky son-of-a-bitch to be given the chance to resign—then there is a fighting chance."

" 'Well!' James screams. He says if the president wants him out then there's no way he can stay, but he doesn't have to take it. He says he is going to leak the whole goddamn report to the L.A. *Times* because he can see now that Keifetz set him up for this whole thing. He says he'll go straight to all the reactionary women's groups in the country—women who outnumber the feminists two to one—and give them the entire lowdown on you and where would his big vote-catching women's leader be then?"

"My God, Dick! What *hap*pened?"

"Heller said he had always hoped he would never have to bring it up, but that he had had FBI surveillance on James for two years and that he even had the numbers of the Swiss bank accounts where James had stashed the money he had grafted from SP secret funds and that he supposed James wouldn't want him to do that."

"My *God*, Dick! And what is Heller going to do about Keifetz?"

"Do?" Gallagher laughed with high delight. "He told Keifetz to set James up. And he told him how he wanted him set up."

"*Whaaat?*"

"Heller wanted James out—and until he was sure you were in the clear he wanted a big Exit sign painted for you, to be able to keep his options open on you."

"Talk about *devious!*"

"Well." Gallagher shrugged. "That's the business you guys are in. The main thing is that he is going to announce you tomorrow."

"An*nounce* me? How? Where?"

"Don't tell me you don't remember you are making the key speech at the national convention for the ERA in the Garden tomorrow?"

She found a chair and fell into it.

"He's going to be telling the women voters of this country that he is going to put your name into nomination at the convention next week. And, baby, let me tell you, the roof is gonna come off that joint!"

"*No!*"

"What?"

She began to weep. "I can't, Dick. I *can't.*"

"No one in this country deserves it more," he said. "That's one thing, but not the big thing, Jean. The women have to get that ERA. They *have to get it!* They deserve it—and we aren't some goddamn Third World undeveloped and hopeless country where the men have to prove the women are beasts of burden to be able to hold their own heads up. We have to hold the respect of the world. We're the biggest democracy where people—including women—are supposed to be equal. You have to run. Because by running you alongside him, Heller is going to get the Equal Rights Amendment into the Constitution. It's as simple as that."

60

Jean was in the VIP room under the platform with Dick Gallagher and Susie Orde. They hovered around the motored wheelchair of the legendary Dame Maria Van Slyke, honorary chairperson of the National Convention of American Women's Organizations for the Ratification of the ERA, when the presidential motorcade was heard to arrive at the stage entrance to Madison Square Garden. Rita Zendt, the national chairperson of the convention celebrated for having destroyed the propaganda lies that if the ERA were passed women would have to use common public toilet facilities with men and that when on duty during a war as infantrypersons would not be allowed to nurse their children if these were born during a concentrated germ warfare and heavy artillery bombardment—came up fast through the broken field of women to announce that the president was arriving.

The presidential party came barreling into the room. The two dozen-odd women assembled gave him such riveted attention and total respect that one would have known instantly, had one not been looking, that he could not have been a woman. He shook hands and butched his way across the room to where Jean was standing.

"They're putting us on right away because I'm running a little late," he said. "I'm going to introduce you today, then I'm going to announce you as being the party's choice for the second half of the ticket."

"Mr. President! Please!"

272

He grinned at her as Mrs. Zendt pulled him away. For him it was a full grin, which held for an eternity of 1.032 seconds then snapped off as if he feared some hidden photographer might get a picture of his teeth, which would somehow associate him going backward from Carter, through Ford, Johnson, Kennedy, Eisenhower, Truman, and Roosevelt. Heller was the first consciously nongrinning president always excepting Calvin Coolidge, the most unconsciously nongrinning one in American history. He was swept away to the platform by Rita Zendt and eight Secret Service men.

Jean looked at Gallagher with dismay.

There was an enthusiastic sustained welcome by most of the convention when Heller came on stage, but three minutes later, when Susie Orde gave the signal for Jean to walk across the platform to her seat, there was a standing ovation which lasted for seven minutes, until Mrs. Zendt demanded attention for the president of the United States.

President Heller accepted the applause, fractionally smiling at the bank of microphones. When the applause gradually died down, he greeted the chairperson, Dame Maria Van Slyke; the attorney general of the United States; the director of the Federal Bureau of Investigation, "whose reason for being here today will soon be clear to all of you,"; and the members of the distinguished convention.

"I will be starkly brief in my address to you," he said. "You have no need for a male for the completion of your business before this national gathering. I am here today for one reason only, to introduce to you the attorney general, Mrs. Jean Spano"—his voice began its booming emphasis—"the next vice president of the United States!"

He turned away from the rostrum dramatically, facing Jean and stepping aside as if to make room for her in the American leadership. The 19,783 women, as they absorbed the meaning of what he had said, leaped to their feet roaring with one great voice. The brass band began to play "She'll be Comin' Round the Mountain When She Comes." Twenty-nine network commentators—TV, radio, and overseas—caught logorrhea.

Jean sat crumpled on a chair at the middle of the platform, staring out at the thousands of yelling females as if they were all her mother, insanely intent upon making her do what she didn't know how to do anymore. The president was applauding like a seal. Mrs. Zendt was shaking her hand and saying something she couldn't hear because of the ear-splitting noise. She saw Dame Maria lift a small bottle of brown liquid high in the air, then knock it back with one great swallow. She felt decapitated, disemboweled. But, as she watched the thousands of overjoyed women pour out into the broad aisles and begin the march and ovation which was to last for the next twenty-eight minutes, despite herself, life began to return to her.

She saw that everything she had ever done in her life had come to her from Mama, and that the time had come to give it back to Mama's memory.

She wanted to be a part of this. And she wanted to be at the head of it. As the whooping and blaring and cacophony went on and on she began to remember Mama's words:

> How I dream, awake and asleep, that one day someone who really cares, as I care, will awaken American womanhood and lead this overwhelming moral force. . . . I would contribute my fortune and follow the woman who would dare to grasp the helm to bring the women of our country into striking unity and thus into the mighty offices where the men of American history have failed. . . . How I would flame with pride wherever I was—in this world or the next— if my own daughter were eager to wear the sword and shield of American moral leadership and move out upon the plains of Columbia to do battle in the vanguard of the great . . . sex which wants to cherish this country and this great life which God gave us.

She trembled with excitement. As if she were watching all of it on a television screen, she saw herself slowly growing—she was Alice; the maniac convention of dissonance and promise as the very small cake of ambition on which the words EAT ME were being beautifully worked out in currants. She felt hubris pour into her veins and rush to her brain. She could suddenly grasp Mama's viewpoint on immortality. She felt immeasurable joy that in four years her friend, Franklin Heller, would have completed his second and constitutionally final term when her own first term as vice president was over, and she saw all at once, as clearly as anyone safely on shore can see a great fire at sea, that she would be the first woman president of the United States of America, despite her mother.

She got to her feet, tall with magnificent posture. She crossed slowly, her hands held out to the president. They embraced before the nineteen thousand-odd women in the hall, for the twenty-one television cameras, and for the forty million women viewers across the nation and over the world. The president led her toward the podium and stepped back.

Jean faced the forest of microphones. She stared out at the wildly cheering audience and saw all the women of the world. She gripped the rostrum tightly and, head thrown back, began to weep her joy. Mama was right. Mama had been sad, unlike these women, and mad, unlike these women, but she was right. She had made Jean a part of all women's hopes and had armed her to fight beside them. When the enormous ovation diminished, she entered the vast sea of acclaim, leaving Mama farther and farther behind among her sandcastles of madness, murder, and her fears of men upon the shore, as she proclaimed with a ringing voice:

"My mother raised me to fight for equal rights for women, but under a definition of her own. None of us here today—not a woman in America—should fight on *only* for equal rights for women but for equal rights for herself among men and other women. When we win that victory the future will take care of itself."

She launched herself upon the ocean of women, ready to drown herself in them, tears of holy ambition streaming down her cheeks. She thanked the president, exulted before the convention, then settled down to deliver a rousing hell's fire political speech, hoping that Mama—wherever she was—was watching and listening.